ONE SHILLING.

THE PIRATES ISLE

BY GEORGE EMMETT.

LONDON: HOGARTH HOUSE, BOUVERIE STREET, FLEET STREET, E.C.

THE PIRATES' ISLE.

BY GEORGE EMMETT.

AUTHOR OF "MIDSHIPMAN TOM," "WAR CRUISE OF THE MOSCA," "ALL'S WELL," ETC.

PIRATES' ISLE.

THE PIRATES' ISLE.

CHAPTER I.

GOING TO SEA.

JACK RAWLINGS was born on the sea. His father was the master of a small coaster, and for reasons best known to himself took his wife with him upon all the voyages he made. Thus it was that Jack had such an early taste for the "briny ocean."

After Jack had passed through all the stages and ills peculiar to all troublesome brats, after disposing of the measles, the whooping cough, and having cut all his teeth, he went pretty smartly through life until he reached the mature age of nine years.

Then he was sent to school, and being too small to do anything except supplying the fourth form with chewed pellets for their pop-guns, the second era of his existence also passed placidly.

He had but few exercises to do, and in this he was helped by the young gentleman by whom he was engaged in the gum-aching duties of masticating stiff brown paper.

When he reached his twelfth year he had managed to master the classics, could write a tolerable hand, and was a fair arithmetician.

John Rawlings the elder was now of opinion that John Rawlings junior knew quite sufficient to begin life; then arose the question—what was he to be?

"I should like to be a midshipman," said Jack, "and wear a cocked hat and a sword."

"Ugh!" grunted the master of the sailing vessel. "What the devil next?"

"I suppose I should be a mate next," said Jack; "then a——"

Here Mrs. Rawlings put in a word or two for her darling.

"Yes, John," said she; "the dear boy will, no doubt, rise in the profession. Yes, it's but natural that he should wish to become a sailor."

"Nateral, woman; what do you mean?"

"Surely you do not forget that he was born upon the sea, and your relation?"

The master of the coasting vessel made a wry face as he answered—

"There are some things a man never forgets, Mrs. Rawlings, and an affair of that sort is one of them. No, I don't forget it."

"You know, John," said the lady, ignoring her lord and master's very sage reply, "you are upon intimate terms with several officers in the King's Navy, and it would be very easy for you to have the dear boy appointed to a man-of-war."

He shan't go, once for all; let that be understood," said the master of the coaster. "I've made up my mind he shall be something more useful than a *walking candlestick* in any man-of war."

"I shan't be anything else but a midshipman," said Jack, dutifully. "If you don't let me be one I'll run away for a cabin boy."

John Rawlings' ruby-coloured nose became very much more inflamed as he took from a nail a piece of an old trace to thrash Master Jack, a proceeding that would have taken place but for the intercession of the boy's mother.

"Do not be so violent, John," she said; "you know the dear boy always speaks his mind."

"I'll flay his hide if he sauces me, ma'am," said the irate father; "and if ever I hear this puppy mutiny again I'll half kill him."

So saying the captain and owner of the coaster bounced out of the room and went straight to the parlour of the Buoy and Anchor and over a glass of grog and his pipe forgot his domestic troubles.

"Don't mind your father's words, my darling," said the lady; "you shall be a midshipman in spite of all he says."

Here Jack's mother stroked her son's curly pate and called him a handsome boy.

I hope this little scene will prove to the reader that Master Jack was pretty well spoiled by an over-indulgent mamma, and was in great danger at times of tasting the piece of twine that hung upon the nail beside the fireplace.

Whatever arguments the lady used with her husband, certain it is they succeeded, for within a couple of weeks Master Jack was delighted by the news that he was to make his appearance on a certain day on board the Albatross, a small gun-brig then lying in dock undergoing repairs for she had been sadly mutilated in an engagement with a French corvette.

Jack's mother was anxious to see her darling in his uniform, and Jack was anxious to appear in it, and when the tailor who had been entrusted with the important undertaking delivered the outfit. Master Jack was soon arrayed, and nothing under instant decapitation or gibbetting would make him wear anything else.

He visited all his relations in it, went to the school he had just left in it, and here his dignity was hurt by a grocer's boy trying to bonnet his cocked hat, and he was further insulted by another taking his dirk for a toothpick.

This was his only visit to the school, but it has been reported that, as a balm for his wounded feelings, he went to bed that night in his uniform, cocked hat and all.

delight was to sport his oak

cocked hat, and sword in the quiet lanes of the neighbourhood, and preparing himself for battle by reading over the events of a well-fought engagement.

One look round to see that he was unobserved, then the dirk was plucked from its scabbard, and Jack calling upon his boarders to follow him, rushed up a bank, reached the top, and was about to place a Union Jack on the summit, when the edge of the bank rolled away, and head foremost went the hero into a stagnant ditch.

Father and mother were both angry, and the former to escape the expense of a second outfit, packed Master Jack off to Plymouth to join his ship.

Jack's sea-chest was painted a delicate light green, and in bold white letters on the front were the words—

"JOHN RAWLINGS, ROYAL NAVY," and on the top was an anchor and crown done with gold.

Dear to Jack was this chest, and he took especial care when he reached Plymouth that everybody should know that he was the important person who owned the name and the words "Royal Navy."

When he had the precious box placed in the boat that was to take him aboard, he sat across it keeping the letters to his feet in order that there might be no mistake "about the young officer and his chest."

On board at last, and the precious chest to his horror was tumbled below along with other chests quite as precious to the owners thereof. He cast one fond look at the golden letters, and then another at the huge white letters, then a rough voice yelled out—

"Keep along the gangway there you youngster; report yourself to the officer of the watch."

Jack did so, and by him was introduced to the first luff, by him handed over to a senior midshipman, who took him below.

Of course Jack went the wrong way down the companion ladder, and his sword getting between his legs nearly sent him head foremost to the bottom.

Between decks he barked his shins against the gun carriages, and as a wind-up knocked his cocked hat against the beams, and was bonnetted in consequence thereof.

He was introduced to his messmates, and laughed at because he came on board in his sky-scraper instead of his cap, but on the whole he had sustained himself pretty well at home, and by the time the Albatross sailed for the Indies, he had begun to realise a little of the that was before him.

Four years were spent by Jack in the gun-brig, then he returned to England and gladdened his parents' eyes by the great change that had taken place in his appearance.

Four years had changed him very much. From a pale-faced, light-limbed boy, he had become a broad-shouldered, bronzed, strapping fellow—the very *beau ideal* of what a sailor ought to be.

He loved his profession in spite of its drawbacks, and hoped to be again upon the ocean. He had seen some service and many distant climes, but only enough to create a desire to see more.

The gun-brig was recommissioned in less than three months, and despatched with sealed orders for a cruise in the South Seas, and one of the first on board was Jack Rawlings.

He laughed a little when he thought of his mishaps when he first went to sea, and was highly amused when he saw several youngsters crying, as he had done four years before.

This time Jack's cocked hat and sword were with his luggage, and he wore the neatest of all dresses—the short blue jacket and over vest, the loose tie, and the cap with the anchor and crown in front.

CHAPTER II.

THE PHANTOM PIRATE.

DURING the voyage out, the fact of the captain's having sealed orders became known to the crew, and many were the surmises conjectured by the men, and the officers were no doubt quite as curious upon the matter, but did not like to risk their superior's anger by any reference to the mystery.

There was one man on board who could not rest when he heard about the mystic packet, emblazoned with the Royal seal, and he would have given ten years of his life to have broken open the cover and seen the contents.

This was an Irishman—a broad-shouldered, herculean fellow, as good and brave a seaman as ever trod the deck.

He was, in consequence of the caterer of the midshipman's mess being laid up with a fever, promoted to the office until that important functionary should recover, and while in this capacity he took a strange liking to Jack Rawlings.

About two months after the Albatross left England Jack was in charge of the middle watch, and the night being particularly fine, and the sky such as can only be seen in the tropics, the young officer was seated on a gun-carriage enjoying the calmness of the scene.

The ship was going steadily through the water, every sail set to catch as much as possible of the westerly breeze, and the middy, as he looked from time to time at the pyramid of white canvas, softly whistled for the wind to rise, for they were now near the latitude where the cover of the sealed packet was to be opened, and the destination of the vessel to be announced.

In the midst of a prolonged note, Jack was not a little startled by Riley McGowan coming to his side, and, in a frightened whisper saying—

"For the love of heaven, Mr. Rawlings, don't be after that now, its like tempting the old one to do us a mortal mischief."

"What's the matter, McGowan? Surely you are not so foolish as to believe the silly yarns of your messmates."

Riley shook his head gravely as he answered,

"It's neither here nor there what I believe, sir, but there's one thing, maybe, not even yourself, asking your honour's pardon, but believes in."

"And what's that one thing, Riley?"

McGowan sank his voice to a low whisper as he answered—

"Did ye ever know any good to come to a ship like this one, your honour?"

"What is the matter with the ship, Riley?—she is strong, well armed and well manned."

"That's not what I mean, your honour."

"What do you mean, then?"

"It's the letter, Mister Rawlings, that big thief of a letter, with a seal like a plaster."

"You have seen it, Riley."

"Faith, yes, bad luck to the hour my eye first saw it on the captain's table, for it's not a minute's rest I've had since then."

Jack Rawlings laughed at the seaman's weakness, and Riley McGowan continued—

"You may laugh, sir, but the devil a word of a lie in what I am going to tell you, and it's this—that big letter has set upon my chest ever since I saw it."

"Sat upon your chest?"

"That's it, your honour; it's when I've been asleep it's done the same, and like a big weight it's stuck there, and the devil a finger will I even move."

"You've had the nightmare, Riley," said Jack, "through eating too many of the good things left in the mess."

"Saving your presence, sir," said the seaman, "it's but little the young gentlemen leave for Riley or anybody else to eat after dinner. It's hungry enough they are at all times, and more hungry when there's little to be got besides the regular allowance."

"Well, Riley," said Jack Rawlings, "the mystery of the sealed packet will soon be over, for we are near the latitude where the seal is to be broken."

"Bedad! an' I thought so," said McGowan; "that's the very thing that we all said before Teddy Billimore saw the ghost in the chains."

"What the devil next?" exclaimed Jack. "You must all be mad."

"'Tis true, every word, you know, about th ghost, for Teddy's seen it more than once, and the first time it was white, and had a red letter in its hands. The next time it was black, and the letter was all on fire like, and when Teddy, who was a bit afraid, called out to it, the ghost grins at him, shakes the letter, and tumbles head over tip in the water, and with a fizz just like as though the ghost had been a big cinder —a big, red hot cinder you know that had been thrown into the water."

"You can tell Teddy," said Jack, "if he sees any more ghosts his grog will be stopped for a month."

The ship's bell pealed out merrily across the silent sea, and the time for the middle watch to be relieved having arrived, the bo'sen's shrill whistle was soon followed by the usual—

"Tumble up there, ye skulking lubbers—tumble up."

Early the next morning the captain of the gun-brig was busy looking over the sailing orders, and finding out the vessel's position on the chart.

A sigh of relief escaped him when he arose from the table, and putting the papers in a locker, he said—

"Within twenty-four hours the sealed packet will be opened, unless the Ariadne has left these waters in pursuit of the lawless vessel."

He went on deck, and gave orders to the men on the foretop to keep a sharp look-out for a sail.

The captain expected a sail. The news soon reached the crew, and the most unmanageable skulkers came up from below to aid in discovering the vessel.

Teddy, the ghost-seer, was in the centre of a knot of messmates, and they were asking him to again relate the spirit's visit, in order that they might ascertain whether the coming of the stranger had anything to do with the visits from the land of shadows.

Teddy made no reply. He shifted his quid to the left side of his mouth, and merely shook his head in a most mysterious manner.

He had nothing to say beyond the event

NEARING THE PIRATES' ISLE.

already given, and this he would not repeat in consequence of the stoppage of his grog, for Riley McGowan took especial care to inform him of this description of spirits caused from the effects of spirits of another kind.

The mysterious shake of the head had more effect upon the crew than a dozen yarns, and they explained to each other that their mess-mate had seen such awful things, too bad to be repeated.

"Most likely," says one. "Teddy knows that the vessel the captain expects is not a ship after all, only the ghost of one."

"May be," says another, "The Flying Dutchman himself. Who knows?"

"Sail ahead," sung out the man on the fore-top, "a sail ahead."

The tiny speck soon enlarged, and it was seen there was something supernatural in her appearance, for no vessel built by mortal hands could travel so fast through the water.

Besides there was an unnatural whiteness about her sails, and many went so far as to declare they could see through the ghostly canvas the sea and sky in the stranger's wake.

The vessel, when near enough, hoisted the

British flag, then a private signal, and Jack Rawlings, who stood at the signal-locker, in obedience to his captain's orders sent up a blue and white flag, the one being a black stripe upon a white field.

The stripes answered with similar flags, and the Captain of the Albatross, walking to the poop, said to his officers—

"This is the Ariadne."

Great was the strength of the fears occasioned by the tars who had seen so much that was unreal in that stranger's appearance, and Teddy Billimore made a great impression upon his messmates by saying—

"I told you I never let my jaw tackle loose unless there's nothing to do better. I know this night was something of the sort that you chaps were talking about; but if I'd have told you so you wouldn't have believed a word of it, so you see I let you have your own way."

Saying this, Teddy went to the forecastle, and his messmates believed in him more than ever, but for the grog question, and inexperience he would have that day lost his fame, for he would have seen more in the appearance of the Ariadne than the most superstitious of his messmates.

The vessels' yards were swung fore and aft, and the hulls were straining before the waters, then a boat dropped from the stranger's side, and the flashing of steel in the sunlight told them on board the Albatross the marines were presenting arms to their captain as he passed on his way to the boat.

Two lieutenants and several officers of inferior rank accompanied the captain of the Ariadne to the Albatross, and when they came aboard, Jack Rawlings was told to pass the word for the whole of the gun-brig's officers to assemble in the captain's cabin.

Here after a complimentary greeting between the two commanders, the captain of the Albatross looked round, and awaiting till his officers were present took up the sealed packet, and said,

"This packet I received when we were about to sail, and the directions on the cover will explain why I signalled for the officers of the Ariadne to come aboard."

He paused a moment to arrest his hearers' attention, then read these words—

"For the commander of H.B.M. gun-brig the Albatross, the seal of this packet is not to be broken until the Albatross reaches the latitude marked on the printed sailing orders, and then only in the presence of the officers of H.B.M. corvette the Ariadne, until thirty clear days shall elapse from the day on which the Albatross reaches the latitude marked in the

printed sailing orders, then the commander of the Albatross will break the seal and act upon the orders contained therein."

"So far, gentlemen," said the commander of the Albatross, "I have been able to obey the orders of the secret department, now I will carry out the order of those we serve."

As he spoke, he broke the seal, and there was a hushed whisper of expectation, and the younger portion of the assembly craned their necks forward, as though expecting to behold something very mysterious jump out of the packet.

"Enclosure No. 1," said the Captain, opening a paper and reading the following sentence—

"You will ascertain from the officers of the Ariadne (should you meet with that vessel) whether they have succeeded in descrying a vessel so long known to our mercantile navy as the Phantom Pirate. Should you not fall in with the Ariadne open enclosure marked No. 2."

"As I have fallen in with the Ariadne," said the Captain, I shall be glad to learn whether her officers have succeeded in descrying the Phantom Pirate whoever he may be."

CHAPTER III.

A MYSTERY.

THERE was a few minutes' silence before the Captain of the Ariadne spoke, and during this brief space of time his officers looked from one to the other in a strange manner.

"What the vessel and crew known as the Phantom Pirate is," said the Captain of the Ariadne, "has been our object for the last two years and a half to discover. But up to the present moment we are as wise as the first day we came upon this service."

The Commander of the Albatross raised his eyes to the speaker's face, as he asked—

"Have you seen the vessel?"

"Yes," was the startling answer; "it has passed by us in the glare of the noon-day sun, in the shadow of the closing day, and in the darkness of night—passed like a real phantom, not a single evidence of the manner in which her sails were worked—and disappeared as suddenly as she came upon us."

The isolated life led by a seaman makes his mind prone to receive suspicions of the supernatural. The boy, going to sea for the first time, hears nothing scarcely during his earliest watches but the tough yarns spun by the seamen of the watch; and out of any of these stories it may be safely estimated that one of two has something supernatural about it.

These early impressions are never thoroughly

eradicated; hence it was that the officers of the Albatross were so impressed by the Commander of the Ariadne's words.

"You have given chase, then to this vessel," the Captain of the Albatross said, "and fired into her?"

"Yes," was the reply, "I have done both, and followed her as near the island as I dared, consistent with the safety of my vessel and crew."

The Captain of the Albatross looked up for an explanation of these words, and the look being interpreted, the Commander of the Ariadne said:

"You will better understand the nature of the case when I explain to you the position of the island, which is called the Pirate's Isle. It is the largest of a collection of islands that seem to me rising out of the depths of the sea."

The Captain of the Albatross placed his finger upon a red mark that stood prominently out on a sheet that lay upon the table.

"These," he said, are the islands at present."

"Yes," answered the Captain of the Ariadne, "and these blue lines mark, or are intended to mark, the circle of sunken reefs that surround the island, but they are not sufficiently indicative of the extent of the danger that menaces a ship attempting to near the isle."

"Yet the vessel that bears such a public reputation finds a passage through the reefs."

"The ship sails on, but that shadowy resemblance of one passes through the white foam, no matter to what part of the island we have followed her. This I have remarked fifty times at the very least, and never has the phantom bark deviated one point out of her way when we have been compelled to sheer off to prevent striking upon the reefs."

"When," the Captain of the Ariadne asked, "is it the strange sloop disappears?"

"Directly we clear the reefs, and when we expected to behold her wreck, she is gone, vanished utterly."

"There is no inlet you think in which the fellow can run."

"None whatever."

"Have you ever tried to approach the island and take soundings with the boats?"

"I have to leave the latter, and the vessel we tried and failed; there was not an opening sufficient to admit the passage of even a small boat. Once," added the Captain, bitterly, "eight volunteers, led by a hot-headed midshipman, left the vessel when we were at anchor, determined to discover the mystery of the pirates' disguise, and neither men nor boat have have been heard of since."

"Had the Phantom perceived you long before the event?"

"Not very long, and we had fired not only cold but red-hot shot into the hull as it skimmed over the white foam and the reefs beneath."

"This is a strange story," said the Commander of the Albatross. "One more question and I have done. Have you ever seen the vessel leave the island."

"Never."

Here was a pause. The story had taken more effect upon the seamen's minds than they cared even to admit to their messmates.

"There is a report among the sailors," the Captain of the Ariadne said, breaking the silence, "that I should not mention where those gentlemen as well as myself have found its truth by experience."

The officer paused, as though loth to proceed; but the Commander of the Albatross said, "pray continue and do not conceal anything from us."

"I will not. When we have edged in as much as we dared to the island, and just after the phantom ship had disappeared, there was upon every seaman's oar a strong smell of sulphur. This, as you may be well assured, did not tend to lessen the horror our men had of meeting or seeing the phantom pirate."

"I can quite understand that," said the Captain of the Albatross, "and I think, gentlemen, it will be as well the crew are kept in ignorance of these strange details."

It would have been as well; but, unfortunately, Riley McGowan was in the next cabin, his ear glued to the wainscot, and his hair standing bolt upright, while his knees knocked together and kept time to the chattering of his teeth.

"Mother of Moses!" gasped Riley. "It's the devil's craft, and when Old Nick drags it down to —— oh, Lord!—the brimstone comes up, and strong smells the nasty stuff. Bad luck to the day you came aboard the Albatross, Riley McGowan, for it's the last time you've seen sweet Kilkenny."

Unconscious of the close proximity of Riley McGowan, the Commander of the Albatross sent one of the midshipmen to prevent the men in the Ariadne from holding any conversation with the crew.

The second enclosure was then taken from the packet and read. Its contents were very brief:

"Should you meet the Ariadne," it began, "you will find, in enclosure No. 3, full instructions as to your duties until the pirate is captured, or a vessel sent out from England relieves you. The secret department wishes you to understand the reason of these conditions that have been passed to keep your destination from being known has been to prevent the pirate from gaining any intelligence that a fresh vessel has been sent to capture or destroy him."

The next enclosure was the order for the Ariadne to return to England, and when the Captain of the corvette heard the welcome news he could not restrain his joy at being relieved from an unpleasant duty.

The Ariadne left the gun-brig soon after that, and the Captain, when he took his leave, said—

"I hope you will be more successful than we have been in solving this mystery."

"I hope so," was the reply; "but I fear not, for there is something more terrible to fight against, as far as the men are concerned, than an ordinary foe."

"So I have found it, for I truly believe my crew would sooner face a three-decker, than spread a sail to overtake this mysterious ship."

The officers shook hands and parted, and the Captain of the Albatross returned to his cabin, to make himself master of the contents of the yet unopened papers.

The orders were explicit : the pirate was really a mortal, and not a phantom as the mystery that attended her movements would lead even the strongest mind to infer. She was not to be fired upon by the gun-brig upon the first meeting of the two vessels.

The man-of-war was to assume the appearance of a trading vessel, and so lure the pirate to her side, then the Captain of the Albatross was either to sink or capture the mysterious foe.

Appended to this enclosure was a notification that a reward of one thousand pounds would be distributed among the officers and crew of the Albatross upon that vessel's return to England with proofs of her success.

When the Ariadne was hull down on the homeward passage, the crew of the Albatross were mustered and addressed by their captain.

"My lads," he said, "we are entrusted with a very important duty by the Lords of the Admiralty, and in a few brief words I will explain their views."

There was a slight shuffling of feet and murmuring as the seamen eagerly listened to the important revelation.

"I've spoken to-day to the officers of a vessel," he said, "who have been for two years and a half over these waters trying to capture a pirate ship. They have failed, and the Lords of the Admiralty, well knowing the stuff the crew of the Albatross are made of, have sent us to do in a week what the other ships now have been unable to do in two years and a half."

Here was a sop for Jack, or should I say Jacks, and they liked it, for they gave three cheers for the gun-brig, three for the captain, and six for pirates.

"That's it, my lads," said the captain; "that's the sort of sound I shall soon hear when we are abeam of the unruly pirates."

"Bravo."

"Well, my lads, the Lords of the Admiralty have been pleased to order a distribution of one thousand pounds amongst us when we return to England after capturing the vessel; so splice the main-brace and pray for the coming of the enemy.

Jack was nothing loth to do the main-brace business, which means pouring grog down his throat, but when they heard from Riley Mc Gowan the sort of enemy they had to encounter, and Riley did not lessen the horrors, you may be sure, the sailors did anything but pray for the appearance of the foe; in fact, if the truth must be known, they were in an awful stew.

It was near the evening when the Albatross came in sight of the cluster of islands—the largest of which was the residence of the Phantom Pirate.

The men and officers scanned the waves of white foam that played over the sunken reefs and those most learned in the matter of navigation declared it was utterly impossible for their boat to find an entrance through the reefs.

While this matter was being discussed the look-out suddenly startled all hands by the intimation that a sail was in sight.

"To your quarters, men," said the captain, "and keep from the enemy's view."

The vessel anchored under the bulwarks ; as the vessel approached, and when she became near enough to obtain a good view of her hull and masts, the officers saw she was a corvette.

There was something ghostly in the appearance of the stranger, as she bore rapidly down upon the island, and seemingly without being conscious of the presence of the gun-brig, for her course was such that she must cross within a fathom of the Albatross's bows. Riley McGowan was intently watching the stranger, and as she came near he yelled out—

"By the great men of Munster it's the divil's ship, for there's not a bit of a foam in her wake."

So it was—the corvette glided through the water without the least spray under her cutwater, or the faintest ripple in her wake.

The effect was magical. The men, who would have faced a battery loaded with grapeshot, ran like frightened hares and hid themselves below, and their pace was accelerated by Riley shouting—

"Do you smell the brimstone bags?"

There was no mistake about the sulphurous fume that was wafted across towards the ship; and even the officers, whose education made them less superstitious than the men, turned pale.

The cause of all this commotion kept strictly on her way; and when gliding across the gun-brig's bows, Jack Rawlings, seized by a sudden frenzy gripped the spokes of the elevated wheel, and passing it down, said—

"Man or devil, I'll run him down!"

The wind was dead aloft, and the gun-brig shot forward, and, in obedience to her helm, the bowsprit came opposite the stranger's elevated side.

Then—and every man who saw it shivered from head to foot—the brig passed through the shadowy outlines of the phantom ship.*

Clean through her bulwarks, decks, masts, and sails, and emerged at the other side, and the corvette kept on her over the sunken reefs, and disappeared when close to the shore.

The spokes of the wheels dropped from the midshipman's hands, and, with a moan of terror, he fell to the deck.

CHAPTER IV.

ON THE ISLAND.

WHEN the spectral ship melted away there arose a suppressed cry of terror from the horror-stricken seamen—not a man was able to turn his eyes from the spot where the shadowy outlines of a graceful vessel had disappeared.

The officers were, for a time, as completely terror-stricken as the men—their faces were as blanched, their lips as much apart, and their faculties as spellbound as those whose minds were so much inferior in intellect.

No one stirred to raise Jack Rawlings from the deck, and he lay like one who had been cut down by the Great Destroyer's scythe, his face of an ashen hue, his eyes firmly closed, and his limbs huddled in a heap at the foot of the wheel.

And, during that awful pause, the ship went on her way. The wind kept her sails taut, and her rudder, swinging to and fro, as the prow of the vessel fell off or stood in nearer to the isle, from which came the strong evidence of a sulphurous taint, pervading the strange and awful spot of land.

The ship was running with her head towards the reefs. She was not more than a hundred

* This seeming impossibility is an actual fact, as will be proved in the course of this story. Critics will please defer their remarks until the mystery is explained.

fathoms from where the wavelets ebbed and flowed over the jagged tops of the terrible reef that threatened to rend the stout planking, and send so many brave men to their grave.

It seemed impossible they could escape, for none knew, or seemed to know, of the danger, until the captain, by a mighty exertion of will over mind, sprang to the poop, and aroused the dormant faculties of the crew.

"To your stations!" he cried. His voice, breaking the solemn silence, caused the men to start into wakefulness. "To your stations, every man! We have not a moment to lose. If we are to save the ship from the reefs, all hands wear ship."

The captain seized the spokes of the wheel as he gave the necessary words of command to carry out the evolution.

It was a narrow escape from certain destruction, and the captain's coolness and presence of mind in keeping the movements of the rudder in unison with the power of the wind as the sails were shifted, did much to save the Albatross from being a wreck.

Once clear of the reefs, there was time to attend upon Jack Rawlings, and he was carried below by the big Irishman, who lamented as he went down the companion-way over the hard fate that had caused him to leave sweet Kilkenny to serve on board a brig that was sent to chase ghostly vessels and demon crews.

The surgeon saw Jack, and to Riley McGowan's anxious inquiries, he answered—

"Mr. Rawlings is merely prostrated from excessive excitement. He will soon be well."

Riley sat by Jack's cot until the young gentleman opened his eyes, and with a shiver, asked,

"Has it gone?"

"Gone?" said Riley; "faith, it went away long since—bad luck to the devil's ship and his island too."

Jack sat up, and, looking at the seamen, said—

"Don't be a fool, Riley McGowan."

"Faith thin, Misther Rawlings, it's nothing else we all are but fools, or we should not be here."

"Where are we?"

"In sight of the beastly place, Misther Rawlings. God speed the day when we have to go away from it."

"Riley," said Jack, "didn't I drive our vessel through the pirate?"

"Faith, you did, sir, every inch through; but if I may be so bold as to speak—

"Go on."

"I should say," continued Riley, "that

you made the old fellow angry for doing the same."

"What old fellow, Riley?"

"The old one, to be sure, sir; for there was a smell of brimstone after that would have choked a black man."

"Nonsense."

"Faith, Misther Rawlings, it's nothing of the sort, for all hands, up to the captain, have been nearly choked by the smell."

"It's your fancy, Riley."

"Was it your fancy, Mister Rawlings, that made you tumble all of a lump on the deck when ye drove the ship through the devil's craft?"

Jack Rawlings was silent, and Riley McGowan chuckled inwardly at having so completely caught the young officer on the hip.

"I don't want to offend you, sir," McGowan continued, "but it's certain I am that you think the same as everybody else does about this business."

"Pray what does everybody else think?"

"That the old devil himself is at the bottom of the mischief, and he's only waiting to get a hold of some of us, and carry us to the place where the brimstone is burning."

"You are wrong this time, Riley."

"Well then, if I may be so bold, what does your honour think about it?"

"I scarcely know yet," said Jack; "but of one thing I am certain—that is, the ship's company are all wrong in their opinion."

Riley shook his head very gravely.

"Well, Mr. Rawlings," he said; "that we have all seen the ghost of a ship, and felt the brimstone nearly choking us is true enough—is it not?"

"Yes—well."

"If," continued Riley, "your honour can tell me that everything is right after we have done all, then it's glad enough I shall be to hear it."

"I cannot exclaim the cause of these strange things, Riley; but of one thing I am certain—that is, that we are the victims of a clever trick concocted by the rascally pirate."

"Riley McGowan!" yelled one of the middies from the top of the companion way. "Riley, you ——"

"All right, Mr. Simpson. It's here I am, and not a bit deaf."

"Come here then."

"It's coming I am as hard as I can."

"Look here, Riley," the middy said, when he caught sight of the caterer, "where's my dinner?"

"Your what, sir?"

"My dinner."

"Devil a know I know. Haven't you had it?"

"How could I have it when I was stuck up in the foretop?"

"I served out the full allowance," said Riley, dolefully, "and the young gentlemen must have eaten it. By the powers, there's nothing stops the appetite of the young gentlemen—no, not if Old Nick himself was sitting on the spanker boom and all his imps dancing round him, would it take the appetite from their stomachs."

"Well," roared the hungry middy, "am I to starve?"

"Shure, I'll go and see," said Riley; "but it's little there'll be left I'm thinking."

Those who are acquainted with a midshipman's mess will easily understand the row that followed between the caterer and the hungry boy.

"I'll report you to the captain,' said the middy; "upon my soul, I will."

"Faith," that won't bring the dinner back," remarked Riley. "Besides, it was yourself that helped to eat the mess of the young gentlemen whose turn it was on deck."

"When did I do so?"

"The day before yesterday that ever was," said Riley: "so what's the use of blowing up poor McGowan who can't help it; it's glad I shall be, when the caterer gets well, for it's worried to death I am by the young gentlemen."

The dinnerless middy went on deck grumbling, and Riley McGowan disappeared in the gun-room regions.

Jack Rawlings lay in his cot, pondering over the strange scene in which he had been a principal performer.

There was a peculiar look upon the youth's face when he had well reflected over the matter.

An expression of mingled enthusiasm and dread, and from his lips fell the words—

"I'll do it, no matter what the consequence may be."

He left his hammock and went on deck, and observed the captain, who stood with folded arms and gloomy brow. Jack Rawlings approached his superior, and respectfully touching his cap, said—

"I have an offer to make, sir, that if acceded to will. I believe, do much to clear up the mystery that environs the island."

"An offer, Mr. Rawlings?"

"Yes, sir," answered Jack; "it is my intention to visit the shore, and endeavour to solve the cause of the pirate's disappearance."

The captain paced slowly to and fro for a

few minutes, then, facing the midshipman, said—

"I accept your offer, Mr. Rawlings, if you can obtain several volunteers to make the venture reasonably safe."

"Half-a-dozen men, sir," said Jack, "will be quite sufficient. Have I your permission to go for'ard and try to obtain the number?"

"You have."

Jack went to the forecastle, and meeting the boatswain on his way told him to rouse up the seamen for some duty on deck.

"Mr. Giles," said Jack, "will you tell the men I want a few volunteers to accompany me to the island?"

The boatswain looked at the young officer, then at the deck, and exclaimed—

"Surely, sir, you would not fly in the face of the devil and all his imps?"

"I would discover that gentleman's tricks," said Jack, "and if I don't obtain any volunteers I will go without."

The old boatswain went on his way muttering something about not being able to put old heads on young shoulders.

"Look here, my lads," he said, when the majority of the men had "roused up," and made their appearance on deck, "Mr. Rawlings is going on a visit to the island, and he wants a few hands to go with him."

There was not a man courageous enough to step forward. Had there been a battery to storm or a vessel to be cut out from under an enemy's batteries, there would have been no lack of volunteers.

But a visit to the devil's dominions was too much for the tars' nerves, and there was not a single response to the motion.

"Bless my eyes!" said the boatswain, "you don't mean to say there is not enough men to be got out of a ship's company to go with a midshipman upon any expedition—no matter if it was to drink a can of grog with the devil."

There was a hitching up of trousers, and a turning of quids, but no mortal assented to accompany Jack upon his venture.

"Well," said old Giles, twirling his red hair about with his horny hand, "I am blessed if I a'nt ashamed of you, that I am, when I think that a young fellow with not a hair on his face is plucky enough to go ashore on that ere island, and not a man, and you are all full-grown men, with big whiskers."

"Haul in the slack a bit," said an old tar, "and just tell me how it is you don't go with Mr. Rawlings to the island."

The bo'sen was taken aback for a moment,

and when he recovered he gave the old tar a bit of his mind, thus—

"Ben," he said, "you are a seaman and know what's what; I am surprised at you;" then he paused in his answer, "why, bless your eyes, how the deuce do you think the ship could go on without me?"

"I'd volunteer to do your duty," said the old sailor, "if you particularly wish to go ashore."

"You are a blessed lot of longshore lubbers, and not worth a—bless."

When the old seaman wound up he gave a shrill call upon his whistle, and at its conclusion said—

"Be smart, or by the Lord Harry, I will try what a rope's end will do."

"Stay, Mr. Giles," said Jack Rawlings, coming forward, "I will address the men, and explain more clearly my object in wishing to go ashore."

"Very well, sir," said old Giles, "but I'm afraid you'll find them just what I've said they are."

Jack Rawlings smiled at the old fellow's words, then turned to the seamen and said—

"Look here, my lads," I am going ashore on the Pirate's Isle, and I want half-a-dozen of you to accompany me, what do you say?"

"Well, sir," said the old salt, "if you ask me or any of the lads to go and scale the rock of Gibraltar, if so be the rock was in the Frencher's roads. Why damn me! we'll do it, but to go ashore where the place is kept by the old one himself we can't be expected to volunteer."

"But my good men——"

"I know what you say sir, sir. You'll say the old one is not there, but asking your pardon, I say he is, or else there would not be such a smell of brimstone—oh, lord!" Then while speaking it, there was a puff came, bringing more than would fill the sails of a seventy-four.

The breeze was blowing from the direction of the Pirate's Isle, and even Jack Rawlings was compelled to admit the fact of a strong smell of sulphur escaping it.

Well, my lads," said Jack, rather disappointed at the result of his appeal, "I suppose I must go myself."

"Bedad an' you won't," said the well-known voice of Riley McGowan, "if there is not another man that will go I will, whenever your honour's ready."

"Riley," said Jack, "you are the last man I should have expected."

"Well, sir," said Riley, "it's the honour of the ship I am thinking on merely, for I wouldn't be able to walk down the old street in Kilkenny with the name of our craft forenent my cap and feeling that there once a time when not a man would volunteer to go away from the ship with our young officer."

" I'll make another," said a curly-headed main-top man, stepping out, " now then boys don't all speak at once."

The couple were followed by five more men, and Jack said—

" We shall now muster seven, which will be as many as I require. Come below, Riley, and help me to get my traps ready to go ashore."

Riley McGowan went below, and while cleaning Jack's pistols, soliloquised—

" It's a fool I know I am for going, but I couldn't see Mr. Rawlings go by himself; besides it's tired enough I am of being caterer for the men ; there's no satisfaction—it's ' Riley, you thief of the world,' from one ; ' Riley, you greedy brute,' it's from another ; then if I go down at night there's a lot of them turn at me —yes, I'll go, if it was only to get out of the job of feeding a lot of hungry—yes, Mr. Rawlings, I'm coming in a minute."

" Look sharp," said Jack, " the boat is ready."

The ship was about a mile from the island, when the party of adventurers put off from her side, and by the time they had pulled to the outer line of surf the sun had begun to set.

Jack stood in the bow, giving the rowers directions, when and how to pull, and after striking on the tops of the sunken reefs for several times, they reached a clear expanse of water.

A moment's survey told the young seaman, that he might expect to find the island smoother by this inner circle of deep water, and putting to the yellow beach, he said—

" Pull, my lads, we shall be safely ashore in a few minutes."

The boy's voice and manner, and the love of a change from the dull monotony of ship board, caused the men to pull as willingly to the shore as they had been unwilling to leave the ship.

CHAPTER V.

A DISCOVERY.

JACK RAWLINGS ran eagerly up the sloping beach, followed by Riley McGowan and the ship's crew.

They reached a rocky eminence, and took a survey of the terrible island, and a strange place it seemed to the seamen.

The beach was covered with shell-fish, and near the margin of the sea were several un-wieldly-looking turtles digging at the yielding sand.

Turning their eyes inland, the seamen beheld huge masses of rugged rock, which seemed to frown grimly upon the silent party.

Scarcely a tree or shrub was visible. No drooping tropical foliage gladdened the eye—all was black and sterile, even under the red glow of the scorching sun.

" There does not seem much here to invite anyone to prolong their stay," said Jack Rawlings ; " so the sooner we explore the rocks the better."

They moved inland, Riley McGowan in front, and having reached a point where a cleft in the gigantic masses of rock revealed a portion of the interior of the isle, Riley gave a howl of terror and rushed back to his companions.

" By the great man of Munster," said Riley, " it's destroyed we shall be if we go a step further !"

" What's the matter, McGowan ?"

" Matter, Misther Rawlings ! Look between the hole in the rock, and it's little cause you'll have to ask what's the matter."

Jack's eyes followed the direction of the sailor's extended hand, and saw several colum of light-coloured smoke issuing from ground.

" There's nothing to be afraid of, Riley," he said. " This is what is termed a volcanic island."

" A what, Mr. Rawlings ?"

" A volcanic island."

" And what's that ?"

" Oh," said Jack, trying to be as explicit as possible, " there's a fire under the ground."

" Bedad, an' a big one too," said Riley, hanging back ; " and plenty of little devils I'll be bound to keep the fire a-going."

" Well, we'll keep out of the way of the fire," the young officer said. " This way, my lads, up this rock."

The mass of stone was nearly perpendicular, but to the sailors the task of ascending was one of comparative ease.

Jack stood upon the summit for several minutes, and looked around for something to guide him in his search for the pirates' cave, for he felt sure there was such a place on the island.

The second search was as unprofitable as the first had been. There was no sign of the island having been trodden by the foot of men—no dilapidated remains of a hut, no appearance of anything human excepting themselves.

The tameness of the birds and the few animals that were noticed as they neared the coast

JACK RAWLINGS AND THE MASTER-AT-ARMS DISCOVER RILEY M'GOWAN ALONE IN HIS GLORY.

were in themselves a conclusive proof that the lower creation had not been taught to fear the presence of man.

Looking over towards the centre of the island, Jack Rawlings saw on the summit of a huge rock something that bore a slight resemblance to a flag.

He strained his eyes to make out what it was, and Riley McGowan, who was watching the young officer's face, asked—

"What is it, sir, that you are looking at?"

Jack pointed to the distant object, and exclaimed—

"I can scarcely give it a name, Riley, for when the sun was upon the rock the object that is above it looked not unlike a white flag."

Riley took an attentive survey as he said—

"Well, so it may be as you say, sir, a flag, but to my mind it's a power too stiff!"

Jack soon saw the truth of Riley's words: the distant object, although not a portion of the rock above which it stood gleamed out under the sun's rays, lay not in folds, as would have been the case had it been a flag.

It was perfectly slanting, and to all appearance the pole, which Jack had mistaken for a flagstaff, was much thicker than is usually used for the purpose.

2

"What is it?" asked the sailors, and Riley said—

"The Lord knows ; but anyhow, the best way would be for us to go and see."

"Yes," said Jack ; " there is yet a couple of hours before the twilight sets in ; let us go and see."

They gave the column of smoke a wide berth when crossing the island, and Riley, as though he expected to see a legion of demons suddenly approach, warded them off by muttering—

"It's but little time to say my prayers since I've been aboard the Albatross. On the run it is I've forgotten them ; but if I once get safe away from this place, I will not forget to say them every night of my life."

The hill upon which stood the object that had attracted the seamen's attention, stood on the opposite side of the island, and within pistol shot of the white line of foam that marked the margin of the ocean.

The rock at first appeared to be perfectly perpendicular, and for a time even the active seamen stared before they essayed the ascent.

"It's like a cat clinging to the side of a waterbutt," said Riley, " that we shall be, if we try to go up there."

"The ascent," said Jack, " seems very difficult, but as the flagstaff, and whatever it is on the top did not grow there, we shall be quite as able to reach the top as those who "——

"Bedad, here's a way up," said Riley. " See, Mr. Rawlings, these steps have been cut out of the solid stone."

Steps Riley had termed some slight notches in the face of the rock, and the young midshipman, when he had examined the marks, said—

"This is the work of man, and these holes have been cut out with an instrument made for the purpose."

There was but little need for this explanation, for the most unskilful eye could detect the cutting of the steps had been a thing of time and labour.

That it was the look-out place of the pirates who had so long befouled the English ensign, there was but little doubt, for the rock was the highest on the island, therefore more easily seen from the sea.

"Now, my lads," said Jack, " let us make our minds up to find out that for which we came ashore."

He led the way, and when the summit of the rock was reached, he stood spell-bound until his men came to the top, and Riley McGowan startled him back to life by a scream of horror.

The object they had taken for a flag was an oblong board fastened near the top of a stout spar.

It was the work of a sailor ; that was told by the peculiar way in which the rope was fastened that held the board to its support.

At the foot of the spar was a number of bleached skeletons, the white teeth and eyeless sockets giving a terrible appearance to the skulls.

The whole of the men stood silent for some time, and Jack, shading his eyes from the ghastly remnants of humanity, looked to the oblong board as though expecting to find a clue to the cause of the death of so many men.

The board still bore traces of an inscription having been written upon it, but what that inscription was could not be explained.

The words had not been cut in the board, although several sailors' knives lay heaped with the skeletons.

They could not have used paint, for it was impossible to obtain that article in such an out-of-the-way spot.

What could the letters have been written with ? The defaced inscription was of a strange colour, and Riley, whose hair stood bolt upright with fear, came near the post, and, after a brief survey, said—

"The ink that has been used was blood, the pen a man's finger, and no blessed mistake about that, Mr. Rawlings."

"I am of your opinion Riley," said Jack, " also, that if we could read this inscription it would explain the appearance of these skeletons here."

"Faith it would, so let us try."

They did so, but the wind, rain, and the sun had left nothing but the following letters visible :—

```
C  E   L    R     R
L  LE     NO      P
L  P   M   HIP    A
   PC  D          M
L   R   ALL       E
    G     T    E
```

Nothing intelligible could be gleaned from the remains of the inscription, although Jack and every man tried to do so, each man reading in his own way, and but adding to the confusion.

"We can't make anything of this," said the midshipman, " and as it is too late to make any further search, we will return to the ship and come ashore to-morrow."

The seamen slowly descended the rock, Jack and Riley McGowan in rear, and, in consequence of the irregular formation of the ground, hidden from their companions.

They stood near the foot of the rock, when

the earth seemed to suddenly open beneath Jack Rawlings and Riley's feet, and with one wild cry, and a piteous clutch at the air, the young officer and his companion closed as it were into the bowels of the earth.

CHAPTER VI.

WHAT THE CAPTAIN HEARD WHEN THE BOAT'S CREW RETURNED.

JACK STUBBS, a sturdy, athletic foremast man, was the most prominent in declaring his belief, that the pirate of the island was a bloodthirsty miscreant, who was fully able and willing to exterminate them all.

Brave as any lion when any physical danger was to be met, the sailor was as timid as a child at the least mention of anything supernatural. No story of ghosts or demons could find a more credulous listener than Jack Stubbs.

"Look'ee here, mates," he said to his five companions, who had drawn a little ahead of the midshipman and McGowan, "if this 'ere blessed pirate 'ud only show himself as a man should, I'd grapple and board him in the twinklin' of a rope's end; but d'ye see ——"

Before Stubbs could conclude his speech a cry from behind startled the sailors. It was the voice of Riley McGowan.

"What's the matter now?" said Jack Stubbs, turning as he spoke. "Hullo! Why, where's he gone?"

Well might the foremast man and his comrades have stared, for not a trace of Riley or the young midshipman was to be seen! Nothing but the bare volcanic rock and the stunted undergrowth.

Jack Stubbs's swarthy, sun-burned visage turned a dirty white with fear, and every hair of his thick black beard seemed to bristle up, and separate itself from its companions.

The effect upon the rest of the crew was no less strong—the superstitious awe that had been gradually creeping over them reached its climax, and their belief that the island was haunted by demons fully confirmed.

Jack Stubbs tried to speak, but only succeeded in uttering a long, deep-drawn—

"Oh!"

It was several moments before any of them could either move or speak, so greatly had the sudden disappearance of their comrade and the midshipman affected them.

At length one of them succeeded in whispering, faintly—

"What's to be done now, Jack?"

If Stubbs had had his own way he would have yielded to the dictates of fear, and fled as fa-

as his long legs would carry him to the boat; but he felt that it would not do to leave the island without some effort to discover the fate of Riley and Jack Rawlings.

So, plucking up his courage, and drawing a pistol from his belt, he flourished it in the air, and said in what was intended to be a resolute tone—

"Never desert a comrade, lads; man or devil we'll try and save 'em."

The four sailors inspired by this heroic sentiment, uttered a cheer, a rather faint one, and demanded to be led to the attack.

"Don't you be in a hurry, this must be conducted scientific," said Stubbs, who was by no means in a hurry to lead the van.

"Here you, Bill Boltrope, you go on ahead a bit and see if the coast is clear."

Bill, thus addressed, looked doubtful, and anything but delighted at the honour thrust upon him.

"I think, Jack, as how we'd best go altogether, I likes good companionship myself."

The foremast man turned a look of contempt upon his companion.

"You're in a funk, Bill Boltrope, in a blue funk."

"And what if I am?" retorted the sailor; "there's cause to be, ain't there? 'sides you're frightened yourself every bit as much as me."

"I'd scorn it," returned Jack Stubbs, indignantly. "If I am frightened away, I——"

He checked his speech suddenly, and gazed with dilated horror-stricken eyes upon the ground in front of him, whence issued a jet of pale blue smoke that was suddenly followed by a flash of fire, and a report which shook the ground beneath their feet.

As if actuated by one impulse, the sailors turned and ran with all the speed of terror towards the sea.

It was no longer a question of courage, but only of the longest and strongest legs. It is but justice to say that Jack Stubbs and Bill Boltrope outstripped their companions by several yards.

Down the incline over the rocky ground, their eyes dilated with terror, their ears strained to catch the fancied sounds of pursuit, went the sailors. If any earthly prize had been in question, it is doubtful whether their speed would have been nearly so great. As it was, the distance that separated them from the boat was covered in a very short time.

With the quickness of thought, four seized an oar each, while Jack Stubbs took the helm, and then, urged by the frenzy of fear, the blades dashed into the water, and the boat moved slowly away.

"The Lord be praised," ejaculated the foremast man, fervently, for the first time looking back at the island. "By the bones of my grandmother, I thought we were done for that time."

"Did you smell the sulphur, Jack?" asked Bill Boltrope, as he pulled at his oar with all the strength of his sturdy arms.

"Why, I can smell it here," returned Jack; "but I say, Bill, did you see the demon?"

"No," said Bill, almost catching a crab in the intensity of his astonishment, and driving his head into the stomach of the man behind him. "No, I didn't see the demon—what was it like?" he continued, recovering his seat and his oar.

"Something awful," faid Jack Stubbs, fully believing in the truth of what he said, and again casting a glance at the island. "A tremendous thing, all black, with peepers as big as the cabin deadlights, all flaming red, horns pretty near as long as the jibboom, and a tail like the mainmast. Why you must a seen it, Bill!"

"Well, I think I did see somethin', Jack, but —"

What more the sailor would have said was cut short by a sudden shock, that shook the boat from stem to stern, and threw all the men from the thwarts, Jack Stubbs pitching forward and diving his head into the lower part of Bill Boltrope's guernsey.

Instantly recovering himself, Jack scrambled to his feet, ejaculating—

"Oh Lor, Bill, it's that blessed demon holdin' us; Lord, if you would say a prayer."

"I—I don't remember one, Jack," said the sailor, his teeth chattering with fright, "it's all over, Jack."

For a few moments the superstitious sailors waited in terrified expectancy of seeing some horrible spectre appear, but as the minutes flew by and nothing more happened than an occasional bump of the boat on the rock, which the night had converted into a demon, Bill and his mate took heart, and, in desperation plunging his oars into the water, headed for the brig, which lay lazily rocking to fro upon the waves about a quarter of a mile distant.

For their powerful arms, nerved by terror, the quarter of a mile was soon passed, the heavy boat cutting through the water with the rapidity of lightning.

Stubbs at every touch of the keel against the rocks, by shouts, urged the sailors to renew exertions, though they needed it but little.

The mysterious disappearance of their companions, and the volcanic eruption on the island were quite sufficient to make them desire place a large reach of blue water between the and the demon pirates.

The instant the boat touched the ship quarter, the sailors seized the ropes and scrambled upon deck, where the crew were assembled, eager to learn the adventures which had befallen the in their search.

But they were compelled to defer the gratification of their curiosity, for the captain, who was on the quarter-deck, ordered Jack and his companions aft.

Pale, and not yet recovered from their fright, yet with a full sense of the importance of the news they had to communicate, the sailors approached the presence of their commander scraping their feet, and touching their forelock respectfully.

"Well, my lads," said Captain Cameron "you have soon returned; what have you discovered?"

"Well, sir——" began Bill Boltrope, when Jack Stubbs gave him a violent dig in the ribs with his elbow, indignant at having his claim to priority intruded on.

"Begging your honour's pardon, but I commands the boat, and it's my place to speak."

"You command the boat," repeated the captain; "Mr. Rawlings was in charge—where is he?"

"I was going to tell you, sir," said Jack with another scrape, "if this here swab—always saving your honour's presence—hadn't put his oar in."

"And where is McGowan?" broke in the first lieutenant, who was standing by the captain "he went in the boat with you."

"Yes, sir, but——" said Bill Boltrope, who was again stopped by Jack Stubbs's elbow.

"This here unmannerly lubber won't larn manners, saving your honour's presence. P'raps you'll be kind enough to clap a stopper on his jaw tackle, sir, till I've spun my yarn?"

"Make haste then," said Captain Cameron "and you, Boltrope, be silent until you are wanted."

The foremast man cast a look of triumph at his comrade, and went on.

"Well, d'ye see, your honour, when we managed to clear the reefs and come to an anchor on the beach, d'ye see, we landed, Mr. Rawlings and the rest of us, and looked about a bit to see what the place was like, and a queer looking, Lord-forgotten crib it was, saving your honour's presence."

"Sich a smell of sulphur," murmured Bill Boltrope, unable to suppress his feelings.

Jack resumed. "Well, sir, we cruised about a bit until Mr. Rawlings, who was a bit ahead, he spies what he took to be a flag, and sings out for all hands Well, I runs up."

"I got there first," put in Bill Boltrope.

Jack Stubbs answered with a dig at his comrade, which was adroitly avoided, and the foremast man went on.

"Well, d'ye see, your honour, we made sail for the flag, a bit cautious like, not knowing whether this thundering thief of a pirate, begging your honour's pardon, hadn't meant it for a trap, but when we fetched it, oh! such a sight!"

Jack paused, and drew his breath heavily at the recollection of the horrors he had seen.

Bill and the others joined heartily in a chorus of sighs and groans.

"What was it?" asked the Captain, whose patience was exhausted by the long-winded narrative of the foremast man.

"I'm a coming to it, sir. Well, what we thought was a flag turned out to be a board fixed on a pole dy'e see, and lying round it was a heap o' skeletons."

"A regular mountain," said Bill Boltrope.

The captain and the lieutenant looked gravely at each other, and then motioned Jack Stubbs to proceed.

"Well, d'ye see, your honour, on this board was some writin, at least', so said Mr. Rawlings, for I'm no scholard, saving your honour's presence, and he tried to make it out."

"Did he read it?"

"Ay, that he did, sir, and it said the most awful things."

Bill Boltrope groaned.

"It said that the pirate would murder everybody who went on the island, and he left these skeletons as a warning."

"Are you sure," said the captain, looking doubtfully at the sailor.

"Certain, sir; warn't it, Bill?"

"Ay, that it were," groaned Bill.

"Well, sir, we were coming back to report progress, when, just as we fetched the beach, I hears a cry, looks round, and Mr. Rawlings and McGowan had disappeared clean out of my sight. We was going back to look for 'em, when, all of a sudden, a flash a fire comes out in the earth, and a monstrous devil."

"A what!" said Captain Cameron, angrily, "Be careful what you are saying."

"It's true, your honour, every word.—ain't it, Bill?"

"Every word," said Bill, "I seed it myself."

"That will do," said Captain Cameron sternly. "Do not think to impose upon me by your idle tales. The matter must be looked into. You may go."

Jack Stubbs and his comrades retired crest fallen, but relieved themselves by spinning a most tremendous yarn in the forecastle, while the captain and lieutenant deliberated on the best course to pursue.

The result was, that the gun-brig remained near the island for a few days, and then, finding that there was no trace of the missing men, and that further cross-examination of Stubbs and Boltrope only produced fresh marvels, Captain Cameron hauled up the anchor, and weighed for the nearest station there to report progress, and await for fresh orders from the Admiralty.

CHAPTER VII

IN THE GORILLA'S CAVE.

RILEY McGOWAN was the first to find the bottom of the fissure in the rock, and as he scrambled to his feet, Jack Rawlings, who had clung to a tough shrub for a few seconds, loosened the roots, and fell upon Riley's head, and knocking him, as he expressed it, into the middle of next week.

"Bedad, sir," said Riley as he sat up, "that was a fearful tumble. Bad luck to the deceiving bits of trees that grow over the hole."

"Its lucky we are no worse," said Jack. Had we trodden upon a similar piece higher up the rock we should have been killed before we reached the bottom."

"It's a quare thing how we tumbled through, Mister Rawlings," said Riley, whose mind naturally gave the pirate who owned the island the credit of having laid a trap for their discomfiture, "for we have crossed plenty of places like the one we tumbled through."

"Now, Mr. Riley," said Jack, "you are mistaken; for we could not have trodden upon a similar place, or we should have gone through."

"It's not contradicting you, I'll be, sir; but the old one has had something to do with this, or I'm not Riley McGowan, born and reared in sweet Kilkenny."

"Nature, Riley," said Jack, "is alone responsible for our tumble, so do not fill your head with supernatural rubbish."

"But see," said Riley, "it's——

"I will explain," said the midshipman, "the opening in the rock has been caused by a volcanic eruption, and since then the edges have thrown out sufficient vegetation to hide the fissure, the plants joining a close network, have afforded a resting place for the sand blown down by the wind, and washed off the face of the rock by the rains. This, to our eyes, seemed as firm as any other part of the rock, and we trod upon it. The consequence was, the branches of the shrubs gave way, and we fell through."

"Faith, it may be so," was the doubtful answer. "So the sooner we get upon our pins and find the boat's crew the better, or—murder, here he comes!"

Riley rolled over on his face as a subdued report came upon his ears, and a cloud of sulphurous smoke filled the opening in the rock.

"Don't be a fool, Riley," said Jack, who could not help laughing at his companion's fear, "that's merely a slight eruption that is always occurring in these islands."

"And the brimstone, sir. It's a fool you must take Riley for. No, Mister Rawlings, although you have a power of learning, you can't say it's not brimstone that's smelling enough to choke the devil himself, who is stirring it up."

"Sulphur," said Jack, "almost every schoolboy can explain the cause of these seeming marvels."

"Maybe they can," said Riley, "but it's a long time they'd be in making me believe it."

"It's all over now," said Jack, "so get up."

"Is the brimstone gone?"

"Yes."

Riley scrambled to his feet, and giving a scared look round, asked——"

"How are we to get up again?"

"The very problem I was trying to solve Riley."

"And what's that prob—pro——"

"A puzzle, Riley. I am puzzled about the way we should get up again."

"Queer things," said Riley, "is enough to turn a boy's brain. Then you use queer words that's only used by the quality. Faith, if ever I see Kilkenny again, it's puzzling the schoolmaster himself I should be with my learning."

"Very likely," said Jack, smiling. "Now, Riley, stand up, and I will climb upon your shoulders, and try and reach the top."

The midshipman climbed from Riley's back to his shoulders, and standing erect, endeavoured to reach the top of the fissure.

"It's more than a foot above my hands, Riley," he said, "so we must try another plan."

"Only a foot?" said Riley. "That's not much. Jump down, Mister Rawlings, we'll soon manage that."

Jack leapt lightly to the ground and asked.

"How, Riley?"

"I'll stand on your shoulders, Mister Rawlings."

"What difference will that make?"

"Shure, I'm nearly a foot taller than you, sir, and if I'm atop"—

Jack burst into a hearty fit of laughter, and said—

"Why, Riley, we shall not be any taller by changing places."

"No more we shall, sir," said Riley; "it's not thinking of what I said made me say it."

"Never mind; something must be done, or the men will be on their way to the ship."

"What's the something, sir?"

"We must call out to attract their attention, and stand from under, in case anyone should fall through."

"Bedad, an' I will do that; now then, sir, for a hail," Riley said, and yelled—

"Albatross ahoy—ahoy!"

There was no answer, save the echo, repeating the words in a subdued, strange manner—

"Ahoy—ahoy—oy!"

"Do you hear that, sir?"

"Yes, Riley; that is the echo of your hail, rolling to every hollow of the rock; and by the sound I should think there is a cave not far away."

"Are you shure, sir, it's the echo?"

"Certain; what else do you imagine it is?"

"Maybe the pirate making game of us—maybe the old one laughing at us as he stirs up the brimstone."

"Hail again, Riley, and don't be a fool."

"Albatross, ahoy—ahoy!" yelled Riley; "Albatross, ahoy—ahoy!"

"Ahoy—hoy—hoy!" was repeated from the hollows of the rock.

"Where can the rascals be, Riley?"

"Perhaps, sir, he's got 'em on his fork."

"Riley, you are a jackass."

"May be so, sir; but perhaps you'll tell me where they are."

"In all probability," said Jack, "they have not missed us yet; and when they do, it may be some time before they discover where we disappeared."

"What's to be done, then?"

"Nothing," said Jack, "except to wait patiently until we are found."

"And suppose we are not, sir?"

"We need not suppose anything of the sort, until the time has gone past for all hope"—

"Don't talk like that, Mr. Rawlings; for if the boys don't find us here, it's done for we shall be entirely——"

"Croaking again, Riley?"

"Faith, it's enough to make any one croak, isn't it, sir?"

"Not until we are left without any chance of being rescued, Riley."

"Then," said McGowan, "it will be but little use to croak or any——What's that? Mother of Moses, what's that?"

"What?"

"Didn't you hear it, Misther Rawlings?"

"I did not. What was it like, Riley?"

"Like? well, it was like the voices of three bosuns—all of 'em with bad colds—and grumbling because the sails were not reefed sooner."

"A simile with a vengeance, Riley."

"Was it, sir? I thought maybe it was something more like a wild beast."

Jack Rawlings roared with laughter at his companion's mistake, and the sound of the fresh young voice caused a strange echo.

"By Jove, Riley," said the midshipman, "you are right. There is something growling like three boatswains with bad colds. What is it, I wonder?"

"The Old One," said Riley, really serious, "sure enough; don't you think so, sir?"

"No, I do not, McGowan."

"And why not, sir?"

"Because," said Jack, "the Old One, as you call him, if he were allowed to appear upon the earth, would choose a spot a little more inhabited than this island."

"Faith, that's something likely. Bedad, I think he would. But you said, Misther Rawlings—you said if he we were allowed to appear on the earth, didn't you?"

"I did, Riley."

"Well, sir, isn't he allowed to come upon the earth?"

"Of course not. The old rascal is chained up."

"Chained up is he, sir?"

"Yes, Riley."

McGowan reflected for a moment, and began to feel a little more assured; but suddenly his thoughts took a new direction, and he exclaimed—

"Who's to know, sir, but that he's broken his chain?"

"Even so," said Jack, "it's not likely he would take the trouble to come here just to catch you and me, Riley."

"Why not, sir?"

"Because," said Jack, "he could have us at any time if he felt so disposed, especially you, Riley, he could have."

"And how's that, sir?"

"Because you have not been an honest man lately, Riley."

"What's that, sir? I've not been an honest man?"

"True, Riley. Now, you have been a rogue ever since you became caterer to the gun-room mess."

"Hear that," said Riley. "Why, it's honester than ever I've been in my life I've been since I looked after the young gentlemen's mess! Faith, I should like to know who would be able to get anything out of the young——"

Here Riley paused, for another low growling noise reached the crevice in the rock.

"Hear that?" the midshipman said, enjoying the fun. "The Old One is listening to you, Riley."

Half angry at the young officer's "chaff," half afraid that his words were true, Riley made no answer, but sat listening for the wished-for sound of his messmates' voices.

"It's strange," thought Jack, "the men have not returned. "What can have occurred? Surely they would not return to the ship without us?"

As the time wore on, this thought became unpleasantly suggestive of the truth, and Jack's mind began to take in the wretched prospect of being left upon the sterile volcanic island.

"Riley," he suddenly exclaimed, "exert your lungs, and this time in earnest, or I fear we shall be left behind by your messmates."

Riley needed no second bidding. He jumped to his feet, and shouted—

"Ahoy! ahoy! Messmates, ahoy! It's down a hole we are, and can't get up!"

The cave echoed his words; then the low hoarse growl they had heard before was repeated—this time louder and with an addition that sounded as though the unseen brute, or whatever it was, did not dwell alone.

"Riley," said Jack, "your messmates have deserted us, therefore we must make an effort to save ourselves, or we shall die in this hole."

"Bad luck to them if they have," said Riley, "but anyhow, sir, it's as well that we try to get out of this, in case they have been looking us, and gone to the boat."

"How are we to get out, Riley? We are tall enough to reach the top——"

"You have your dirk, sir; let us cut so steps with it, for the rock is as soft as an o cheese."

The midshipman drew his dirk and thrust the point into the side of the passage, and the thrust, although not given with any force, caused the weapon to pass up to the hilt.

"This is not a part of the

Jack : "it is but a hole filled with the drifted sand. Lend me a hand to clear it away, and we shall soon be able to escape."

They worked with a will, the young officer using his dirk, the sailor his hands, and at the expiration of an hour they had cleared away sufficient of the sand to discover a hole in the rock big enough to allow their bodies to pass through.

They were only half way through the hole yet, so they worked on, and at last the passage was cleared, and, thinking the means of escape was within their reach, Jack clambered through followed by Riley.

Emerging upon what seemed the yellow beach, Jack looked around for the ocean, but to his dismay he beheld a series of arches, and the dark entrance to a number of caves.

"Riley," said the young officer, "we are in a trap ; these caves and the peculiar formation of the rock is the effect of a volcano, and heaven knows how we are to reach the shore."

"It won't do to give up," said Riley. "Maybe there is a way up, and we must try and find it."

"We must," said Jack, bravely struggling against the feeling of despair that had come upon him. "It will never do to give up hope while a chance remains."

Their eager search was met by disappointment at every turn, the low arches the high galleries, from the roofs of which depended fantastic points and jagged ornaments of stone, were like a maze. After an hour's winding in and out, they found themselves in precisely the same spot whence they had started.

The young officer and his companion were worn out by their exertions, so seating themselves on the rocky ground for a few minutes' rest, they talked over the chances that were yet in their favour.

"It wants more than an hour to sunset," said Jack. "If we can reach the beach by that time we shall be all right."

"Then you think the men have gone back to the ship, sir ?"

"I do," said the midshipman. "They, no doubt, missed us; but not knowing the exact spot where we disappeared, and not finding us, returned to the ship."

"It would be a dreadful thing to be left on this place."

"It would, Riley."

Jack rose as he spoke, and the search for some means of reaching the shore began again.

They tried all those places that seemed likely to lead them to the desired spot, but the result was that they were left in what seemed a circular hole in the rock.

The light came in from an aperture about twenty feet from where they stood, and, with the exception of the hole by which they had entered, the place was surrounded by dark cavernous openings.

"We must try those dark holes," said the young officer ; "the light holes have not been productive of much good so far. Perhaps some of them may lead to an upward path."

"I hope so," said Riley. "Let's try this one first, sir."

The sailor pointed to a dark opening on the left of where they stood, and, unsuspicious of the danger of entering these caves, Jack said—

"Very well, Riley ; get on."

They entered the cave, and the interior was so dark that it was impossible to distinguish the extent for some moments.

Riley was the first to ascertain the place was tenanted, and when he did so a shout of terror came from his lips, and with chattering teeth he gasped—

"The Lord help us. There's the Old One smoking his pipe."

Jack ran to his side in a moment, and saw, with beating heart, the cause of Riley's terror.

In the gloomiest part of the cave were three huge beasts, looking larger in the gloom than they really were.

One, designated by Riley as the "old one," was sitting upon his haunches, chewing the end of a thin twig Riley had mistaken for a pipe.

By the left side of the half-human looking brute was his mate ; on the right a young specimen of the tribe, and when Jack's eyes were enabled to make out the hideous group, he said—

"We are in a gorilla's cave."

A couple of bats flew out of the den as he spoke, and a huge snake that had been coiled up in a corner reared its head about and began to hiss at the intruders.

Then, to complete their terror, the gorillas began to growl and show their white, hideous-looking teeth.

CHAPTER VIII.

THE WRECK OF THE ALBATROSS.

Soon after the cluster of islands faded from the view of the look-out on board the gun brig, dark masses of clouds gathered in the sky.

The man mistook the evidence of the gathering tempest for the coming of night. He was unused to the swift tornadoes peculiar to those latitudes, or he would have known there was danger—aye, death—in one moment's delay.

Suddenly the rain fell in large, heavy drops

then came the distant roar of thunder, then a blinding sheet of lightning, and, as the officer of the watch rushed below to acquaint the captain with the sudden change in the weather, the storm burst, and struck the brig.

The officers were on deck in a few moments, but too late to save the gallant barque. Here sails were torn from their fastings, the masts creaked and groaned, the guns broke loose, and dashed from one side to the other, threatening destruction to all who came in their way.

Then the sea lashed with a sudden fury, rose in mighty waves, and one striking the brig on the larboard side, caused her to heel over to such an extent that her yards were under the white-topped waves.

Full twenty fathoms of the raging billows were traversed by the vessel in this manner, and when a giant wave struck her and her masts arose, the wind blew every stitch of canvas into ribbons, and many of the spars were snapped off and carried away.

Amid the tempest's roar and the howling wind there could be heard the cries of the men as they were, one by one, swept into the sea.

On rushed the ship; the darkness of night above the wrathful billows swelling over the decks. On, until a sudden shock caused the hull to shiver from stem to stern; and the waves as though exulting in their terrible work, leaped around, and came in surging masses over her sides.

Then above the howling of the storm came the cry—

"She has struck! she has struck!"

The words passed from mouth to mouth, and the men cowered in deadly fear; the most superstitious amongst them ascribing this misfortune to the evil influence of the Pirates' Isle.

The strong hull stood bravely for some time, then the timbers creaked and groaned, and those who yet clung to life expected every moment that the ship would break into a thousand pieces.

The captain and twelve men were all that remained of the many who had one short hour before peopled the vessel.

And those in such imminent peril that life was not worth one moment's purchase.

Dashing through the blinding spray, Captain Cameron rushed to the side and shouted—

"This way. There must be land close to us. Lower a boat—in a few minutes she will go to pieces."

The sailors had sufficient consciousness left to understand that certain death awaited them when the groaning timbers gave way before the storm, and catching at their captain's words as a means of escaping this doom, they rushed to the side and lowered one of the boats.

The waters were subsiding as they attempted to pull from the vessel's side. Then came a blast of wind, and the boat was thrown up. There was a crash and a cry of hopeless despair as it shivered against the Albatross's dark side; a mingling of fragments of wood, broken oars, and human forms, then all was over. The captain and crew of the brave ship had passed away for ever.

The storm passed away as quickly as it had arisen, and when the morning came, the stricken ship rested peacefully upon the bosom of the rippling waves, and, save for the broken spars and tattered sails, no trace of the late fearful hurricane was visible.

Though the storm-riven vessel was at rest beneath the water line, two points of jagged rock held her as in a vice.

Full a dozen fathoms around the stately hull, their white curling lines of frothy wavelets showed where the deadly reefs lurked.

Within a mile of the broken bowsprit, the barren shore of a volcanic island reared its rocky outlines, and stretching inland could be seen a mass of dark tangled herbage.

And leaning against the shattered stump of the mainmast was the solitary form of the grey-haired master-at-arms, the only survivor of that dreadful gale.

"All gone!" said the old seaman, in a hushed voice. "Can it be possible that I alone have been saved?"

The grey and grizzled veteran, who had gone through many a tempest and well-fought action unnerved, now knelt on the wet decks, and returned thanks for his deliverance from the dangers of the past night.

"I am a sinner," he said, "but in this prayer I am sincere; and, now that I am left, it becomes me to try and ascertain whether all my brave messmates are gone beneath the waves."

He looked towards the shore as he spoke, and in a moment his mind was made up.

"I will explore yon island," he said, "maybe there's one or two of them wrecked ashore, and, though bruised, still alive."

The thought of being alone upon the ocean was dreadful to the old seaman's mind.

"It will be a living death," he said, sadly, "to one who has been so many years used to the companionship of his—— Yes, I must search the island, and should there not be any of my messmates there, I will explore the whole of the isles in these seas. Surely there will be some one to be found who has been cast ashore, if not in the last hurricane, at an earlier time."

With this project before him his heart felt lighter, and became filled with hope; besides, there was the novelty of going from isle to isle, and beholding the wonders of nature.

He knew also that the ship would remain for many months on the reef, that he could always re-visit her, and obtain a supply of food and ammunition.

"Now," he said, hopefully, "to examine the boats, and ascertain which of them is fit for use after last night's terrible storm."

After a careful examination of the longboat, he found it seaworthy, and before the evening he had placed a sail, a half-dozen of rifles, a keg of powder, bag of bullets, and a week's provisions in the stern.

Thus equipped, the old seaman awaited until the sunrise; then alone, and in the full belief that he was working out his destiny, he started upon his lonely voyage.

The sea was as calm as an inland river, and the boat, propelled by a light breeze, glided quickly through the mighty waste of water.

Twice before the night closed in did the intrepid old tar pull his light craft ashore upon two islands.

Each proved like the one he had left, barren and desolate, and still, with the hope of accomplishing the object of his voyage, he drew the boat ashore, and spreading the sails over the sides of the boat, prepared to pass the night.

The first beam of the young day found him once more upon the wide ocean.

Mile upon mile of waters was passed, still no sign of an island that was inhabited rewarded his search.

The exertion consequent upon having the entire management of the boat had thoroughly worn out the brave old sailor's strength, and scarcely had he crept beneath the covering than he fell into a deep sleep.

So far was he lost to all that occurred around him, that the watchful seaman heard not the grating sound caused by a number of canoes striking sharply upon the beach.

Each canoe, as it became stationary, disgorged its freight of savages; and when all were disembarked, they spread themselves around the low-lying coast, and protected only by the skins that hung from their shoulders, threw themselves upon the ground, and save for one whose duty it was to watch over his companions, were soon asleep.

They were a party of savages who had come from an adjacent island to hunt the wild animals.

Unsuspicious of the host of dusky wretches, the old sailor slept on until he was aroused by the canvas being rudely torn from above his head.

Opening his eyes, he beheld to his dismay a crowd of dark faces gathered round the boat, and from their gestures it was plain they were as much astonished at finding the lonely voyager as he was to behold them.

Luckily he had stowed away the rifles and ammunition beneath the loose boards which covered the bottom of the boat, or they might have been captured.

With dire forebodings that his voyage was stayed, he arose to his feet, and before he could leave the boat, a dozen hands were stretched out to grasp his clothes.

Resistance was useless, so the old seaman, calm and defiant, waited, for the death he felt was near.

When every article of clothing had been stripped from him, the savages collected in a group, and held a long conversation respecting their prisoner.

A speedy death he feared not, but from the horribly significant actions of his captors, he knew that they were cannibals, and evidently canvassing the best mode of cooking and eating their prisoner.

This fearful fate bleached the bronzed cheeks of the seaman, whose heart had never quailed before the heaviest broadside or the fiercest storm.

"After beating about all over the world," thought the old sailor, "to come to this. Well, if it is my fate I must die, but, unless I am much mistaken, they will find this old hull anything but tender."

Urged forward by the muscular savages, the old sailor was then compelled to assist in the hunt.

The task soon became arduous, for the sun as it gained power, scorched his flesh, and caused him the most excruciating agony.

From sunrise to nearly sunset the work continued; then the immense heap of game was placed in the longboat, and the prisoner, by signs, was given to understand that he was to hoist the sail and join the canoes.

His heart leaped with joy.

He knew the sailing powers of his boat and as he prepared to leave the island, a wild hope of escape crossed his mind.

Hope that was soon doomed to be dissipated, for a number of the dusky devils, armed with spears, the tops made with sharks' teeth, seated themselves in the boat.

"While there is life there is hope," thought

the master-at-arms; "I am not to be eaten yet, it seems, and if they do not discover the rifles I may yet stand some chance of escape."

Several times during the passage from the island the boat's sail, heavily freighted as she was, had to be taken in to allow the canoes to keep up with her.

This fact gave the sailor infinite joy.

Once on board and the sail spread, he should be able to escape from a fate the bare thought of which caused a cold thrill to run through his veins.

About six hours from their departure from the island the canoes grounded upon a rocky shore.

From the immense masses of stone and its dark colour, the master-at-arms had no difficulty in discovering the latitude into which he had been so unwillingly brought.

When the keels of the vessels touched the shore, the old men, women, and children, belonging to the island tribe rushed to the canoes and the long boat, and began to carry off the produce of the hunt.

The spoil was soon gathered, and the old seaman was left with his grim guardians.

By this time the news was spread that a white man had been captured, and the savages gave vent to a yell, expressive of their joy.

At a signal from one whose waist was garnished with a string of scalps, the captive was taken ashore, and followed by the yelling crowd of cannibals, they went to a cluster of huts, which, evidently, formed the town or village.

Here a short halt was made, and after a brief speech from the chief, the captive was taken further inland.

At every step the hope that had buoyed him became fainter, and when he passed inside the circular space, railed off by long stakes, he felt that death was silently stalking towards him.

A train of horrible thoughts, conjured up by the ghastly sight within the enclosure, caused his blood to run cold; and, for the first time since his captivity, came the terrible reflection that he must fall a victim to the cannibals.

The anguish caused by this foreboding was worse than the thought of coming death, and striking his hand upon his open brow, a deep groan of agony welled up from his heart.

Without a word, his guards placed their weapons upon the ground, while two held him firmly by the wrists, the remainder bound him with tough withs to a tree.

Commencing at his feet, coil after coil was passed round until they reached his armpits.

then uttering a few words to the helpless seaman, they left the enclosure.

The tough reeds cut into his flesh, and at every attempt he made to escape, he was aware of the utter hopelessness of his struggles.

"The Lord's will be done," said the sailor; "but I would sooner have died a sailor's death than this."

He resigned himself to his fate, and with stoical indifference, watched an armed sentinel pace to and fro a few yards in front of where he was bound.

CHAPTER IX.

THE COMBAT WITH THE GORILLA.

THE shaggy denizens of the cave arose as Jack and Riley retreated slowly backward, and when the brutes rose upon their hind legs a terrible feeling of a hitherto unknown nature came across the young officer and his companion.

"God help us, Riley," whispered the midshipman, "for we are in a sore strait."

"It's all over with us, Misther Rawlings, and I shall never see sweet Kilkenny again."

"Courage," said Jack; "I have my dirk, you take that boarding-pike; I will tackle the brute on the right, you take the other."

The young gorilla made no attempt to follow its parents, but remained in the corner of the cave chattering angrily at the intruders.

Outside the cave the adventurers separated, and took up their positions a few yards apart.

Jack stood upon a piece of fallen rock to give him more advantage over his powerful foe, and Riley, planting his feet well apart, gripped the pike and commenced the onset on the brute he had to slay, or be crushed and torn limb from limb by the huge paws and muscular fore-arms.

The male gorilla advanced upon Jack, beating his hairy breast with his huge paws, and gibbering strangely at the pale but resolute young officer.

He paused when within a few feet of the midshipman, as though desirous to examine the two-legged animal more closely before closing with him and crushing his young life with his strong fore-paws.

The unexpected pause in his attack gave the midshipman time to better examine his enemy.

And as he stood there face to face with this denizen of the cave, Jack's hand became steady and his nerve strung to the highest degree.

The animal, as he stood upright, would have measured, at the very least, six feet, with chest and limbs massive, and of wondrous strength in proportion to his great height.

It was an awful moment for Jack Rawlings; that dread pause when he stood awaiting the attack of the fierce brute, whose long white teeth and sinewy limbs were suggestive of a terrible death.

The animal, as though satisfied with its scrutiny, advanced upon the young officer with the evident purpose of crushing him, for the long fore legs, or arms, were advanced ready to grasp Jack by the body.

The creature's hot breath fanned the middy's cheek, and nerving himself for a struggle which he knew would end in the death of one, he withdrew his hand ready to plunge the blade of his dirk into the brute's breast.

"Courage, Riley," he called out, without turning his head, to see how matters stood with his companion; "courage, and we shall conquer."

"It's cold meat we shall be," answered Riley, "if the devils get near us. This brute is foreninst me now, at the point of my pike."

Jack would have replied, had not the gorilla at that moment made a swinging blow with his long paw.

He gave a howl as the middy held his light dirk before his body and caught the blow on the sharp edge.

The inner sinews of the brute's paw were severed by the blow, and, looking at the blood as it dropped from the wound, the animal gave a low, guttural cry, half angry, half in fear.

At length, as though realising what had occurred, he gave a howl and sprang forward to grasp the midshipman.

Jack's heart beat fast as he leaned forward and plunged the dirk in the brute's chest.

The gorilla gave a scream of agony, and sought to grapple with his brave young antagonist.

Nerved to desperation, Jack drew the weapon from its fleshy sheath, and as the animal's blood spurted out of the hole, he stepped nimbly aside to escape the terrible embrace of the long hairy limb.

Jack's quickness saved his life, for the brute, maddened by the pain and the sight of his blood flowing, gnashed his teeth, and sweeping the air with his long paw, missed his aim as the middy stepped aside.

The victory was not yet won, for the gorilla, though becoming weaker every moment from loss of blood, was evidently determined to take the life of his young antagonist, and he shambled forward uttering wild cries of rage.

Suddenly he paused, and placed his paw over the wound in his breast as though trying to staunch the blood.

This was an opportunity not to be lost by the gallant midshipman; his foe's back was turned towards the piece of rock on which Jack had stood.

In a moment the young officer sprang upon it, and with all his strength drove his dirk into the gorilla's neck.

The blow brought the angry brute to the ground; the jugular vein was severed, and though not dead, it was unable to reach the young officer.

With flushed cheeks, and his weapon red from hilt to point, Jack stood and beheld with awe the efforts the gorilla made to rise.

Biting and tearing the sand in his fury, and seeming more like a human being in agony than a wild animal, the brute howled and panted in his endeavours to regain his feet.

It was a terrible sight, but the midshipman had no compassion for the animal's agony. It had been a battle to the death, and he had just won the victory.

"I've got him down," he proudly called out, "and another dig or two will finish him."

"Finish him, sir," said Riley, "or I shall be pinned in a corner."

"All right," said Jack; "but it is not safe to leave him yet, and I cannot get a chance to give him another dig."

The gorilla's movements prevented the midshipman using his weapon, and it was not prudent for him to leave the brute while a spar of life remained, so he stood clutching the dirk ready to renew the strife.

The brute tried to stop the blood flowing, for one of the large paws was placed upon the wounded chest, then, with a convulsive effort which only tended to accelerate his death, he sought to drag himself towards Jack, who stood calmly, proudly, defiantly watching its maddened throes.

The wounds were small, but the middy knew from the large circle of blood-stained sand that he had divided one or more of the large blood-vessels.

For several minutes the brute's terrible struggles continued.

During that time the excessive motion of the body, as the animal tore up the sand with his teeth and nails, had so emptied the huge carcase of blood, that he lay nearly still, a convulsive movement of the lower jaw and the closing and unclosing of the paws betraying that only small portion of that tremendous muscular power yet remained.

Gradually these struggles were over.

A sudden throe passed over the carcase, limbs stiffened, and the gorilla turned slowly over on its side, dead; and the rays of the sun

THE TURTLE PUZZLES M'GOWAN.

ing sun fell upon its dark, shaggy breast and the flushed face of the brave young victor.

"Now," said Jack, "to help Riley. Hallo! he's gone."

There were no signs of Riley or the she gorilla, and Jack, fearing the worst, went in quest of them, expecting every moment to see his companion's mangled body and the savage brute rending it limb from limb.

CHAPTER X.
THE PATH TO LIBERTY.

"I HOPE," thought the master-at-arms, as he watched his guardian pace to and fro, "my pension and back-pay will be given to the wife.

Good Lord that ever I should have to come to this!"

He wrestled with his bonds, and a snapping of the reeds that held his arms was followed by the old seaman finding those useful limbs at liberty.

"Joe Seedy," said the master-at-arm softly, "you are not to die at a cannibals' feast. One fastening is loose; it will go hard if the others do not follow in their wake."

He worked silently and swiftly, and one by one his bonds were loosened and lay at his

Before him was the path to liberty, t' obstacle in his way the dusky spearm?   eet..

                                    ue only
                                    n and the

3

sleeping tribe that lay insensible between him and the sea shore.

"I'll face them," said Joe Seedy; "it's worth the risk. If I'm skewered it will be no worse than I should have been without making the attempt. Now for the sea-shore!"

Creeping towards the entrance of the stockade, Joe was about to emerge and make an attempt to gain the beach.

The first step brought him face to face with an armed black who had been left in charge of the captive.

The long deadly spear was levelled at his breast, and the savage sought to drive him back to the interior.

Rendered desperate, and not caring whether his life was taken or not, Joe Seedy sprang aside, then, with a tiger-like bound, he closed with the cannibal.

There was a short struggle, then a sharp gurgling cry, and the black fell to the earth, his own spear transfixed through his heart.

Then the master-at-arms, with the blood-stained spear in his hand, stood over the prostrate form, and twice plunged the barbed point into the fallen man's body.

The Englishman's muscular power had soon crushed out the islander's strength; the weapon changed hands, and the deadly point drank its owner's life.

With a loud convulsive laugh, Joe Speedy stood over his foe until the last convulsive throb told that death had taken place.

Then he started at a swift pace towards the beach, where his boat lay drawn up to near high water mark.

The sharp-pointed stones cut and lacerated his feet at every step, and the cold night winds froze the blood in his veins.

Those feelings were unheeded.

The tranquil ocean was before him, and the night's silvery gleam seemed to guide and encourage him to regain his liberty.

It wanted but an hour to the dawn, and the master-at-arms, as he neared the spot where the canoes and his own boat were lashed, became sensible of several dusky forms moving about.

Creeping behind a massive stone, he watched their movements, and, after a few minutes' consideration, he muttered—

"They are keeping watch over the canoes."

The moon's rays gleamed upon their toma-

ks and the barbed points of their long

; and as they paced slowly to and fro

rocky shore, Joe counted twenty dark

odds, if I am seen," Joe Seedy

thought; "but if I can once get to the boat in time their number would not stop me"

Between the piece of rock behind which he crouched and the next massive fragment that stood between him and the boat, was an open piece of ground upon which the moon shone with wondrous brilliancy.

To pass this place was the most dangerous part of the desperate venture; and baffled for a time, he stood silently calculating his chance of doing battle with the watchful guardians of the boats.

"It will be daylight soon," thought the sailor, "and unless I reach the boat nothing can prevent my discovery—death will follow that. What is best to be done? I can but die once it is better to die fighting for my liberty than to be taken back to that horrible enclosure, and be slowly bled to death. I'll risk it; liberty or ——Ha! what's that?

A loud noise from the direction of the sleeping hill, and the savages upon the beach turned suddenly round, and ran swiftly past the very stone which hid Joe Seedy from their eyes.

Fully expecting to be discovered and immolated, the intrepid sailor waited, with his spear lowered, to transfix the first who should come within reach of his arm.

Though several of their number passed so closely that he could have touched them, he was unseen; and, to his joy, the islanders ran nimbly to the peaks of the highest rocks, and appeared to be striving to make out the cause of the unusual sounds that had boken the death-like stillness around.

That signal was no mystery to the old sailor. He knew the sound was caused by a hollow tube used by the islanders to summon the tribe when they were required to repel the attack of an enemy for some important purpose.

"They have discovered my escape," growled the seaman. "That fellow must have shammed death after all."

The master-at-arms felt there was not a moment to lose.

The distant flicker of torches and the angry hubbub of voices proclaimed the whole tribe upon his track.

Regardless of the savages on the rocks above him, he darted boldly from his place of concealment, and ran to the boat.

Exerting every muscle, he pushed the heavy boat into the water, then scrambled over the gunwale.

Not a moment too soon did the boat begin to drift from the shore.

The islanders, started by the keel grating

upon the beach, sprang from the rocks, and, with a wild yell, rushed towards the fugitive.

There was no time to use either sail or oars, so the sailor, with set teeth, stood in the bows, one trusty rifle in his iron grasp, another leaning against the side of the boat.

Unaware of the danger that awaited them, the Indians rushed into the water.

Not more than twelve feet intervened between them and the desperate hunted fugitive.

One fellow soon came within reach of the boat—his hand touched the gunwale—a loud report echoed over the rocky, cavernous island, and the savage fell back, his skull shattered.

The fugitive had thrust the muzzle of his piece in his pursuer's face and fired, when the dusky wretch was about to snatch it from his hands.

As quick as thought the second rifle was taken up, and the master-at-arms waited but for a fresh victim.

Awed by the swift and terrible fate of their companion, the natives paused in their headlong career.

It was but for a moment; then, as though actuated by a sudden frenzy, they swam in a body towards the receding boat.

Brief as had been the check, the sailor had set the single sail, and to his joy, the boat began to glide swiftly through the water.

The pursuers gave a wild yell when they beheld the boat slip from their fingers, and those who had brought their spears hurled those dangerous weapons after the intrepid sailor.

He was not touched, but an accident occurred to the ropes that caused the sail to shiver in the wind, and for a few minutes the boat remained stationary in the water.

In a moment the sail was righted by the desperate fugitive, and the boat again shot ahead.

The savages were almost as much at home in the water as ashore, and soon they were up with the boat, and gripped it in their strong hands.

A wild laugh came from the determined seaman's lips as the second rifle was fired point blank at the face of another foe, then clubbing his weapon he sprang upon the bow and sought to beat down those who held the boat.

The loud report and the warm blood of the slain man bespattering their naked forms caused the savages to drop back into the water; then, as though urged forward by the wish to avenge the death of their companions they again seized the boat and tried to scramble aboard.

Nerved to desperation, and fighting for life and liberty, Joe Seedy brought the butt of his rifle upon the head of the the first who impeded the boat's progress.

The black's forehead was crushed in, and falling back with a yell of agony, he sank beneath the wave.

Some yet remained—a dozen foes.

Again the clubbed rifle performed its deadly work and rid him of another enemy.

So the terrible contest continued, until there remained but one whose desire for the white man's life caused him to cling to the boat.

Some of his companions were slain, and the others had retired from the contest; but this, man, who was both young and powerful, scrambled on board and closed with the gallant Briton.

In muscular power the English sailor was superior to his antagonist, but the fatigue he had undergone rendered him weak.

He felt the black's sinewy fingers tighten upon his windpipe, while from the well-greased skin of his opponent he could barely retain his hold.

With the little strength left, and sensible that a film was coming over his sight, the master-at-arms closed his left hand and delivered such a "facer" that the black's nose was flattened.

The right hand quickly followed the left, and dealt such a succession of blows upon the astounded islander's face that he loosened his grasp, and sought to ward off the tremendous club-like fists of the English tar.

No sooner was his throat free than Joe Seedy saw the victory would be his.

Calling to his aid all the skill he had acquired when a boy, he drove the savage step by step backward, until a well aimed right-hander caught the islander between the eyes, and sent him over the boat's stern into the sea.

Unfortunately for the master-at-arms, such was the impetus of the blow, that he lost his balance, and fell into the water after his bruised and gasping opponent.

The black's powers were revived by the immersion, and he struck out, and, as the master-at-arms rose to the surface, seized him by the throat.

Nothing loth to continue the encounter in the water, Joe Speedy in turn gripped his opponent, and for several minutes a desperate struggle was carried on between them.

Their tactics were the same, each tried to force his adversary's head beneath the surface, and the master-at-arms at length succeeded in holding his adversary's face below water until the iron grasp of the black fingers relaxed their hold.

The fugitive loitered not to ascertain whether

his toe yet lived, but turned and struck out for the boat.

He gave a cry of despair when he saw the sail bellying out in the wind, and the boat gliding rapidly forward.

His heart sank within him at this fresh misfortune, and as he struck out madly in the track of his boat the shore became illuminated by a hundred flaring torches.

The tribe were rushing to the beach.

A yell came from their lips when they beheld the white sail gleaming beneath the moonlight, and when the master-at-arms turned his head he beheld a dozen canoes being launched in pursuit.

At the same moment the black who had been so severely handled gave a loud shriek of agony; then came a fearful crunch that caused the cold drops of agony to ooze from the sailor's forehead.

The savage had been bitten in two by a ground shark, the most vicious of the species.

There seemed no escape now from death; he was madly plunging after the boat, which increased her speed every moment.

A dozen canoes were skimming the water, and would in a few minutes be close upon him.

To render death more certain, he knew one of those fearful monsters, a ground shark, would be upon his track.

The strong man shrank with fear, for he felt appalled at the terrible death that awaited him, and from which there was no escape.

CHAPTER XI.

IN THE TIGER'S DEN.

THE island upon which Jack Rawlings and Riley McGowan had been left was the summit of a volcano, whose base was many thousand fathoms in the depths of the ocean.

The chasms, rifts, and rugged base, had at some former period been the means of exit for the boiling lava, and the jagged reefs that just showed above the water that surrounded the isle, were formed by the liquid fire, thick with scoriæ, pumice, and fragments of Juga rock and granite.

Jack saw nothing of this as he ran wildly to and fro in search of his companion. He beheld hillocks formed by the outpourings of the water, he passed rifts in the barren rock where the smoke ascended in whirling wreaths that showed the mighty fire was not yet extinct in the base of the volcano.

He passed over a large hole whose depth gave out a strange bubbling noise and exhaled a stifling sulphurous steam, and the midshipman knew he was near a boiling spring.

Still no sign of McGowan, so he retraced his way to where the dead gorilla lay, and took another survey of the place, and for the first time saw he had overlooked a dark rift, close to where Riley had found the female gorilla.

"They must have gone across here," thought Jack, "and were it to lead to the very depths of this place I will follow them."

A thick vegetation grew upon the sides of the hole, a thick growth of cactus, prickly shrubs, and rank grass.

Jack tested the strength of the roots by pulling with all his strength but found them immovable.

"They will bear my weight," cried the middy, as he swung himself over the edge; "if not, I shall only die a few days earlier than if I never made the attempt to save poor Riley, for it is imposible to live on this accursed place alone."

He went down fathom after fathom, the place soon being as dark as night, and the pent-up sulphuric air causing him to feel sick and giddy.

At last a faint gleam of light was perceptible beneath, and as it grew strong Jack saw with dismay the dark carcase of the gorilla, lying in a muddled heap, and a few yards from it the form of Riley McGowan, to all appearance dead.

Jack dropped lightly to the ground, and examined the gorilla, and saw the boarding-pike was buried in the brute's chest.

He saw, too, the blow had been the animal's death, for the blade had gone through her heart and had broken the skin at the back.

"A mighty thrust," said Jack; "but I fear poor Riley will never give another."

He rolled his shipmate over, and placed his hand over Riley's heart, and to his joy felt a slight flutter—very faint, for it was scarcely distinguishable.

There was no bruise or mark of violence visible on Riley's head or face; so Jack shook him and called out—

"Riley!—Riley McGowan!"

The ex-caterer gave no signs of life, so Jack propped him up with his back against the rock, and went through a narrow opening at the furthest end of the cavernous place to search for water.

He emerged upon a strip of rugged rock, and in front of where he stood he saw a cluster of drooping plants, greener than any vegetation he had seen in the upper region of the sterile island.

"There must be water near these plants," thought Jack; "the rocks would not supply them without."

He was right.

There was water—a deep and clear stream; he stones visible at the bottom, and the silvery ides and dark backs of a swarm of fishes were visible—the carp, in size and appearance—darting hither and thither, disturbed by the shadow Jack cast over the surface of the water.

The young sailor filled his shoe, and proving to himself the facility of capturing a few of the finny tribe, he returned towards the place where he had left Riley McGowan.

There were many openings in the rock, and the interiors were, to all appearance, alike, so much so, that Jack could not distinguish the one he had left.

"While I am debating about the right entrance Riley may die," thought Jack. "Let me see how many are there—one, two, three, four. I will begin at number one."

He entered the first cave, but soon emerged, for the place was in total darkness.

He went to the next. There was a faint light visible at the opposite end, and towards this Jack went.

He had not taken a dozen steps when he was startled by a low, fierce growl, and, thinking, for the moment, it was the gorilla giving its last dying gasp, he went boldly forward.

Suddenly he stopped, and, as though turned to stone, he stood, looking wildly at the dark outlines of some objects he had mistaken for the gorilla and Riley McGowan.

He dropped the shoe to the ground, and felt for his dirk, for within a few yards of the place where he stood, he saw the crawling forms of several jaguars, the cat-like tigers of the southern hemisphere.

The sight would have appalled the bravest man, and Jack gave himself up for lost.

He gripped his dirk, nerved to desperation, but well knowing how useless was his puny strength against the ferocious and strong-limbed animals.

"I will make an effort to hold my life," said Jack; "but I am sure I have looked at the heavens for the last time."

Jack looked from one to the other as though waiting for the strife to begin, but beyond a repetition of the low growling noise the fierce animals seemed to take no notice of the intruder.

His look was but brief; to his sorrow he bitterly regretted taking his eyes from a noble-looking brute who lay direct in his path.

The young adventurer found that so long as he kept his gaze fixed upon the majestic animal he was safe.

But no sooner had he looked around than the beast arose, and sweeping the ground with his tail, he gradually prepared for a spring upon the brave-hearted boy.

"Heaven help me!" Jack said. "Should I by a miracle sheathe my dirk into this fierce beast's heart, I shall be surrounded and torn to pieces by the remainder."

"Though expecting never to escape from the dread place alive, the intrepid boy turned his weapon towards the crouching beast of prey.

He saw the fierce eyeballs glaring with a lurid light as the animal crouched lower and lower until his body became flat with the ground.

Then with a roar that caused the whole of the savage denizens to start angrily from their recumbent positions, the animal bounded upon our hero.

A prayer came from the firmly-closed lips as he was borne to the earth by the animal's weight, and expecting every moment to feel the long white fangs tearing open his flesh, he closed his eyes, as he thought, for the last time in this world.

His dirk was wrenched from his grasp as the fierce brute sprang upon him; and now when he felt a warm shower deluging his face and neck, life seemed to revive in his bosom, and he unclosed his eyes.

The upper portion of his body was covered by the tiger's quivering form, and the midshipman knew the animal was in its death-agony.

Jack, when awaiting the spring which he felt would terminate his life, had held his dirk directly in line with the jaguar's chest.

The ferocious beast, springing forward with a terrible impetus, had come upon the point of the weapon, tearing it from Jack's hands; then, as the huge form bore the gallant boy to the earth, the animal went forward, and the hilt of the dirk coming in contact with a large stone, drove the blade home to the hilt.

The warm stream that fell upon our hero was the life-blood of the fierce brute.

As quick as thought Jack drew the blade from the quivering carcase, and with one foot planted upon the dead animal's body he awaited the coming of the next terrible foe.

The scent of blood aroused their fierce natures, and with deep cries, which caused a dread echo in the rocky lair, the deadly animals gathered round Jack and the fallen form of their late companion.

What followed the next few moments was like a dream to our hero.

He remembered the dread array of fierce fiery eyes gradually encountering his—he heard the roaring of the wild animals as they lashed themselves into a state of fury—then as he staggered beneath the fierce attack of a jaguar, a sheet of blinding fire, followed by a loud report, shook the rocks; and as the untamed animals fled to their lairs the midshipman swooned and fell across the carcase of the slain jaguar.

CHAPTER XII

RILEY MCGOWAN'S PROMOTION.

WHEN Jack Rawlings returned to consciousness he was seated near the margin of the spring, and Riley McGowan knelt over him bathing his forehead and hands.

"Riley," said Jack, "alive!"

"Faith," said the caterer, "its the same question I was about to ask you, for it's a long time you have been coming round."

"Ah," said Jack, "I remember the tigers, and the flash of lightning, and the thunder."

"The tigers, and mighty ugly ones they were," said Riley, "is quite true, but the lightning was nonsense."

"What do you mean, Riley?"

"Just this, Mister Rawlings, when you were ——I suppose I had better begin at the beginning, sir."

"Do."

"When I left you settling your score with the biggest of the two men monkeys, all of a sudden the brute that I had shoved the boarding pike into tumbles back into a hole, and I stuck to the pike and tumbled down too."

"But you were——,"

"Easy a minute, Mister Jack, I fell on the baste, so went not so far; but my skull comes against the handle of the pike and I was stunned."

"That is how I found you."

"Yes, Mr. Rawlings; and when I wakes up, who should I see going out of the place but yourself? So, as well as I could I followed, and as I went on I saw something shining among the rocks. I goes down to pick it up, and bedad, when I came up again, you were gone."

"I had entered the tiger's den, I suppose?"

"Yes, for I went back to the hole, and you were not there; so I went to look after you, and seeing all the places were dark, I felt in my pocket for the tinder-box, and got a light. Ugh! murder!"

"What's the matter, Riley?"

"It's thinking of what I saw when I came in where the wild beasts were, Mister Jack," said Riley; "faith, they were all round you, but I knew looking at you would not do much good, so I made the lightning and thunder, and frightened the varmints away."

"Made the lightning and thunder, how?"

"I told you it was a light from the tinder-box."

"Yes."

"I told you I found something in the rocks."

"You did."

"That something was a powder-flask, most likely lost by one of the poor fellows up by the signboard."

"Most likely, Riley."

"Well, in a moment I screws the top off, pops a piece of lighted tinder in the flask, and flings it amongst the varmints, and dragged you out here."

"It was a good thought, Riley; but for that I should have been torn to pieces."

"Never mind now," said Riley, "we are both all right, so let's look for the ship."

"First," said Jack, "let us have something to eat."

"I should like that, powerfully."

"Look in the spring, Riley."

The ex-caterer did so, and exclaimed—

"Fishes! by the powers!"

"Catch a few, Riley, and we'll have a feast."

Riley caught a half a dozen, and asked—

"How are we to cook them?"

"This way," said Jack; "I'll show you."

They went to the boiling spring, and there, much to Riley's surprise, the fish were cooked, and, despite the smell of brimstone, he did not fail to eat his share.

They ascended the rocks and looked for the gun-brig when the meal was over, but to their horror not a vestige of the vessel was to be seen.

The day passed wearily until one evening, when they were in chase of a large turtle, Riley yelled—

"Here's a boat coming, Mister Jack!"

The midshipman looked out among the reefs, and saw a boat with a sail set making towards the island.

In the boat was a seaman, and as his features became distinguishable, Riley said—

"By the powers, it's old Joe Seedy, the master-at-arms, but look to leeward of the boat, there's a huge chest and a spar drifting in towards the Island."

"Yes, Riley, you try and secure the chest while I look for the boat."

Riley departed upon his mission, and the long boat, after striking several times on the sunken reefs, ran into the clear water, and grounded near where Jack stood.

Great was the surprise of the old master-at-arms when he was welcomed by the young midshipman, and to the latter's anxious queries about the gun-brig he told the story of the wreck.

Then he briefly related his encounter with the cannibals.

"You said," the master-at-arms suddenly broke off in his narrative, "that you are not alone on the island."

"I am not," Jack replied, "Riley McGowan is with me."

"Where is he now?"

"Gone," he said, "to look after a chest we saw drifting in towards the island; but pray go on with your story, Mr. Seedy. You left off when you were swimming after the boat pursued by a great shark and the canoes."

Old Seedy, though the fearful episode had passed away, shuddered as he thought of the dreadful moment, when he was left in such dire peril upon the bosom of the deep.

"That was a dreadful time, Jack," he resumed "I had given myself up to a shark, which I knew was close aboard of me, and had shut my eyes; but even then it was hard to die, so I opened 'em again to have one more look at the sea.

"I looked towards the boat, and then I saw her with the sail flapping against the mast, and looking for all the world like as though she was waiting for me to come aboard.

"That sight gave me new hopes of life, and looking towards the black devils who were coming hand over hand upon the craft—for, d'ye see, they didn't know as I was in the water—I stretches out as hard as I was able to reach her.

"No good. A canoe full of them came up before I had; one ten fathoms, and while another canoe went and took the boat in tow, I was dragged aboard by the hair of the head.

"I didn't struggle. I felt it was all over with me, so sat down and waited for the thrust of the black devils' spears, but that didn't happen. They had something worse than death so easy for me.

"So I was dragged off to the place I was in before, and bound hand and foot, the wretches telling me as well as they could that I should be tortured next day, and made into roast joints afterwards.

Here the old fellow smiled grimly as he thought of the tender dishes his weather-beaten carcase would make for the cannibals' repast.

"There I stopped until night; the blacks thinking I could not get away, went to their huts, leaving only one big fellow to keep watch over me.

"I don't know how it was, Jack, but I passed off all of a sudden just as though I died. I can't call it anything else, for one minute I wa

ing at the big, black fellow, the next, everything went round like, and I forgot my pain and where I was placed."

"What was the matter with you?"

"The savages," said the old seaman, "recollecting that I had escaped bound me so tightly that my flesh was cut. Well, I got all right again in time, and of course my first thought was how shall I escape, as I tried the same dodge as before, and broke the reeds that held my hands, and very soon I was free.

"I could see nothing of the black who had been standing over me, and as the night was very dark I determined to make an attempt to reach the boat.

"I knew where it lay, not more than two fathoms from the tree, and I knew the terror the natives had of my rifles—they were lying safely in the boat.

"My powder, shot, and cutlasses were safe in their hiding-place, and creeping forward as well as I was able to, reached the black.

"To the right of where I had been tied to the tree, there was a small cave-like place in the rock, and as I passed I saw a light inside.

"Creeping to it, afraid to disturb a stone, I peeped in, and saw—what do you think?"

"Your sentry, perhaps."

"What else?"

"I cannot guess."

"Yes; I saw the fellow who had been guarding me, Jack, and I saw him leaning over a fire, roasting two pieces of flesh cut from a human body."

"A black, Mr. Seedy?"

"I don't know, but it was human flesh, and when I saw the cannibal stooping over his horrible feast and, weak as I had felt before, I became as strong as a giant with rage.

"Before he could turn and save himself I had my fingers at his throat, and there held them until the wretch's life had passed away.

"Then I took these weapons as," he pointed to a couple of spars, "emblems of my visit to that fearful island, and went to the boat. There was no one there to stop me, and I was soon out upon the sea: had I been followed they never would have taken me."

"How was that, Mr. Seedy?"

"The first thing I did," said the master-at arms, "was to load a rifle, and as soon as the blacks had laid their hands on my boat I would have blown my brains out."

"A better death," Jack said, "than again falling into their hands."

"So I thought;" but there was no pursuit, and before morning I was out of sight of the
ce.

"For several days after this I must have been in a raging fever, for when I next remember anything I found myself alone upon a beautiful island, the boat nearly full of water from the rain, and my body one mass of blisters from the sun."

The old sailor paused, and remained for some minutes in deep thought.

"I dare say," he said, "I was very ungrateful to the One who had protected my life, for I prayed for death to end my sufferings, but the prayer was not answered, for that night I was bled by the mosquitos, and it saved my life, for I was better the next day."

"I thought," said Jack, "Riley and I passed through some terrible adventures, but you can give us points and beat us easily."

"I will hear yours when Riley returns, for mine are almost finished, for as soon as I was able to attend to the boat, I started again on my voyage of discovery. I took care not to put in at any island until morning, when I saw you and Riley on the rocks."

"By the way," said Jack, "I think we had better go after him, for this island abounds with savage beasts, and Riley may have fallen into one of their dens."

They went in search of Riley, and found that gentleman perfectly happy.

He was sitting on the top of a huge chest; on his head a cocked hat, in one hand a bottle, at his feet another, evidently just emptied, and the second he had just taken; he saw Jack and the master-at-arms, and he said with drunken gravity—

"Captain McGowan havesh a drop of gro—og, shix bottles in the shest, and——"

Here Riley gave a yell, and tumbled backwards off the chest and howled—

"The pirate—the pirate—the devil's ship!"

Jack and the master-at-arms turned, and their cheeks paled with horror, for crossing the reefs was a stately vessel, every sail set and every rope in its place, and through her ghastly canvas they could see the red sun glow.

"The Phantom Ship!" gasped Jack, clutching the old sailor's arm, "the Phantom Ship!"

"The good lord defend us," said the master-arms, "and preserve us from all evil."

"The devil," muttered Riley from behind the est, "and the pirate, it's skeletons we'll be ery soon."

CHAPTER XIII.
THE PHANTOM SHIP.

It was no chimera of the brain. There upon the sun-tipped waves *a large vessel* was plainly visible.

As he stood spell-bound at the strange sight, Jack, with blanched cheek and distended eye, asked in a low whisper—

"What is it? what can it be?"

There came no reply from the stout-hearted sailor; he heard not the question.

Every sense was for the time deadened by a deep feeling of superstitious horror which harrowed his soul, and made the lion-hearted man's form shiver with dread.

True, his lips moved spasmodically, but no sound escaped them.

Fear that he had never felt when, with cutlass in hand, he sprang upon an enemy's deck, now, under the spell of this horrible vision, had stricken him dumb.

True there was a cause for the awful spell that had fallen upon our adventurers.

There, precisely in the spot Jack had pointed out, stood *the phantom ship.*

That it was any other than an unreal vision, the mystic manner in which the semblance to a full-rigged vessel had burst upon their sight put aside all thought of it being anything more substantial than what it seemed.

Nor was the suddenness with which it appeared all. There was a misty, unsubstantial look about the vessel that made her look like a thing of the spirit world.

"Sweet Kilkenny," howled Riley, from behind the chest, "I shall never see thee again. Is it gone, Mister Jack?"

The young officer paid no attention to McGowan's words; every faculty was too deeply engaged elsewhere in the terrible sight, and the longer he gazed at it the more his faculties were enthralled by the dread apparition.

For nearly an hour the phantom ship stood motionless upon the waters, then the frail mystic semblance quivered, and gradually melted away.

When the dread visitor had departed, Jack's fingers relaxed their grasp upon his companion's arm, and he said, in a low frightened voice—

"What can this dreadful sight mean?"

"The divil's ship, of course," said Riley, "sure you needn't ask that, Mister Jack."

The master-at-arms did not reply to the midshipman's question; the power of speech seemed to be taken from him.

Brought up from boyhood among men so prone to believe in superstitious legends as sailors are, Joe Seedy had not failed to imbibe strong feelings of horror at the story told by the captain of the Ariadne, and its never failing power of bringing evil upon those who witnessed it.

Fully believing at the time that the horrible

was no other than the veritable pirate, [Mr.] Seedy at last answered—

"The Lord have mercy on us, lad! That sight will surely bring some terrible calamity."

"It's skeletons we all shall be," said Riley, coming from his retreat, and pretty well sobered; "there's not a morsel of doubt about it."

The master-at-arms went over to the chest, and sat silent for several minutes, his eyes fixed upon the reefs where the phantom ship had appeared.

Suddenly he started from the chest, and gave a lusty shout, and Riley, who made sure the ghostly ship had returned, bolted to his place of refuge.

Jack felt certain his companion had suddenly become deranged, and, with much concern in his voice, he asked—

"Whatever is the matter, Mr. Seedy?"

"Matter, boy! Hurra! hurra! What fools we must be. Why Jack, my boy, that wasn't the phantom ship after all."

"It was not?"

"No, lad, no. It was but the reflection of a ship, that's all. Hurra!"

"The reflection of a ship?"

"Yes, lad, yes; the shadow of a vessel in another sea."

"Of course," Jack exclaimed, jumping to his feet, "How foolish we were to be so frightened. I have often read of it, now I remember, but never thought it could be true."

"True enough, lad; there are more wonderful things than this ship to be seen in the world."

"I think so. Such strange and terrible sights, that in a book we should think them only fiction."

"What's that you say, Mr. Jack?" exclaimed Riley, peeping over the chest. "Is it that's not the devil's ship?"

"The vessel we saw," said Jack, "is the reflection of another vessel."

"It's joking ye are."

"No, Riley, this strange sight is caused by the mirage, and is common enough in many parts of the world."

"Well," said Riley, "I'll believe you; and perhaps, as we are not in such a funk as we were, Mr. Seedy won't mind telling me how he got here."

The master-at-arms repeated his story to the ex-caterer, who exclaimed at its close—

"It's sorry I am the poor boys are all gone, but if that devil's ship wasn't something to do with it, may I never see sweet Kilkenny again."

The master-at-arms and Jack Rawlings tried to make Riley understand the natural cause of the shadowy vessel's appearance, but to no purpose.

"I think I know the chest," said the master-at-arms; "it is the purser's."

"I thought so," said Riley, "for it's full of nothing but whisky bottles and cocked hats."

"Not bad things in their way, Riley, but it would have been better for us had the purser laid in a stock of pea jackets to keep us warm."

"The whisky is better than the jackets, Mr. Seedy—try it."

Nothing loth, the old seaman acceded to the request; then the bottle was handed to Jack, who took a hearty gulp, and being unused to the powerful spirit, he was nearly choked.

Worse than this, in a few minutes he began to feel really drowsy, and was soon glad to yield to his shipmate's advice.

"Have a sleep, lad," said the master-at-arms; "we will rouse you up when we have the supper ready."

CHAPTER XIV.

RILEY MCGOWAN AND THE TURTLE.

"Supper ready—all right," jeered Jack, as he stretched his limbs under the shades of a tree "I hope it will be a good one."

"Come on, Riley," said the old sailor, "we must catch a turtle or two; there's sure to be plenty on the beach."

"Is it good to eat they are, Master Seedy?"

"Nothing so delicious in the world."

"Bedad, then we'll have 'em every meal and twice for supper."

"There you are, Riley. You run over there, and prevent that big fellow getting back to the water. I'll capture this small one, and carry him off."

Riley ran across the rocks, and came up with the turtle—a mighty fellow, of several hundred pounds in weight.

McGowan increased the animal's speed towards the sea, and the master-at-arms, who had, by this time, shouldered his prize, called out to Riley—

"Don't let him reach the water, Riley, or we shall lose him."

The turtle still scrambled over the rocky ground, and Riley, clinging on to the excrescences of the shell, tried to stop him.

"What the devil am I to do?" exclaimed the panting turtle-catcher. "The turtle won't stop, and I can't hold him."

Driven to desperation, Riley, as a last resource, drew his clasp knife.

"That's no good," shouted Joe Seedy; "his coat is like iron. Turn him on his back, Riley."

McGowan, after a little difficulty, succeeded turning the turtle over, and, sitting on the shore, he said—

"Well, you're about the strangest baste in or out of any place. Bedad, it's a power of cooking your back will take before it's soft."

Assuring himself the turtle could not escape, Riley went after the master-at-arms.

When Jack Rawlings awoke, it was a strange sight that met his eyes.

A blazing pile of wood, evidently part of the sea chest, threw a lurid glare upon the beach, and gave such a strange spectral look to the master-at-arms that, had there been a stranger near, he would have taken the harmless old tar for a demon practising some kind of horrid rite.

From the uncouth figure Jack's eyes wandered to the dark object which caused the savoury incense to float beneath his nostrils.

What was it?

It was not an iron pot, nor yet a kettle; yet, by it's shape, it might have passed for either.

Jack looked long and earnestly at the strange object, but could make nothing of it.

At last he raised his head, and said—

"What is that you have on the fire?"

The old sailor desisted in his cooking operation, and looked up.

"You are awake, are you?" he said. "I found you asleep, or I would have shown you how to make a mess fit for an admiral."

"It smells good. What is it?"

"Fish," said Riley, "with a skin as soft as the copper on a ship's bottom."

"It's turtle soup," said old Seedy; "and though Riley persists in saying it will never be soft, I say it will."

"Believe it when I see it," quoth Riley. "What do you think of it, Mister Rawlings?"

Jack surveyed the culinary proceedings, and said—

"Well, I daresay it's all right, but I can't make out the emigrant."

The lad, though well versed in the ingenuity displayed by various unfortunate men who had been thrown by the waves upon a desolate shore, had never heard or read of such an astonishing contrivance as this.

"In the first place," said old Seedy, exhibiting the object of Jack's wonderment, "I knew we wanted something to eat."

"And wanted it quickly; so without wasting time to shoot any of the animals, for the simple reason that he had nothing to cook them in, Riley and I went in search of an old acquaintance, one I knew that would be a good meal, and answer the purpose of a good thick saucepan at the same time."

"Yes, but——"

"Wait a moment. This old friend, you see, is a turtle, and, by the way, Riley turned another on his back for to-morrow. Now can you see the arrangement, Jack?"

"Yes; I wonder how you thought of it."

"Knew it years ago, when I was cast ashore in a worse place than this. Now bear this in mind, Jack, it will be useful some day."

"Like all your advice."

"Glad to hear it. Now, look here; first catch a turtle—see?"

"Yes, I see."

"Then, having lit the fire, place the stones, one on each side, to rest the gentleman on."

"Yes, I understand."

"Then, turn him on his back, as I have done; but before you do this, cut off his head and feet. Then place him over the fire, and wait until it is ready."

"What is that on the shell?"

"Ah! I had forgotten. This is wet clay."

"What is it for?"

"To prevent the shell breaking before the soup is ready. Now then, my hearties, stand clear while I take the soup-dish off the fire."

The turtle, cooked within its own shell, and sending forth such a delicious steam that Jack's mouth began to water, was, much to Riley's disgust, who moved quickly away from the black smoking object brought near the tree, and each adventurer began to partake of the rich invigorating stew.

There was a happy smile upon their faces as they sat down to partake of this strangely-cooked supper, and in spite of the recent dangers they had gone through, as the men progressed, their light laughter pealed out.

And Poor Riley was sadly roasted about his attempt to catch a turtle by the tail.

CHAPTER XV.

A COMMITTEE OF WAYS AND MEANS.

AFTER supper, the adventurers sat close to the fire, for after sunset the wind came in cold gusts from the sea.

The trio formed a curious group; the old master-at-arms, gray and weather-beaten, but as hale and hardy as a man could wish to be.

Riley McGowan, his honest, good-tempered-looking face ornamented with a stubby beard of several days' growth, his rather corpulent form not over well covered with his canvas trousers and blue shirt, both of which had suffered considerably from much wear and tear.

The smartly-braided hat, placed jauntily upon his head, formed a perfectly ridiculous contrast to the uncombed hair, unshaven chin, and illed cloth, and Jack, whenever he turned his head and caught a glimpse of the sky-scraper, as he triumphantly termed the cocked hat, could not help laughing.

The young officer was a good specimen of early manhood.

He was just, as it were, changing from the boy to the man, and, even in their hopeless existence, there was an expression of hope upon his face that told how sanguine he felt that all would yet be well.

The explanation of the phantom ship took a weight off their minds.

The cause of its appearance being understood, would deprive the shadowy object of its terrors.

"Now, my hearties," said old Joe Seedy; "the ghost having been satisfactorily accounted for, I think it will be quite as easy to explain the death of those poor fellows whose bones you saw on the top of yonder rock,"

"Skeletons," said Riley; "killed outright; anyhow you can't make anything else of it."

"Make this," said the master-at-arms; "the captain of the Ariadne told our skipper that his boats' crews went ashore and were never heard of again."

"That's just it," said Riley; "and if——"

"Hold your tongue, Riley," said Jack; "Mr. Seedy knows much more of these islands than either of us, and he can explain many things that seem supernatural to our eyes."

"Maybe he can," said Riley; it's all ears I am to hear it."

"Well, Riley," the master-at-arms said, "will you believe that I have seen an island rise out of the sea?"

"Ye-e-s," said Riley; "when a ghost of a ship isn't a ghost—of course if I believe that, it's anything else I can believe. Go on; tell Riley anything ye like—he'll believe it. Go on."

Here Riley drew the cocked hat over his eyes desperately, resolved to believe everything the master-at-arms and Jack wished him to believe.

"Have you really seen an island rise out of the sea?" Jack asked; "it must be a fine sight."

"It is," the old sailor said; "I was only a youngster when I saw one of these strange and sublime spectacles. I passed the spot a month after, and beheld an island not less a than a mile in circumference, and between seventy and ninety feet high—that is, the immense mass of volcanic matter was that height above the level of the sea."

"You saw all this, Mr. Seedy."

"Ay, lad, not only saw it, but walked over it; and what is stranger, six months after I was within musket-shot of the place, and instead of an island there was nothing but a small reef not ten yards in length."

"It had nearly disappeared?"

"Yes; sank as strangely as it had come, and, save for the smoke that issued at times from the sea, it was almost impossible to make out the place where this wonderful phenomenon appeared."

"Marvellous!" said Jack, "most marvellous."

"It is, lad. Such sights as those do not fall to the share of those who stay at home all their lives."

"I question," said Jack Rawlings, "if one half of those who have never been beyond England would believe such things."

"Perhaps not, lad, perhaps not; but those who see must believe."

"Bedad," said Riley, "I am believing it, and the divil a sight I've seen of it yet; but anyhow, I'll believe it—go on with some."

"I'll tell you what it is, Riley," said the old seaman, "there's not the least doubt but that you will see several of these strange sights."

"I don't want to see them—I believe it. Go on about the poor fellows up there not being skeletons—say what you like, I'll believe it."

"What I have to say about them," said the master-at-arms, "is this—the boat was most likely knocked to pieces on the reefs, and the poor fellows died from a fell disease, for at times the black fever sweeps across these volcanic isles."

"If this is the case," said Jack, "I begin to have an idea that His Majesty's ships of war have been nicely bamboozled by the tales of the ignorant merchantmen."

"How do you mean?"

"You know it was in consequence of the representations made by the owners of the merchant ships sailing in these seas that a man-of-war was stationed here to overhaul the rascally pirates, whose spectral ships frightened the peaceful seamen—and so forth. And, after all, the phantom pirate is caused by the mirage, and the shadow being thrown upon this island has given it a bad name."

"That's about it, lad. But, if we get away from here, we can tell them a little of the truth; but, while we stay, it will be as well to make ourselves as comfortable as we can."

"Quite so."

"The muskets and ammunition I have in the boat will be very useful; but the first thing we must do is to catch a shark."

"A shark!"

"Yes. The gentleman will supply us with all we require in the way of tools; and, as we musk knock up a hut, a few shark's teeth will be indispensable."

"For what purpose?"

"For marline spikes," said the old seaman. "With them we splice the tough loop-rope and all that sort of thing."

"Go it," said Riley. "When shall we begin the hut?"

"To-morrow, first thing. You can be getting on with the hut, Riley, while Jack and I go in search of a shark."

"You'll find it all done when you come," said Riley; "it's a fine builder I am."

Jack and old Seedy laughed, and telling Riley to keep up the fire, they went to the boat, and brought away the muskets and ammunition.

"I think we can have a snooze now, old Seedy said. "To-morrow we shall have plenty to do."

The adventurers were soon fast asleep, and were in this blissful state for some time.

Jack Rawlings was aroused soon after midnight by a succession of unearthly cries, so much like a human being in distress, that he started up, every nerve thrilling with excitement.

"Mr. Seedy," he said, anxiously, "awake! there is a terrible noise amongst the trees."

Old Seedy raised himself upon his elbow and listened for a few seconds, then growled out—

"It's those cursed howling monkeys. I did not know we had any upon the island. All right, go it!" This was added when a yell louder than had come before reached their ears; "I'll settle a few of you to-morrow night."

"I suppose," said Riley, "it's singing a song they are, the bastes—it's a long pole I should like to stir them up with, bedad—I've seen monkeys before—heaps of them—but never heard any make a noise like this."

"Very likely not," old Seedy said, "these are quite a separate species."

"Oh, are they? then we'll soon have some of the others."

"I thought all monkeys were much alike," said Jack, "are they not?"

The old seaman told him that the howling monkeys were huge, and of a reddish colour, and had long beards.

The difference between those midnight disturbers and their species was, the howlers never quitted a large tree they had chosen for a home; and, he added, that one tree alone would contain upwards of a hundred noisy creatures.

Jack determined, during his stay upon the island, to give those tenants immediate notice to quit; for old Seedy told him that he would have this serenade every night for at least nine months in the year.

Leaving Jack and Riley to this comfortable reflection, the old seaman went to sleep.

Not so Jack, whose mind had been excited by the commencement of the howling, and it was a long time before he could shake off the strange fancies that came to his brain.

At times the howls were subdued and sullen, and seemingly some distance from the centre of the hill.

Then, as he closed his eyes, the most unearthly discord would suddenly come upon his ears; so sharp and plain that he felt assured that his tormentors were grouped around the fire.

"I cannot endure this," he muttered angrily; "I will send a charge of small shot among them; perhaps that will have the desired effect."

Loading his gun, he fired in the direction of the noise.

Never in the whole course of his life did Jack Rawlings so much regret anything as that.

The loud report of the rifle, so far from silencing the disturbers of his repose, caused an unwelcome addition to the concert.

The myriads of birds that were at roost among the trees, startled by the noise, began to flutter their wings, and give utterance to the most dreadful cries.

Then came the deep, subdued growls of the jaguars and pumas, as they were prowling about in search of food.

Then the wild hogs—the tapirs—began to grunt and snort at the unusual sound, and Jack's friends, the howling monkeys, seemingly disgusted that others should join in their serenade, increased their yells threefold.

Jack stood for a moment and listened to the horrible discord, then he flung the gun from him, and stopped both ears with his fingers, and in that position he went to sleep.

CHAPTER XVI.

SHOOTING A SHARK.

RILEY appointed himself cook, and by the first stage of the sun he was at work measuring up the turtle.

Old Seedy was busy cleaning the muskets, and Jack, not having anything particular to do, went to have a morning dip.

He had not gone very long, and when he returned his face was very pale.

"What's the matter, lad?" the master at once

THE FIGHT WITH THE SAVAGES.

asked, and Riley said, "Seen the Old One, Mister Rawlings?"

"It was nearly a case," said Jack; "I went to have a dip, and as near as a toucher got between a crocodile's jaws."

"We must be careful of the pools in these islands; they are very dangerous."

"Bedad," said Riley, "here's a boy who won't bathe. Come on, the breakfast is ready, me boys."

When the meal was over the master-at-arms and Jack started upon a foraging expedition, and left Riley alone in his glory.

On their way across the isle the adventurers passed the crocodile's pool, and Jack, with his finger upon the trigger, looked out for the scaly gentleman who had so narrowly made a meal of his young form.

The monster was not visible, and old Seedy, guessing the import of Jack's anxious gaze said—

"Don't be in a hurry, my lad; we will have him yet."

"I hope we shall," said Jack, "for I shall never look at this pool without a shudder."

"Enough to make you, boy; had the scaly

fellow once got you between his teeth, there would have been but short time to have said your prayers."

They passed on. The scenery at every step was bold and beautiful in the extreme, and several times Jack paused to gaze upon the glowing expanse of nature.

"This is very lovely, Mr. Seedy," the boy said; "so beautiful, that one can scarcely feel a regret at leaving the world."

"It is, boy, it is; but I have seen more beautiful sights than this, and yet have pined for home and friends."

"I suppose," said Jack, " this is but natural; perhaps I shall get a little home-sick when the novelty of this life has worn off a bit."

"Hallo!" exclaimed the old tar; "this looks something like the place we want."

They had just turned a projection and come suddenly upon a large extent of sand, still wet, and varied by small lines of rock and tangled seaweed.

"Yes; but the last time I was here this place was covered with water."

"It was high tide at the time, my lad. Bear ahead. It strikes me there is just the spot we want over by those stones."

He pointed with the butt of his rifle towards a number of irregular pieces of rock, and, as he looked to the priming of his piece, he continued—

"Those stones, Jack, have been upheaved by one of these volcanic eruptions that are common in these parts. See, here are some small pieces that have been carried away by the receding tide, and, unless I am at fault, at the foot of those high pieces of stone we shall find a nice nest of gentlemen who will provide us with all we may want in the way of arms and tools."

By the time he had ceased speaking, they reached the objects of his remarks.

Between the bases of the pointed rocks they found a deep chasm, and old Seedy, standing by the brink, said—

"Ten fathoms of water, at least. Throw a stone in, Jack."

The lad obeyed, and watched with interest its swift descent.

The pebble had not sunk more than three yards, when a long, greyish-looking object darted out from beneath the shadow of the highest piece of rock.

Jack uttered a cry of alarm, and hastily brought his rifle to his shoulder.

"A shark!" said the old sailor. "I thought we should find one here, Jack."

Jack did not reply; he was too closely watching the dreaded monster as it rose within an inch or two of the surface; then, as though angry at being lured from its retreat, the dreaded creature caused the water to seethe and bubble by a few movements of its powerful tail, then darted back to its lair.

When it had disappeared the young castaway drew a deep breath, and said, slowly—

"Yes, Mr. Seedy, it is a shark, and a large one. I cannot understand it scarcely; but every quiet-looking pool in the island is the dwelling-place of some terrible monster."

"This is very easy to understand, Jack. This fellow has been left here by the receding tide, or else stays by choice."

"Choice! How do you mean?"

"Yes; it may be more profitable to his hungry stomach to stay here than go out to sea and search for food."

"The wretch!" Jack said; "I wonder if any poor sailor has ever fallen a victim to his jaws."

"Most likely, lad. I should think he is an old one by his length. It must be, at the least, eighteen feet from stem to stern. Throw in another stone, Jack; we will try what we can do for the gentleman."

Another stone was thrown in, and, as the voracious creature again darted out, the old sailor said—

"Fire at his head, Jack. Don't miss him, boy, whatever you do."

Drawing a deep breath, Jack drew the butt of the rifle firmly to his shoulder, and fired.

CHAPTER XVII.
LANDING THE PRIZE.

THE ball sped true to its mark, and the water, which had been of a pale greenish tint, became crimsoned with the fierce animal's blood.

"Bravo!" shouted the old tar, lustily; "well hit, lad! Load again—that's it. Always be ready, in case we might be attacked in rear."

Jack carefully reloaded his weapon.

"Come here, lad," said his companion, seating himself upon a stone near the brink, "and see the fun out."

"Rather dangerous fun," thought Jack.

Even in watching the furious monster's death struggles, it seemed to Jack Rawlings an unnecessary piece of cruelty not to put an end to him at once, so he said—

"Can't we put him out of his misery, Mr. Seedy?"

"No lad," said the old sailor, "never use two charges of powder when one will do; besides, you would not hit a better part, were you to fire a broadside at him."

The water by this time had been beaten into a foam by the shark's tail, and as this dark-coloured froth began to subside, the shark was seen to float upon the surface of the little land-locked bay.

"He is dead!" Jack exclaimed. "See how quiet he lies!"

"Not yet, my lad. That won't happen till we see his ugly white belly uppermost."

The creature was so still that Jack thought for once his companion was mistaken, but, as he was about to give the thought utterance, he saw the large fins moving gently.

"You are right, Mr. Seedy," he said; "the reptile is not yet destitute of life."

"No, my boy; old Joe Seedy has not been on the sea, man and boy, fifty-five long years without knowing a little about these varmints."

He then explained, in his homely way, to his companion that the muscular power which is necessary for a fish to have over the swimming bladder was just departing, thus it was that the huge carcase floated.

"You see, my lad," he said, in conclusion, "this varmint hasn't the power to compress the swimming bladder, so he can't go the bottom. It's a wonderful thing, isn't it, Jack? Ha! there he goes. This way, lad."

They ran to the rocky edge of the pool as the lifeless brute rolled slowly over, and the red sun gleamed upon its white breast.

The next thing to be considered was how to bring the vanquished monster ashore.

An easy task, had our adventurers been in possession of a goodly coil of strong rope; but as they had neither rope nor anything that would answer as a substitute, the victory they had achieved seemed fruitless.

While old Seedy stood gazing longingly at the shark, and a puzzled look upon his weather-beaten face, Jack had a happy thought.

"We can do it," he said. "Hurra! Come and give me a hand."

He bounded swiftly towards a grove of tall trees, and before old Seedy could well understand the cause of this sudden act, Jack was busily at work hacking at one of the lower branches.

"Catch hold of the end, Mr. Seedy, and bend it down."

The master-at-arms gave a peculiar laugh, and said—

"What on earth is Jack up to?"

He held down the branch, and in a few minutes it snapped off close to the gnarled trunk.

Jack soon lopped off all the superfluous shoots,

and when he had finished he held it before old Seedy's face, and said—

"There, Mr. Seedy, won't that do?"

The old sailor rubbed his chin reflectively, and smilingly said—

"Well, Jack, you'll soon be ahead of me. Dash my old wig, I should never have thought of that."

The object of his admiration was the shorn bough, which had at its smaller end a good sized and tolerably strong crook.

Proud of his old companion's words of praise, Jack led the way to the brink of the miniature bay.

Fixing the crook in the shark's gills, they began to draw their prize towards the shore.

It was an easy matter while the dead shark was upon the water, but when they had succeeded in landing the huge ugly head and part of the shoulders they were brought to a stand-still.

The dead weight was too much for their united strength, also too much for the green bough which had done them such essential service, and the adventurers, much to their regret, were compelled to desist.

Old Seedy looked wistfully at the huge carcase, and, as usual when in a delemma, he began to stroke his chin.

"This won't do, Jack," he said. "We mustn't leave the beggar here, or the tide will carry him into the sea."

"We can't land him, that's certain," said Jack, "perhaps Riley's assistance will turn the scale in our favour."

"No," the old fellow said, "the dead weight is too much. I have it! You be off and fetch Riley, also the two pair of axes that are in the boat."

"All right, but—"

"I'll keep the beast in his proper position: if we leave him he may float away."

"Ay, I see," laughed Jack; hold on until I return, and if Riley dissects him as well as he tried to dissect the turtle, we shall be all right."

Jack found Riley very busy. The ex-caterer had planned out the hut in a very creditable manner, and the midshipman told him so.

"You see," said Riley, "it's just this way, Mr. Rawlings. I thought, as we had to rig out a caboose, it would be as well to have it near the sea, for there's no knowing when the brimstone that's all about the place may begin to blaze up and fry us up, if we don't get out of the way—and it's out of the way we shall be able to get, for even brimstone can't set fire to the water."

"Don't you be too sure, Riley; have you never seen sheets of fire on the top of the water?"

"No, Mr Rawlings, but I'll believe it—it's anything I'm open to now, so go on."

"Some other time, Riley," said Jack. "I want your assistance now to help us with our prize."

"Have you caught one, then?"

"Get the axes out of the boat, and come and see."

Armed with these useful tools the ex-caterer and Jack hastened to where the shark was partly beached.

"Now, then, my hearties," said old Seedy, "we must be quick with the gentleman, or the tide will take him out to sea."

The shark was at least thirty feet long, and of proportionate width; and Riley, when he surveyed the monster, exclaimed—

"By the powers, but that's a tall fish! Are you sure he is dead, Mr. Seedy?"

"As mutton, Riley."

"As if he isn't," said McGowan, "it's mutton we shall be when he opens his mouth. Anyhow it's by the tail end ye might have brought him so ~ ~ our legs.".

"   won't bite, Riley," laughed Jack, putting   mad in the shark's mouth; "so fire away and let's get him ashore."

The master-at-arms and Riley went to work with the axes, and soon severed the head and shoulders from the brute's body.

Then a strong pull and a pull together brought the carcase further ashore, and another piece was hacked off.

"Now, my hearties," old Seedy said, "I think we can leave the remains of the prize."

"The Lord be praised for that same," said Riley; "it's broken me arm with chopping at such a hape of flesh.".

"Very useful if ugly," said the master-at-arms, "so you will say when you will see all the things we can produce from his ugly carcase."

"Bedad," said Riley, "it's more and more we larn every day; but maybe, Mr. Seedy, ye will be kind enough to tell me some of the things ye intend to make."

"The shark's jawbones," said the master-at-arms, "will make capital saws; the bones will make needles, spear-heads, and nice points—the flesh boiled down will supply us with oil—and the skin when dried will answer the purpose of leather."

"Oh," said Riley, "by the piper that played jigs to Moses, it's a wonderful man ye are, Mr. Seedy!"

The adventurers went to work and by suns the dissection of the shark was completed, an Riley, as he took the saws for his useful propert said—

"It's a dacent hut I'll have up in no tin now; it's beautiful they cut. Look!—Wh the devil's that?"

An old and seemingly withered trunk gre near where they stood, and Riley drew one the saws across the bark, and from the incisio thus made there flowed a white fluid.

The master-at-arms gave a cry of deligh when he saw the sap oozing, and as he eager drank some from the hollow of his hand, Jac Rawlings asked—

"What is that you are drinking, Mr. Seedy?

"Milk, my lad; taste it."

"By the great man of Munster," exclaime Riley, "it's mad I shall go!—Milk!—and o of an old bit of a stump like that. Bedad, it a cow we'll be after calling it next."

"Quite right, Riley," said the old seamar "this is milk, and the old stump gives milk a pure and as freely as a cow."

"The Lord be good to us! said Riley; "it roast beef we shall be finding next, I suppose growing on the trees."

The midshipman tasted the sap, and after little trouble, Riley did the same.

"It's milk," he said; "milk, as true as th great St. Patrick swam across the sea with hi head under his arm."

Carrying with them as much of the shark a was necessary for present purposes, the adven turers went towards the place they had selecte as their habitation.

"I think," said Jack, to the master-at-arms I have read something about this tree before."

"Most likely, lad; the great Humbold mentions it under the name of Galactroden drum."

"Yes, I remember he does——"

A yell came from Riley at this moment, and his companions, making sure he had been attacked by a beast of prey, dropped their bur dens, and cocking their muskets, ran to the rescue.

CHAPTER XVIII.

A WONDERFUL SIGHT.

WHEN Riley uttered the shout his companions stopped aghast, nor was their astonishment diminished when they beheld the ex-caterer with staring eyes and cocked hat upon the back of his head, standing like a statue gazing out to sea.

"What's the matter, Riley?" asked Jack, laughing.

The Irishman answered with a roll of the eyes, and a gasp, and pointed to seaward.

It was now the turn of the old salt and Jack to express astonishment, for a wondrous sight was before them.

The sea, about two miles from the shore, was violently agitated; vast jets of water were rising in the air, surmounted by sulphureus smoke.

The surface of the ocean boiled and bubbled like a witch's cauldron, and then came a succession of loud reports, masses of stone rose like rocks falling into the blue water some hundred yards away.

The first momentary terror passed, Jack grasped the truth of this strange phenomenon.

"Volcanic action below the sea!" he cried. "Don't grunt and gasp in that fashion, but look at the wondrous works of nature like a man."

"Be jabers, I can't," moaned Riley, sitting down; "it's draming I am."

"Dreaming, Riley. Nonsense," rejoined Jack. "Come, Mr. Seedy, help me to restore our benighted friend. What is your opinion of the scene before us?"

The old sailor, who had been gazing thoughtfully at the disturbed water, paused for a few moments ere he replied.

"There's an island coming up," he said at length. "I have heard of them many a time, and seen such a sight once, and only once, before, in my lifetime. See, now, a dark mass like the back of a whale appears."

"Come, Riley," said Jack, clapping the ex-caterer on the back, "look up."

"It's a sorry day as iver I landed here," moaned the wearer of the cocked hat. "Phantom ships, sharks, and islands rising out of the say."

"How grand the sight!" mused Jack. "The troubled waters announce that birth of an island. Mr. Seedy, is not the sight majestic?"

"It is, Jack," was the reply. "Mark how the smoke disappears, and a mass of earth grows slowly and grandly from the ocean. Here comes a mighty wave aboard us. Run lad, up the hill here."

Our hero saw it was time to be moving, for a mass of water half a mile in length, and upright as a wall, was rolling towards him.

It required no experienced eye to tell what it would strike the shore with terrific force and roll far up the beach.

"Up, Riley," he cried, "and run for your life."

"Shure it's not worth running for," moaned the terror-stricken fal——

"Nonsense!" Jack returned. "Mr. Seedy, lay hold of his other arm."

They grasped the ex-caterer by the arms and raised him to his feet.

"It's a dhrame," he muttered, "and shure, Riley, you'll wake directly."

"In another world," interposed Jack. "Here it comes."

With a roaring, angry sound, the mass of water beat upon the sands and spread far up the beach, carrying the dismayed Riley and his companions before it.

Fortunately for them, it bore them towards a piece of rising ground, which divided the foaming wave and gave them an opportunity to escape from its violence.

Jack, still firmly clutching Riley, struggled to his feet, and old Seedy, giving his trousers the hitch peculiar to sailors, declared that "he never was nearer to slipping his cable."

"Here comes another," cried Jack, pointing to a second advancing column of water.

"We are safe, lad," returned Seedy; "'tain't half the size of the other. Stand by, lad," he said to Riley, who obeyed him by falling full length upon the ground, as a low rumbling sound came forth apparently from the bowels of the earth.

"Bedad," gasped Riley, "it's all over."

"The danger is," replied Jack, who stood pale but firm.

"It's not danger that Riley fears, divil a bit, but when I b'lieve all about yer phantom ships and milky trees; but a biling say is a little more than Riley McGowan can swallow."

"But it's true," said Jack; "we have it before our eyes."

"Every schoolboy knows that in warm latitudes the phenomenon is nothing unusual," interposed Seedy; "but it does not fall to the lot of every man to witness it. Two minutes have sufficed for the bearing up of an island not palpable to our eyes. Look, Jack, how it swells and grows! the warm soil breaking into rugged heaps."

"I can hear the sound as they rend asunder," Jack rejoined; "listen, Mr. Seedy."

"I hear," the old salt resumed, after a moment's attention; "your isle is a pile of stones, different from the soft soil I imagined it to be. If I mistake not we are above a bed of stone, and this sand and earth is but a superficial covering."

"Then caverns may abound here."

"They do, undoubtedly, and it must be our task to seek and find them."

"It's not much ye need seek here,"

Riley; "sure there's wonders enough without running after any more."

"But if I mistake not," replied Seedy, with a smile, "we shall find something worth the looking for; all rocky countries abound in wealth—the choicest minerals are gathered from the roughest stones. We need not be alarmed by yon strange sight; the various changes of nature are designed to please, not to terrify."

They looked in the direction of the newly formed island—Riley with his cocked hat on the back of his head, and a quizzical, doubting expression of face, which seemed to say that he must look further into the matter before he entirely believed in it.

Jack's face was glowing with enthusiasm; he was an enthusiastic admirer of nature, and all that he saw was to him an interesting book.

The last page, the volcanic island, was the strangest of all, for there stood the pile of rock heaved up from the sea, with no sign of the late commotion beyond a slight haze hovering near—the last remnant of the sulphurous smoke.

Old Seedy watched his face, and instinctively divining that he was wrapt in wondering meditations, forbore to break the silence, until Riley McGowan with a grunt led the way homeward. Then he took the boy by the arm, and they descended to the level beach.

"You think it probable, Mr. Seedy, that wealth abounds here?" Jack said as they strolled away.

"Certain of it, my dear boy; there are indications of ore near, but whether gold, copper, or tin, I am unable to say."

"Wealth would be of little use to us here," Jack intimated.

"But we shall not remain here for ever," replied the veteran, "and wealth, if we can by any means obtain it here, will be a good friend to us when we have an opportunity for leaving here."

"True, sir."

"Besides, metals may be turned to a thousand useful purposes, even here."

McGowan, who had been lounging before halting for a moment occasionally to scratch his head and whistle softly, interrupted the conversation with a loud cry.

"What's the matter?" cried Jack, springing forward.

"Be Jabers!" returned Riley, "it's a mighty big crack I nearly ended my life in."

He pointed to a rent in the earth about twelve feet wide by sixty long direct in their path.

"I have observed this before," said old Seedy, as they stood together upon the brink, and peered into the chasm, "but the violent erup-tion of this morning has widened it considerably. The rocks at the side will prove it is an old formation, and it is only the surface of the earth, the roof of the cavern in fact, which has fallen in."

"It is not very deep, Mr. Seedy."

"Thirty feet at the outside. I propose we descend."

"I should be delighted," replied Jack; "we can easily drop from rock to rock, and if Riley will fetch and fix a rope our return will be just as easy."

"I'm off for that same rope," muttered Riley, "it's myself that is getting tired of believing, lumps of ground sinking ashore, and lumps rising at say; all is a puzzle, and if there's much more of it I'll be after giving notice to quit."

"Don't be long Riley," shouted Jack.

The ex-caterer waved his hand and toddled away.

"Now give me your hand, Jack," said old Seedy, "first drop upon that piece of stone, from that to the one below with the surface covered with glittering particles, the next leap will leave you safe and sound on the floor below."

Jack followed these instructions, and in half a minute he was at the bottom of the cavern.

The veteran quickly followed, and the two surveyed the place with curious eyes.

There was nothing very alarming in its appearance—an ordinary cavern with rough unhewn rocks jutting its sides, the floor strewn with leaves, sand, and other particles brought thither by the wind.

"One of the rooms fashioned by nature," said old Seedy. "She shapes them strangely."

"But no work of man could be so handsome," rejoined Jack. "I like this ruggedness, it is beautiful, it is grand, and how these stony walls glisten!"

His companion, who had been thoughtfully examining a piece of rock he raised from the ground, replied—

"Ay, and glistens with the right stuff—gold—and, what's more, we are not the first discoverers of this place, nor has nature been the sole architect, for these rocks have been blasted and worked by man."

Jack stared at his informant with distended eyes.

"Years ago, perhaps," resumed old Seedy. "But man has been here, and here by some power he rent the rocks asunder; this piece I hold proves it. Look, Jack, here is the mark of an iron tool. You would ask me how I know the nature of the weapon. See, a portion of it, a grain still remains upon the surface; the rest of the metal mingled here is gold.

At this moment a slight rustling in the rear startled the two discoverers. It was the rope now lowered by Riley McGowan, who was looking down upon them with a very philosophical expression.

"Come down, Riley," cried Jack.

"Why?" demanded that worthy.

"We have made some wonderful discoveries."

"Bedad, yez are welcome to them."

"Then you won't come?"

"Not if I know it."

"Let him be," said Seedy, with a smile; "Riley is not a naturalist, he is not formed to solve the riddles of nature. Now for a little further investigation of this place; here is a nook we have not peeped into."

As he spoke, he turned by a jutting rock, and gazed for a moment into the darkness beyond. He started up with an exclamation which drew Jack to his side.

"Am I not right?" he said; "there are two barrels, nature doesn't fashion them, and here, behind, lies an old Dutch boot, the wearer dead and gone many a day; now, Jack, give a hand, we'll roll these tubs into the daylight."

Their first effort to move them were useless, and when they united their efforts, and endeavoured to shift one barrrel, it suddenly fell away to fragments, and a heap of various stones, intermingled with gold, fell at their feet.

"A duke's fortune," said old Seedy. "The men who worked here two centuries ago at least, knew the value of these precious stones."

"Are they very valuable?" asked Jack, breathless with surprise.

"Touch the smallest, and you touch a hundred pounds; touch the largest, and the value I cannot name."

Jack drew a deep breath, and gazed intently at the treasure.

"Time," resumed his companion, "has rotted these staves, and the wood can be powdered with the thumb and finger; here for the present as the casket is broken, we must leave the jewels; but they are safe enough; we will ascend for the present."

They looked up for Riley, but his broad humorous face was no longer visible; they shouted to him, but no reply came; and having tested the rope and found it fast, they both ascended to the light of day.

CHAPTER XIX.

AN UNPLEASANT POSITION.

"Where the deuce has Riley gone?" said the master-at-arms. "I thought he was here."

"He was before we came to the top of the rope," said Jack, "but I suppose he has gone to prepare supper."

"Most likely; so we will hurry on, Jack, for it is getting very dark, and there's no knowing what pleasant animal we may tumble over."

"Just so," said Jack, "there was something run past me as you spoke."

"Be careful, lad—this way—quick, or we are lost!"

There was no time to be lost, for a number of dark forms issued from the forest, and the old seaman, who knew the danger they were in, at once ran to the nearest tree.

They were not long ascending to a place of safety, and only just in time, for a full-grown puma made a spring at Jack's legs as he scrambled up the tree.

"Not this time, my friend," said Jack, coolly, "I am glad to say."

Looking down from the fork of the tree, the adventurers saw a dozen pumas walking round the base of the trees, their blazing eyes turned from time to time to watch their prey.

"Hang it!" old Seedy said; "we must have been a pair of fools, Jack."

"What for?"

"To leave our muskets below."

"Yes," Jack said, "we could have stood a siege had we our muskets and spears."

They had fashioned several spears—the shafts were of willow, the blades of shark's teeth; a couple of these weapons they took with them.

It was not a pleasant position for the adventurers, and as they beheld the number of wild animals encircling them, there seemed a great probability that the siege would last some time.

The myriads of sparkling fireflies as they glided over the soft ground, and up and down the lower limbs of the trees, gave a sufficient light to render the dark bodies of the prowling beasts distinctly visible.

There could be seen the sleek tigers walking with noiseless tread around the base of the tree, and ever and anon lifting their heads as they sniffed the dainty meal above.

A group of strong-limbed lions stood a few paces from the huge tree, their massive forms and blazing eyes looking strangely vivid by the dancing sparkles of light.

The night wore on, the adventurers rarely exchanging words; both silent, watchful, and not without a sense of dread, which the brave at all times feel when left to the calm reflections of a great and terrible danger.

No knight of yore had a stouter heart or greater indifference to danger than the young sailor. Had he been hemmed in by the skulking crew who stood beneath, he would have battled with them without one thought of the probable issue of the conflict.

The affair now wore quite a different aspect; the body and mind became chilled—one, by the cramped position they were in, the other by the certainty that unless the midnight prowlers returned to their lairs they would be starved out, or compelled to descend and become food for the forest children.

At times a subdued growl would escape old Seedy's lips as he found his position becoming irksome.

The least movement in the tree was greeted by the watchful animals as a sign that their prey was about to descend, and in an instant every head would be upturned and a circle of blazing eyes looking doubly cruel in the dim light.

From the depths of the forest came the wild startling cries of the peccaries and tapirs as they rushed through the dense tangled brushwood pursued by their fierce and more voracious brethren.

From the banks came the noise of the crocodiles as they plunged into the water to stifle the prey they had seized.

Mingled with these sounds came short, angry growls from the wild beasts below, the plaintive cry of the water-fowl, and the dull croaking of a colony of frogs filled the air with sounds that were neither pleasing to the ear nor soothing to the mind.

It was near daybreak, and a white vapoury mist began to arise from below.

Jack, whose limbs were cramped, and his eyes ached, from their long vigil, uttered an exclamation of joy as he saw the white smoke curling up from the dark rocks.

Old Seedy, who had been sitting cross-legged in the fork of a large limb, looked up and asked—

"Are they going away?"

"No."

"Ugh! I thought you were by the noise you made. What was it?"

"Look! Do you not see that vapour rising?"

"Well?"

Old Seedy's temper was evidently soured by his night's roosting.

"I thought," said Jack, "that we might possibly escape under cover of the mist, which seems to increase every moment."

"Did you think these fellows below are fools enough to let us escape, eh?"

"They will not see us. We can creep to the point of one of the lower branches and drop to the ground."

"Can we," growled the old tar. "No, Jack,

here we must stick until those devils are either too tired or too hungry to stay longer."

"I had hoped," Jack said, "that they would have gone away when daylight came at the very latest."

"I'm afraid not, boy—afraid not. We shall see."

There was a long pause, and as Jack's eyes wandered from point to point, he beheld a faint streak of light in the east.

"The day is breaking, Mr. Seedy," he said, joyfully. "Look, look!"

"Ay," the old fellow grumbled, "it won't make much difference to us, I expect."

Jack was silent; he knew by his companion's manner that conversation was irksome to him.

He fell into a drowsy reverie, wondering who the men were whose chests they had found in the chasm; and, not without reason, did the midshipman dwell upon the probability that a similar fate was before them.

Jack's reverie was cut short by an angry growl from below; then old Seedy's savage voice broke upon his ears.

"Growl away, you ugly skulking devils," the old tar said; "had I my musket here, I would shoot two or three of you varmints."

The growls and old Seedy's voice ceased, and Jack closed his eyes and began to doze until the daylight caused him to awake with a start.

The sun's resplendent rays had pierced the thick grey vapour until it seemed like a thin gauze veil hanging in festoons above the giant trees.

Little by little the graceful foliage of the surrounding trees became visible, then the green slopes and verdure-clad valleys, and like a curtain slowly rising to disclose a well-set scene, beneath the edge of the mist could be seen blue sparkling streaks of the interminable sea.

The joyous chirp of the small birds as they fluttered from branch to branch, the heavy flapping of the gaudy parrots' wings, and their sharp peculiar cry, the hum of the insect world as they awoke beneath the sun's genial warmth, gave life and additional beauty to Nature's wondrous panorama.

Forgetful of the crowd of hungry animals beneath, Jack drank in the beauty of the scene, and his gaze wandered from one beautiful object to another still more beautiful; his thoughts were of the hour he last saw England's white cliffs.

He thought over every circumstance that had befallen him since that moment; and though but a few months had passed, what a wondrous change had taken place!

He could scarcely realise that so short a time

had passed ; it seemed an age of excitement—new scenes and wild adventures had been compressed into a few weeks.

A new world had opened to him, and he marvelled when he thought how great had been the change.

The low fierce growls of the prowling beasts of prey broke upon his ear, and then he thought —how sadly came the terrible impression upon his mind !—that ere many hours passed he would probably fall a victim to the long white tusks of the greedy brutes, whose dogged, silent watchfulness had not for one moment ceased since they followed the scent of the adventurers to their place of refuge.

Little marvel the brave heart became heavy. It was hard to be cut off at the onset of a life of adventure—a mode of existence so congenial to his temper and courage.

"I can't stand this any longer, Jack. I'm—— if I can."

Old Seedy was excited and angry, or he would not have used a word that would be bad in these pages.

Jack made a drive with his spear at a noisy macaw who was screaming above his head, as he said—

"What can we do ? They are determined to stop."

The beasts had laid themselves flat upon the ground their vicious faces upturned, and their hungry eyes watching the slightest movement of those they evidently looked upon as a legitimate meal.

"Do !" old Seedy growled : "can't you assist me, lad ? Come, think of a plan to regain our muskets."

Perched twenty feet above the desired weapons, the young sailor had not an easy task assigned him.

"If we had a line," he said, "I think we might manage to recover one."

"With a line, of course—fish for them, eh ?"

"Exactly."

Old Seedy rubbed his left ear, and said, with less asperity in his voice than he had before used—

"Yes, lad, that is the thing ; but as we have not anything like a line——"

"Mr. Seedy !"

The old man looked up at the lad's animated face, and ejaculated—

"Well, boy."

Jack pointed with his hand to a long willow-like bough, as he said—

"How would this do, if we can manage to get it off ?"

The old man scanned the long supple branch attentively ; at length, satisfied with his scrutiny, he said—

"Ah ! I see there is a small shoot at the end that would make a good crook. But is it strong enough, lad, that is the next thing ?"

"We can but try it."

"True ; how to break it off ? I wish I had my old knife. The Lord help us, what is the boy doing ? Hi, Jack, are you mad ?—there, oh, heaven ! I thought so. Hold on, my lad, for your life while I skewer that beggar."

Whizz through the air old Seedy's lance flew, and with a dull thud passed clean through the back of a large tiger, whose teeth were within a few inches of our hero's legs.

The beast writhed and growled savagely and strove to scramble forward as the long quivering weapon pinned him to the earth.

The cause of this terrible, and to the actors, this momentous episode, was Jack's attempt to break the long branch from its parent stem.

The boy had scrambled above the doomed limb, and placing his spear between his teeth, then with both hands tightly grasping one of the uppermost branches, he placed his feet upon the supple limb he wished to detach.

For this purpose he jerked himself upward, his feet for a moment being suspended between the two branches ; then falling with the whole weight of his body upon the lower branch, it snapped off close to the trunk.

Jack had expected more resistance, and to his and old Seedy's horror, the supple branch which he grasped bent like a cane, and before he well knew what had befallen him, he felt that he was descending right into the jaws of the hungry fraternity who had so long and patiently awaited his coming.

Not a sound escaped his lips, though the boy could hear the sharp snap of a tiger's teeth only a few inches beneath.

When old Seedy's lance cleft the air the tiger was in the act of crouching for a spring, and but for that timely and well-aimed blow there would have been an end to the gallant fellow's adventures and perils.

The tiger transfixed, old Seedy, fearful that a second brute would be more successful in dragging the boy from his perilous position, descended the tree with wondrous speed until he came within reach of Jack's head.

Then lying horizontally along the trunk, he seized Jack by the hair and drew him upwards.

The supple limb which had so nearly caused Jack destruction, relieved of part of its burden, rose slowly, and as Jack clutched at a stouter branch, flew upward, and resumed its place.

Without commenting upon his hair-breadth

escape from a deadly peril, Jack simply said—

"I think I detached that branch."

The old sailor, who had not recovered from the fright Jack had given him, blurted out,

"Detached it, eh? Why—why, do you know that skulking devil I have pinned nearly had you by the leg?"

"Yes, I know that" (this was said with all the *sang froid* imaginable); "lucky you picked me up in time, Mr. Seedy."

The old tar was staggered by the boy's coolness, and as he gazed at the flushed face, he said, proudly,

"Jack, had you served long on board ship you would have worn a pair of gold epaulettes on your shoulder. Yes, you may laugh: but it's true, and an admiral's cocked hat in the bargain."

Jack laughed heartily at his companion's earnest face, and said,

"Like Riley's hat, I suppose. Ha! ha! ha!"

"You young madcap! There you are laughing as though we were safely on the deck of a good ship"

"Have you forgotten the hungry, ugly, sneaking gang that is below?"

"No. Where's the long stick I broke off?"

Like a monkey he climbed from bough to bough until he reached the rod-like branch, which hung to the tree by a small thread of bark.

To detach the branch was the work of a moment, and, stripping off the leaves and every useless shoot, Jack began to descend the tree.

Arrived at the lowest branch, the boy thrust his spear into the trunk, and began to lower the long rod.

Stretched at full length along the massive stem, and gripping only with his legs, he tried to fix the crooked extremity of the long branch in the trigger-guard of the nearest musket.

The circle of animals took but little notice of Jack's movements, and, looked if possible, more intently at the lithe figure stretched along the branch of the tree.

The task was not easy of accomplishment and not until Jack had several times raised the rifle a few inches from the ground was the desired result attained.

Old Seedy had eagerly watched every movement and when he beheld the weapon slowly rising towards his companion he uttered a short cry of joy.

"Well done, lad, well done! Gently. Ha! it nearly capsized then. So—that's it. Hurra! I have it."

During the time he had been speaking the precious weapon was in Jack's grasp, and th boy rising from the fearful position necessary t attain this desirable result, handed the rifle t old Seedy.

"No, my boy," he said; "no, you got th piece, keep it, and pepper away at thos beggars."

Jack gave him the thin branch, and while th master-at-arms was busy fishing for the secon rifle, the boy settled himself firmly upon th stout stem, and carefully examined his weapon

He drew the hammer back several times t assure himself no injury had been sustained b the trampling of the brute's heavy feet, the carefully loaded,

"Shall I begin," he asked, as his bright ey glanced along the dark barrel, "or wait fo you?"

"Blaze away," was the answer. "I canno get a grip upon my piece."

Jack could not resist smiling at the exertion his companion was undergoing.

One of the besieging force, a powerful full grown lion, was watching intently the swingin to and fro of old Seedy's body, as he tried t affix the crooked end of the stick in the trigger guard of his musket.

Jack covered the royal brute with the muzzle of his piece, then drawing a deep breath, he drew the butt close to his shoulder, and pulled the trigger.

The animal uttered a wild cry, then sprang upward; a moment the fore feet clawed wildly at the empty air, then with a dull thud he fell to the earth lifeless.

The bullet had entered close beneath the shoulder, and cleft the heart.

"Number one," said the young adventurer as he began to reload. "Come, Mr. Seedy, you will be late for the sport."

"Ugh!" grunted the old fellow, "I can't get the plaguey thing up."

Jack rammed home the bullet, and asked—

"How's that?"

"Don't know, Jack. The rifle cants over when I begin to haul up."

Jack laughed at this woful speech, and again drew the rifle to his shoulder.

The fall of the lion had caused a movement among his companions, but whether of fear or rage it was hard to determine.

The whole of the brutes had risen to their feet, and as their white fangs glared horribly, and their tails swept the ground, a succession of low growls came from their massive throats

Again the boy sped a bullet from the fatal piece.

This time a full-grown tiger was hit, but not

mortally wounded, for the animal, as the blood trickled from its neck, stood as though spellbound with rage at the sharp cutting pains, then suddenly raising itself upon its hind legs, made a grip at the weapon old Seedy had at last raised from the ground.

One blow from the animal's paw sent the rifle flying far beyond the reach of the long branch, and as an expression, more remarkable for its force than politeness, came from the old seaman's lips at being thus treated after the trouble he had taken, the tiger turned suddenly upon one of its companions, and attacked it with terrible fury.

Such a fearful roar came from the assembled beasts, as the combatants hit and clawed each other, that the forest resounded with the terrible echoes.

"Give her another, Jack," old Seedy sang out, as he dashed the stick he had been using to the ground. "Aim well, lad; the coward brute has knocked my rifle beyond the tree."

The sharp crack of Jack's piece followed those words, and as the "ring" of the ball yet sounded in old Seedy's ears, the growling combatants rolled over and over for a few yards, then became motionless, save for a convulsive movement of the flanks.

CHAPTER XX.

UNEXPECTED VISITORS.

"BRAVO," said the master-at-arms; "that shot has passed through the pair of their heads."

Jack was excited with the slaughter he was making among the enemy, and without noticing his companion's words, he loaded as quickly as possible.

The denizens of the forest that yet remained unhurt, seemed suddenly to comprehend that something wrong had taken place among their fellows.

Round and round the carcases of the four dead brutes they walked, then, halting for a moment, sniffed at the yet warm blood, then, as Jack's rifle rang out for the fourth time, they gave a yell, and making towards the forest, soon decamped.

The last shot Jack fired had broken a puma's leg, for the animal limped after his companions, the off fore leg held up, and blood dropping at every step.

Old Seedy gave a loud huzza as the enemy turned tail, and without waiting to consider whether the four animals that lay so still were beyond the power of doing mischief, he rapidly descended the tree and clutched his rifle.

Jack was on the ground a moment after his companion, and with flushed face and sparkling eyes, he stood proudly regarding the fallen forms of the powerful brutes.

"They'll remember the crack of a rifle," said old Seedy; "eh, Jack? Four warm skins f our hut; we need not fear the cold."

"There is no doubt about that," said Jac "therefore I suppose we can leave the carca here until we have seen Riley."

"Right, lad, let's be off."

They found the ex-caterer in a state of alarm at their absence; and when he saw them he closed his building operations, and said,

"It's glad I am that yez have come back, for I thought some more beautiful things had reappeared, and maybe ye were both tossed over the moon by the cow-tree."

The midshipman and old Seedy laughed at their companion's quaint speech.

"The cow-tree, Riley," said the master-at-arms, "although capable of giving milk, cannot use the branches like a pair of horns.

"That's a blessing anyhow," said Riley; "now I suppose it's hungry yez both are."

"Yes," said Jack, "have you anything to eat?"

"Heaps of good things."

The tiger-slayers soon made havoc with the contents of the larder; then the master-at-arms, who was tired out with his long vigil, sought the shade of a drooping tree, and he soon fell asleep.

The midshipman tried to follow the example, but his brain was yet excited by the previous night's adventure.

"I'll go and help Riley," Jack said, "for I cannot sleep."

He found McGowan busily employed cutting the flesh of the shark into thin steaks, and placing them on the sunny side of the rock.

"Hallo, Riley," the midshipman said, "what are you up to?"

"Getting a stock of eatables ready for the voyage, Mister Rawlings."

"The what?"

"The voyage. Wasn't it agreed that two of us should go to the ship and bring off all sorts of things."

"Oh, yes, I had forgotten. "But don't you think, Riley, those flakes would dry better if they were on a line."

"Bedad, so they would, but the devil a bit of anything have I—not so much as an inch of cotton."

"There's some in the boat, Riley."

"Shure to be some there; bedad, I never thought of that, but I'll soon have some!"

"I will go with you, Riley, for I feel a little

knocked up, and a bathe in the sea may do me good."

They went to where the long-boat was beached, and upon turning the angle of a rock Riley came to a sudden halt, and exclaimed—

"Look there, Mister Rawlings, and first tell me what those two black things are that's hopping about round the boat."

"Two savages," said the midshipman, "naked savages, Riley."

"An' so they are, except for a bit of white calico undher their breasts. How the devil did they get there?"—

A small, rudely-fashioned canoe was drawn up on the beach. This Jack pointed out in answer to Riley's query.

The dusky visitors seemed much surprised at the make and shape of the long-boat, and after walking round it several times they began to overhaul the contents.

Riley, when he saw this, began to roll up his sleeves.

"Bedad!" he said, "it's not anything unearthly yez are, but flesh and blood, so here goes."

"Riley——"

"Come on, Misther Rawlings, or it's the contents of the boat they will have."

"There's some truth in that, Riley, so the sooner we are in attendance the better, for these islanders are great thieves."

"Whurroo!" yelled Riley, when within a few yards of the blacks, "whurroo, ye divils!"

The savages evidently took this as a war-cry, for they faced the white men and returned the cry. They were about to run to the canoes no doubt, to get possession of their arms.

In this they were defeated, for the ex-caterer and Jack were upon them in a moment.

The savage attacked by Jack had possessed himself of a goodly cudgel, but the fellow attacked by Riley had only his fists.

Jack luckily wrested the stick away from his antagonist at the same time that Riley managed to get his man's head in chancery.

"Hurrah!" shouted Riley, "I've got ye this time. Go it, Mister Rawlings, don't be afraid of using the shillelagh."

The dusky visitors eventually found themselves in the wrong place, for the savage engaged with Riley now called out something to his countrymen, and before the midshipman or the ex-caterer could point, the dusky visitors had bolted and regained their canoes.

"By the powers," said Riley, "but this is better than ghost ships, and islands coming out of the say; shure, there was something to keep a boy's hand in practice."

"Judging by the poor devil's nose," said Ja "I should say you did find something to pun at."

"They won't come here again in a hurry said McGowan, "bedad they have had enou for one day."

"So it would seem, Riley."

CHAPTER XXI.
IN SEARCH OF THE SHIP.

WHEN the master-at-arms heard of the visit the savages, he merely said—

"There's nothing to be alarmed at, for the islanders go almost incredible distances in the canoes. I am rather glad they have given a look-up."

"How's that, Mr. Seedy?"

"Just this, lad, it shows that this is t proper time to make our voyage to the ship, a return before the night birds set in."

"It's a quare thing," said Riley, "that can't all go; what's the use of leaving one of behind?"

"For the safety of the whole of us," said t old sailor; "for unless the boat is ready the time we return, we shall all be frozen death, for the winter is as cold as the summ is hot."

"Bedad, if that's it," said Riley, "I'll stay an build the shanty."

For three days after this the adventure were busy preparing for the voyage, and Rile though rather sorry to lose his companion even for a few days, worked willingly to ge them afloat.

He was well aware that the island they wer upon was more in the track of a passing shi than any of the numerous groups on thos seas.

"Bedad," he said," "it's all for the best th I'm to be left behind, for I can ve doing m share of the work here."

The dried flakes of shark's flesh were stowe away, to be used only in the event of the stor of salted pig failing; but that seemed scarcel possible, as there was more than they woul have consumed in a month.

Their only difficulty had been in constructing vessels to hold water.

But this was overcome by making bags capa ble of holding from two to three gallons, from the skins of the wild beasts slain during tha fearful night they sat in the tree.

A small shark bone formed the needle for thi purpose—the thread was drawn from a piece o he boat's sail.

THE MASTER-AT-ARMS MAKES A DISCOVERY.

Four of these water skins were placed in the boat with the provisions.

Everything being ready, old Seedy hoisted the sail, and, wafted by a gentle breeze, the adventurers' boat glided slowly by the island.

Reclining at full length upon a soft pile of skins, Jack looked wistfully at the small black speck standing out so boldly against the azure sky—he looked and felt as though he was leaving his home.

He was going, Heaven only knew whither, leaving peace and tranquillity for an unknown place, or mayhap, to be engulphed in the treacherous ocean, which now like an inland lake bore the boat forward.

Until the land became a mere hazy outline, he kept his gaze steadfastly fixed upon the place where he had passed both lonely and happy hours.

Then as the dim streak became blended with the far distant horizon, he raised his hand, and a peculiar appearance some twenty fathoms ahead of the boat caused him to exclaim—

"Look! What is that? Is it?—yes; it must be—a sail!"

Old Seedy turned quickly, but before he could

catch even a glimpse of the welcome canvas, our hero said huskily—

"It's gone; yet I could have sworn I saw— Yes; look! There it is again!"

The old seaman's face flushed slightly at the object, which to the uninitiated had the appearance of spread canvas, but his practised eye soon saw the real nature of this, to him, unpleasant sight.

"Sail, lad," he said, in a tone that showed how heartily he wished the strange appearance anywhere but in the vicinity of their little craft. "No; it's a whale spouting."

As he spoke a second white object suddenly arose from the water, then a third.

Jack saw the look of gloom that passed over old Seedy's face augured danger from the presence of the spouting jet of white vapour.

"What is it?" he asked eagerly. "Your face tells me that all is not right."

The old seaman shook his head, yet never for a moment suffered his eyes to wander from the object of his dread.

"All wrong, lad," he said—"all wrong. If they come this way, one fluke of the tail and up we go. I hope," he mentally added, "the boy's feelings were not prophetic of what I feel almost sure will happen."

Several dark objects were plainly visible above the water, then the sea, which lay so placid all around, was seen to swell into white-topped waves, as though under the influence of a sudden squall.

Amazed, yet interested at the strange sight, Jack watched with suppressed breathing the swift approach of the horde.

"A large shoal," muttered old Seedy," "and coming right upon us. Look out, lad!"

The warning was only in time, for Jack had been so intent with the movements of the whales that the possibility of being cast overboard had quite escaped his mind.

He had but time to clutch the side of the boat, when the frail craft was turning to and fro in the swell caused by the passage of the whales through the water.

"They escaped death by the merest trifle.

Had the whales kept the same course they were pursuing when first sighted, nothing could have saved our adventurers' boat from being thrown on her beam ends by the fan-shaped tails or the huge back of one of these leviathans.

They had, much to the old sailor's joy, swerved a little as they came within a couple of fathoms of the boat, though the sea was agitated by their swift passage through the water to such an extent that the boat was at

times lost in the trough of the sea, and at other times perched upon the crest of a white-topped frothy wave.

The exertions of both were required to keep the frail vessel from foundering, and though the timbers were untouched, neither felt safe until the waters began to subside and they were once more going free before the wind.

"A lucky escape, lad; had one of those beggars fluked us, there would have been an end to our voyage."

Looking round at the boundless tract of water, Jack found that all traces of their visitors had departed.

The boy had beheld, for the first time, a gathering of the ocean's strange and monstrous inhabitants, and with that thirst for knowledge which is inherent in every intelligent mind, he asked his companion to solve the mystery to him of that vast gathering.

Old Seedy had during his career on board a whaler, and with more intelligence than could have been expected, answered every query both readily and intelligently.

The old man was a keen observer of Nature, and, as a boy, he had often been struck with the singularity of her works.

Even then, although but a child in years, he had often puzzled grey-headed men by the shrewdness of his remarks, and the quick perceptive power he displayed of learning the habits of the strange denizens of the deep.

With them it was sufficient to know that, we will say for example, a whale rose to the surface at certain periods; or that a shark was usually attended by a number of pilot-fish and suckers. He wanted to know why it was so— a question his shipmates, although they had served many years at sea, could not answer.

Curtailed as he was in the outset of his desire to attain a knowledge of the ocean's strange denizens, the wish became stronger, and he patiently watched every trivial circumstance that took place among the finny tribe until he had acquired a better and more profound insight into the sea's natural history than many who are looked upon by the world as great and learned naturalists.

Such a man was a fitting companion for the brave, intelligent boy, and, as the sequel will show, the knowledge Jack thus obtained was a mighty power, and saved him more than once from the icy clutch of the grim destroyer's hand.

"I never could have imagined," the young sailor said, "that we should have been in such peril in consequence of these whales nearing us."

"Peril, lad!" the old sailor said. "Did you think those great brutes were as harmless as a shoal of herrings?"

"No; I have heard that, when attacked, they often upset a boat, but never knew there was any danger to be apprehended when not interfered with."

"There is, boy, great danger; and I, too, well remember a circumstance that happened when I was a boy aboard a whaler. What think you of a stout ship being sunk by one of them?"

"How do you mean: lifted out of the water and upset?"

"No, lad; the biggest among 'em couldn't do that. But the one that I am speaking about was the cause of our vessel sinking, and sending forty poor fellows to Davy Jones's before their time. You look surprised, lad. Shall I tell you how it occurred?"

CHAPTER XXII.

THE MASTER-AT-ARMS RELATES A WHALING STORY. JACK'S face brightened. It was not often that old Seedy indulged him with a yarn, or rather, truthful recital of perils that he had passed through, and strange hardships and sights, that would have been discredited by many, who, forsooth, called themselves wise, and sent forth huge volumes of the wonders of nature, without having seen one iota of the many strange things they profess so well to understand.

There has been, and no doubt there are at the present moment, many rough, unlettered men before the mast who could enlighten the world with many truthful and wondrous stories of nature's mystic works, and, were they believed in preference to the many great naturalists, whose field of observation consisted in the limited extent of their own gardens, or a heap of musty books, the ignorant and untravelled would be nearer the truth than they can ever hope to be by poring over their calf-bound volumes.

"Every word of this, lad, is as true as we are in this boat," old Seedy said, as he began his recital; "and this is how it occurred. The whale ship of which I was aboard was in the Southern Ocean, looking out for whales.

"One morning, as the captain, or the mate—I forget which now—was on the look-out, we all stood by the boats, ready to let fall the moment he gave the signal."

The old seaman paused, and drew his hand across his eyes, and Jack saw, by the working of his features, that the recital recalled unpleasant memories in the veteran seaman's mind.

"Don't tell it," the boy said, thoughtfully, wishing to spare his companion any painful feelings; "the recollection is too much for you."

The old fellow gathered the corner of their little sail tightly in his hand, and making an effort to appear cheerful, said—

"Yes, lad; I've begun, and may as well go on. Now, Jack, I always see his pale face and blue lips when he said ' good-bye' to me."

Jack's interrogative look was answered by the narrator of the sad story.

"He was my brother, lad"—old Seedy spoke, as though making an effort to choke back the husky sensation that almost stayed his words—"the only one I ever had. Well, well, he went, I hope, to a better world, for he was too good—much too good—to—to——"

Old Seedy paused, and a tear trickled down each weather-beaten cheek.

Jack felt for the poor fellow; he could understand, although he had hitherto been alone and friendless, the strange yearning that clings to the heart of those who have lost for ever one that was dear to them.

Again he expressed his wish for his companion to abtsain from recalling the details of that fatal day; the old man's answer was a quick gesture of the hand as though to imply silence.

"Where did I leave off?"

His voice was firmer now, and the nervous twitching motion of the lips had passed away.

"We were waiting for the look-out to give the signal."

"It came.

"Little did the gallant ship's company think the welcome word was their death warrant.

"It was," he resumed, after a slight pause, "although when the cry came from above, ' she spouts—she spouts!' we gave a cheer and, like magic, down went the boats and the whole of the hands complete; six were soon pulling like mad towards the huge animal; who could be seen blowing about every half minute.

"We were not long getting alongside the whale, then, as he was about to sink, the captain called out, ' peak your oars!' Up goes the shining blades, and, afore you could count one, I had sent the harpoon deep in the brute's carcase, for," he added proudly, "I was then harpooner, and, if what they record and tell me is true, as good as any man who ever drove a lance into a whale."

"After he was struck, the mate calls out, ' Stern all!' and we backed out of reach of the monster's tail, and, giving him plenty of line, down he went, sixty fathoms of good rope fastened to the harpoon.

"We followed the brute until he rose to the surface, and the headsman stood ready to give him the finishing stroke; but, quick as thought, his tail went up in the air, and as it descended our boat was struck, and the next minute we were splashing about in the water.

"That would not have mattered much, as the other boats were not far off, had it not been for a shoal of sharks which were swimming about near us—they always do when a whale is struck—in the hope, I expect, of getting the blood which runs from their wounds.

"Be that as it may, they were soon seen coming towards us, and before the boats—which came, you may be sure, as quickly as man could pull—arrived, three poor fellows were bitten in halves by the powerful teeth of the rapacious sea monsters.

"Poor fellows! they were saved from many long days of suffering by their dreadful fate, although none at the time knew the great danger that was creeping towards us.

"This accident," old Seedy continued, "stayed the pursuit, and the whale, maddened with the pain of his wounds, appeared at times to spring out of the water, throwing up a mountain of white spray with the convulsive flappings of his fan-like tail.

"Never shall I forget it, lad; that dreadful moment when the men in the boat which was in advance of us called out, 'He's struck the ship.'"

"Those who heard the cry could not at first believe the dreadful truth."

"Alas, the matter was soon beyond dispute. We were not more than ten fathoms from the doomed vessel when we saw a detached portion of the cutwater floating towards us."

"A minute after the whale rose to the surface, and, as true as I'm a living man, the powerful brute made a furious charge upon the ship's larboard bow, and with his immense head crushed the planks; it seemed as easy as we would break an egg-shell.

"The ship filled, and before we could reach her she had lurched over on her side, and down she went with all on board.

"There we were, lad, hundreds of miles from land; no food, no water, and our home engulphed by the treacherous ocean. There was nothing left for us but to die; and before we sighted a ship the whole of the crew, except myself and the second mate, had perished miserably in mid-ocean; among the first was my poor brother."

Then old Seedy sat with his elbows on his knees, and as he abruptly finished this sad story, he covered his face with his hands, and wept.

Jack felt the unbidden tears rising in his eyes, and quitting his seat, he came beside the grief-stricken man, and placed his hands upon the old seaman's shoulder.

"Mr. Seedy," he said, in gentle, soothing tones, "you have lost your brother; let me fill his place in your heart."

The veteran sailor upturned his gaze, and, looking fondly in the boy's face, he took the small hand between his own rough palms and pressed it affectionately.

"You shall," he said—"you shall be my brother; next to him I have loved you more than aught else in this world."

"And I have told you; you have been my friend, now we will be as brothers."

The setting sun had thrown a dull red glare upon the ocean before the master-at-arms recovered his wonted cheerfulness, and when the young sailor had won him from the deep melancholy which so heavily weighed upon his heart, he asked a few questions about the leviathans of the deep.

"Do they always," he asked, "swim in such vast numbers as those we saw a short time since?"

"Not always, lad; that must have been a pod of young whales."

"A pod," Jack cried, with a marked stress upon the word; "it seems a strange one to use in reference to the great quantity."

"By a pod," old Tom said "I mean a great number of young whales, which, under the guidance of some old ones, learn to swim and seek their food—as least, I expect this is the cause of the vast numbers of young I have seen, each herd attended by one or two old ones."

"Strange," Jack saie, musingly, "these creatures have no power of speech, yet they are as capable of being instructed."

"Nature, lad—nature," said old Seedy. "Here comes the darkness. Help me to make an awning of the sail, then you can turn in while I keep watch."

The sail spread over the boat's stern formed a comfortable covering, and kept the night damps from falling on the adventurers.

Jack, tired and unused to fatigue like his companion, was soon asleep, and old Seedy, with an extra skin thrown over his shoulders sat just within the sail, keeping solitary vigil.

The hours glided slowly onward, still the old seaman sat with his head buried in his hands listening to the gentle ripple of the waves as they kissed the sides of the little craft.

The recollections connected with his brother's death, so long dormant, now recalled by the recital of the whaling adventure, saddened the hardy seaman's spirit, and he felt the honest love of his rugged heart more firmly fixed than ever upon the handsome boy who slept so near him.

So the long night passed, and morning's cheerful beams shone upon the grey-headed seaman whose position had remained unchanged, but whose faculties were lulled to mute forgetfulness by the soft murmur of the rippling waves—the gentle murmur which had from childhood lulled him to sleep, and whose heaving breast had been his home both in sunshine and storm.

CHAPTER XIII

RILEY MCGOWAN'S "DRAME."

THE ex-caterer watched the boat that contained his companions, the single sail faded in the distance, then he turned sadly from the shore, and went towards the partially-built hut.

"It's a nice mess I'm in now," muttered Riley, as he seated himself upon a log. "It's all alone I am, except the skeletons upon the top of the hill, and it's there they'll stop I hope."

Riley took up the hatchet and began to chop from one of the branches he wanted to use, and when he had fixed this in its place he looked to the priming of his musket and drew his cutlass from its sheath.

"It's a sleep I'll have," he said; "and in case any of them black devils come here agin it's ready for them I'll be."

Curled up under the shadow of a big tree, Riley was soon asleep and dreaming of all kinds of horrible things.

First he thought all the bleached bones of the men who had perished so mysteriously became strung together, and the ghastly figures came down from the hill top and began to help him to build the hut.

He awoke with a start just as they were using hammer and nails, and, seeing the sun shining upon the surface of the ocean, Riley pulled his cocked hat over his eyes and said—

"It is only a dhrame, the Lord be praised."

He was soon asleep again—this time to be troubled by the appearance of a number of savages landing upon the island.

He saw them draw their canoes upon the beach, and one fellow with a large ring through his nose, came and pointed out the spot where Riley had hidden the last bottle of the precious whisky.

The savage tasted the spirit, then gave a yell, and ran off to join his companions.

Riley watched them kindle a fire, then he went and roused up the master-at-arms and Jack Rawlings, whom he thought slept in the hut so quickly finished by the skeletons.

"It's boarded we are, Mr. Seedy," said Riley; "look this way and ye will better see them."

The master-at-arms and Jack seized their muskets, and taking up a position behind a piece of rock, witnessed the swarthy indians of the Pirates' Isle."

"I'll tell you what it is," said Riley, as he took up the naked cutlass, "it's a council of war we will have."

"Yes," said Jack, "and an ambuscade; for our only chance is to get these fellows within range of our fire."

"It's quick about it I hope ye will be," said Riley, "or every drop of the whisky will be gone down their dirty throats."

"You fire first, Mr. Seedy," said Jack, "and knock down the fellow who touched the bottle."

The master-at-arms fired, and Jack, pointing with his finger, exclaimed—

"Well done—that's one down!"

"Let me get at 'em," said Riley, brandishing the cutlass, "it's mincemeat I will make of every mother's son."

"Wait until I fire, Riley," said the middy, "there's too many for us to attack at once."

Jack fired, and the savages gave a yell and started to their feet.

With this noise ringing in his ears Riley awoke, and to his dismay he saw on the beach a dozen savages, who had just landed from their canoes.

"It's a dead man I am now," exclaimed Riley, "for one part of my dhrame has come—and that is the worst part—for it would not have been so bad had the master and Mister Rawlings been here as I saw them in my sleep."

Riley presently returned to doze again in the niche, taking with him his musket, cutlass, and hatchet, and a full supply of ammunition.

"It's a long time," he muttered, "they'll be in getting me out of the hole, bad luck to every mother's son of them."

As Riley retired to his fortress, the savages with bent bows and arrows on their strings, came up towards the interior of the island.

CHAPTER XXIV.

A BATTLE WITH THE SHARKS.

THE sun was shining on the sea's glassy surface when Jack awoke from his slumbers, and started up to a sitting position. He glanced towards his companion.

A remorseful feeling came to his heart when

he beheld old Seedy still in the same position as when he had bade him good-night.

Rising softly, he crept forward and placed his hand on the old seaman's shoulder.

"Mr. Seedy," he said, "this is not right; you have kept watch the whole night. Why did you not rouse me?"

The veteran started at the boy's light touch, and instantly his senses, which had been buried in oblivious slumber, returned.

"I could not have slept, lad," he said; "besides, there was no need keeping a good lookout. We are far from land, and a hundred miles away from the track of any vessel."

"Still, Mr. Seedy," said the boy, "you ought to let me share the labour of the voyage with you."

"So you shall, lad—so you shall. Now begin and help me to get breakfast."

He jumped to his feet while speaking, and with Jack's assistance the sail was hoisted and securely fastened, and as they went aft to partake of their frugal meal a light wind carried them swiftly forward upon the bosom of the trackless waste of water.

The breeze fell about noon, and the sea became as smooth as the polished surface of a mirror.

The middy noted the anxious expression upon his companion's face when this sudden calm fell upon them, and following the old sailor's inquiring glance as he swept the horizon, he asked—

"What is the matter, Mr. Seedy? You look anxious since the boat became motionless."

"There is nothing much yet, boy, but there may be something. Look there!"

Old Seedy pointed to a bank of heavy dark clouds that was at that moment gliding slowly over the sun's burning disc.

"I see them, Mr. Seedy," Jack said. "What does it mean?"

Shading his eyes with his outstretched hands, old Seedy took a long and deeper scrutiny of the rapidly accumulating harbingers of a coming storm.

"That's what I can't answer yet," he said, in reply to Jack's query. "It may be only a gathering of rain clouds—it may be the prelude of a heavy squall; if so, the Lord help us—this boat will never live it out."

The middy knew his companion was not in the habit of magnifying any approaching peril—far otherwise.

Knowing this caused a vague feeling of uneasiness to enter the gallant boy's heart; and there was a cause he should feel thus.

They were alone on mid-ocean, and nothing to shelter them from the coming storm, their boat a frail structure that would not withstand the buffet of a large wave.

Checking the chill feeling that came creeping over his faculties, Jack stood beside his companion, and in silence they stood watching the slowly gathering storm-clouds.

Rolling upwards as though they rose from the ocean, the dark masses drifted across the sun; then as the wind came stealing gently across the water, the sail bellied out, and the boat like a high-mettled racer when goaded by the spur, shot forward.

The white foam curled before her sharp prow in feathery streaks, and from time to time a shower of minute spray swept across the faces of the anxious pair.

"To the helm, boy!" shrieked old Seedy, when this change took place. "Keep her to it, and, please the Lord, we may yet escape."

Obeying this order with an alacrity that showed how deeply Jack shared his companion's excitement, he seized the tiller, and kept the boat's head in the direction pointed out by a silent gesture of old Seedy's hand.

Ten minutes passed in this manner—both silent; one grasping the sail ready to let fall should circumstances require, the other watching every movement of his companion's hand.

The wind which wafted the boat so swiftly through the water, also brought the storm clouds upon their track, and their only hope of salvation lay in being able to out-speed the mass of murky clouds.

"I think," old Seedy said, as he suffered the single sail to go free, "we shall do it, lad. Ha! look, it has burst!"

Jack turned his head, and beheld the atmosphere about a mile to leeward now having a thick misty appearance and the water beneath appeared to bubble and froth upward.

Presently the minute spray increased in size, until the white-topped billows could be discerned rising and falling as the water was lashed by the sweeping gusts of wind.

Jack knew by the misty appearance of the horizon that the rain clouds had burst, and the water was falling upon the ocean in such force as to darken the air through which it passed.

He knew also that the white-crested foam and the undulating movement of the distant part of the sea was caused by the wind suddenly sweeping downward.

Yet, strange to say, although these evidences of a terrible tempest were raging within a mile of their little boat, all around, save to leeward, was calm and beautiful.

The young officer now understood the meaning of his companion's exclamation when he said their only hope of safety was the possibility of outstripping the gale.

"You don't think there is a possibility of the storm reaching us now," Jack said, as the boat glided swiftly onward; "the clouds seem to me to be drifting this way."

The master-at-arms steadied himself by holding the mast, and took a long look at the seething water and deluge of rain that was falling.

"No, lad," he said, "I think not. The gale is nearly over now, and the clouds that you imagine are coming this way are gradually disappearing, the Lord be praised."

He concluded in such a faint murmur that Jack felt the danger, despite these assurances, was not yet over.

He asked his companion if such was not the case.

"You are right, lad," was the answer; "there is yet danger, but not one-twentieth part of what threatened us when the clouds began to gather."

The danger, from whatever quarter old Seedy expected it, did not come; and soon after the sun shone out with a double brilliancy, the wind fell, and the sea again became calm.

"We must take a spell at the oars," said the old sailor. "I am suspicious of these seas; one minute a cat's-paw, the next a hurricane. Bend to it, lad; perhaps we may sight an island before dark; there are plenty hereabouts, or I am much out of my reckoning."

The rudder was made fast, and Jack took the stroke oar.

"Are we far," he asked, "from the wreck?"

"Not far, lad; but there are so many islands hereabouts that we may touch at a dozen before we find the one we want."

They pulled for some time in silence, and Jack, who was watching the tiny wavelets, suddenly suspended his rowing, and uttered an exclamation of surprise and admiration.

"What is it, lad?"

"A fish," was the reply. "Here, Tom; look! I never saw such a beautiful creature."

Resting for the time upon his oar, old Seedy leant forward, and looked in the direction indicated by his companion's finger.

When the veteran seaman beheld the little creature, which swam close to the stern, so far from sharing Jack's admiration, a warning cry came from his lips.

That there could be anything to fear from the pretty little creature that glided so gracefully through the water was ridiculous to entertain. Yet, Jack knew well there must be a cause for his companion's warning cry.

What was it?

Old Seedy was by this time standing upon the thwart, his keen grey eyes directed first one side of the boat then the other, and finally, as they turned to the stern of the boat, he exclaimed—

"I thought so—here he comes. To quarters, lad; hand me my rifle."

As quick as the words left the old fellow's lips, Jack was upon his feet, and snatched up the rifles which had been placed beneath the gorilla's skin.

He gave one to the master-at-arms, and the other he held ready for use.

Following the direction of his companion's fixed gaze, he beheld a sight that for a moment sent an icy chill to his heart.

Making direct for the boat was one of those dreaded monsters of the deep, the white shark, the most furious and dreaded of the terrible species.

Every moment brought the monster nearer the boat, the huge black body was visible beneath the dorsal fin, which, like a sail, showed the speed at which the unwelcome visitor was approaching their frail embarkation.

Though startled by the sudden and unexpected appearance of the ocean monster, Jack's brain was busy trying to solve the connection between the shark and the beautiful little fish that had been visible so close under their lee.

He noticed that the object of his admiration had suddenly disappeared, and well knowing the voracity of their grim visitor, his first thought was that the small azure-coloured fish had swum away terrified at the shark's approach.

His surprise was great when he beheld the small fish swimming a few yards ahead of the shark, and looking, to all appearance, as though it was guiding the monster to the boat.

He also forgot the danger they were placed in, by his anxiety for the little creature; nothing he thought could save it from the capacious jaws of the shark; but as he feverishly watched, he saw to his increasing surprise that the terrible animal took not the least notice of the tempting morsel so close to his jaws.

There was a mystery in this he could not fathom, and much as he wished to understand it, there was no time to ask any questions.

The boy well knew that had they been upon the deck of a stout vessel there would have been nothing to fear, even from this, the fiercest of the shark tribe; he also knew that, situated as they were, only a couple of feet above the water, there was every possibility of their terrible pursuer springing out of his element, and either seizing the boat or one of themselves.

He had heard many such stories told on the gun-brig's forecastle, and, bravely as he had hitherto faced ordinary danger, his cheek now paled at the prospect of an encounter with this the mariner's most inveterate foe.

There was not much time given him to prepare for the fight, for the shark, whipping the water violently with his forked tail, made a charge at the boat's stern.

The adventurers thought their last hour had come when the huge creature struck the boat, and sent it forward with the swiftness of an arrow.

Both were hurled, bruised and bleeding, between the thwarts, and before they could regain their feet a crunching of wood was heard.

"Great Heaven," old Seedy ejaculated; "he has torn the stern out. Jack, my boy, it is —— "

His young companion was upon his feet in an instant, and as he arose he saw the terrible jaws above the gunwale; then as the crash of breaking timber sounded upon old Seedy's hearing, the boy called out—

"No, no, it is only the rudder."

The voracious brute had seized this useful appendage by his triple row of teeth and torn it away from the fastenings.

The shock given to the small boat threatened to swamp it, and as the fierce brute rushed through the water with the piece of board between its teeth, the sailors had regained their feet and stood ready to defend their lives.

The shark crushed the rudder between its formidable teeth and scattered the fragments, then with a sudden flap of the forked tail, dashed for the second time towards the frail craft.

The hideous fin rose above the water, and the teeth seized a portion of the gorilla's skin which hung over the stern.

But before the skin could be whipped away, old Seedy's rifle rang out, and to the young officer's joy, the huge monster's jaws relaxed, the tail whipped the water into a white foam, then a convulsive throe traversed through the creature's body, and he rolled over dead, the sunshine gleaming upon the white breast.

A shout of joy came from Jack's lips at this sight, and he ran aft to assure himself that their deadly and dangerous foe was no more.

"Dead as a herring!" old Seedy said; "that shot hit the most vulnerable part of the monster's carcase."

Jack saw a thin ensanguined streak rising to the surface from beneath the shark's head, and as he gazed with glad yet dread feelings upon the ocean-terror, he said—

"The ball has entered his head, Mr. Seedy."

"No, boy," was the reply, "the nose—fair in the middle: that is the place. Though they ar so strong, a blow with the butt-end of a muske will kill any of them, if you hit the right spot.

"Heaven be praised! you have done so, Mr Seedy, or the brute would have dragged ou boat beneath the water."

"Very likely, my lad, very likely. Now don' forget, when you want to kill one of thes reptiles, hit it between the nostrils, and it's al over with 'em."

Jack, whose eyes had been fixed upon the dead shark, suddenly cried out—

"Look, look! See is here another coming.'

Old Seedy hastily, but carefully, reloaded his rifle, and, looking to leeward, he saw the dorsal fin of one of the species cleaving the sunlit waters.

Jack suggested taking to the oars, but his older and more experienced companion overruled this.

"It ain't a bit of use," he said, "trying to get away; we must let him come, and serve the varmint as this one has been served. You know the spot, 'tween the nostrils; let him have it. I'll reserve my fire, in case you should miss."

As Jack, with compressed lips and flushed face, watched the second shark coming towards them, he saw, as in the former case, one of those beautiful little creatures, the pilot-fish, swimming a few yards in advance of the monster's snout.

There was a mystery in this that surprised the boy, and had there been time he would have asked his companion the meaning of this affinity between a creature so small and beautiful as the pilot-fish and the ugly-looking, ferocious white shark.

When the huge fish came within a few feet of the dead carcase, his fins became quiet, and the small, evil-looking eyes were seen examining the lifeless form of his late companion.

The snout was within six inches of the surface, and Jack, taking careful aim, pulled the trigger.

Whether the wounded animal went to the bottom and died, or whether he shot away and rolled, belly upwards, out of reach of the fire, the adventurers could not determine.

But after the shot from Jack's rifle the monster disappeared.

A red streak coming to the surface at right angles from that which came from the already slain animal, proved that the boy's shot had taken effect, though not so fatally quick as the old seaman's.

Too much elated at being thus rid of th enemies, the ocean wanderers did not tro themselves respecting the fate of the shark, aking to their oars, they began to move swiftly through the glassy-looking surface of the sea.

The late exploit called forth no comment from the rowers. Deadly peril and hair-breath escapes were too much a matter of daily occurrence to cause a second thought.

But Jack, as he laboured at the oar, could not dismiss from his mind the recollection of the shark and its beautiful little satellite.

When they paused to rest for a few minutes from their labour, the boy took the opportunity to clear up the matter.

"Mr. Seedy," he said, "when you saw the small fish that came leeward before the shark, you seemed amazed. Had the little thing any reference to the other's appearance?"

"Ay, lad," was the reply, "it had. That was the pilot-fish; they always go in front of a shark."

"Does not the vicious brute ever eat them?"

"No, lad; the little things are too useful. Didn't you see the pilot fish, after looking at the boat, go away?"

"Yes—now I remember, I did."

"Then you saw it swimming in front of the shark, and guiding the brute to our boat?"

"Guiding the shark?"

"Ay, that's just it, lad—nothing else. It saw us, maybe, and went back to its protector. I've heard—but that I can't say is true, 'cos not seeing it; but those who saw it told me—that when the pilot-fish is in danger of being devoured by an enemy—for in the sea, my lad, the fish prey upon each other, the shark excepted—he sometimes gets killed by a thrust from sword-fish."

"Wonderful!" the boy said, deeply struck by these words.

"Yes, it is wonderful, lad—very wonderful. Let's see—I was saying about the pilot-fish being in danger."

"You were."

"When this happens, the shark opens his mouth and lets the little creature stay inside until the danger is past. Then they come out again, and swim in front of their master's snout."

"It is strange, these things—very strange."

"Yes, lad, to those land-lubbers who know nothing of the wonders of the deep; but to the sailor, he so often sees them that they become matters of no interest.

Old Seedy settled himself upon the seat, and seemingly glad the boy's cross-questioning was over, began to feather his oar.

Jack took the hint, and the light craft was soon gliding swiftly forward.

CHAPTER XXV.

BREAKERS AHEAD.

DURING the conversation related in the preceding chapter, the huge carcase of the white shark had drifted in a parallel line with the boat.

The monster was within a fathom of the frail structure his triple teeth had so nearly destroyed, and our hero, as he called his companion's attention to the proximity of their late foe, exclaimed—

"As I live, there is a number of fishes growing out of the shark!"

"Growing out of the shark, lad. No; they are suckers, and have nothing to do with the big varmint, except to make him useful."

The boy had ceased rowing until old Seedy had turned the boat's head towards the floating carcase; then he bent to his task with a will that soon brought the boat alongside their late foe.

By the time this movement was accomplished the shark had rolled partly over, and the suckers were under the water, but near enough to the surface to be visible.

The fish to which old Seedy had given the peculiar name of "sucker" was about ten inches in length, and differed slightly in conformation with its fellows by a peculiar apparatus upon the top of its head; it appeared not unlike a second mouth, for when old Seedy bent over the edge of the boat, and forcibly detached it from the shark's side, Jack beheld a row of small teeth in the strange conformation.

Old Seedy struck the peculiar-looking fish a sharp blow upon the edge of the boat, and soon terminated its existence.

"You see, lad," he said, holding the curious-looking creature by the tail, "this fish ain't got much of a pair of fins, so it can't swim fast, but it ain't to be beat for all that."

Jack took the object in his hand, and minutely examined the apparatus which nature had provided as a counterbalance to its feeble powers of progression through the water.

"That thing," old Seedy said, "causes it to stick to the belly of a shark, a ship's bottom, or a floating plank. It ain't particular as long as it gets carried about."

Jack placed the fish in the bottom of the boat, and, more than ever mystified with the singular inhabitants of the ocean, resumed his seat, and again plying the oar, thought over the many wonderful things he had become acquainted with since he had been left upon the island.

The dangers he had passed were all forgotten

in the all-absorbing wish to penetrate yet further into the mysteries of animated nature—a wish that could not be eradicated by twice the peril he had gone through.

Old Seedy seeing the boy's abstraction, said—

"It's strange work, Jack, ain't it? and it makes you thing of curious things. Eh, lad?"

"More than strange, Mr. Seedy, more than strange."

He replied thus to his companion, and again relapsed—a quietude only broken by the jerking of the oars in the rowlocks.

Nearly on hour they rowed thus silently; then the voice of old Seedy awoke the boy from his reverie.

"It's time to take a rest now, lad," he said; "so pass me over your oar, and come for'ard."

Jack resigned the oar to his companion, and stepping lightly over the thwarts, stood in the bow.

The golden sun threw its rays across the sea's vast expanse when our hero took up his position.

Nothing was to be seen around save the azure-tinted sea in the wondrous yet monotonous aspect presented by its vast magnitude.

"Keep a good look out, lad," said the old seaman; "if the wind keeps down, we shall sight the island before night."

It needed not his companion's words to incite the boy to look for the promised land, and shading his eyes—for the slowly sinking sun shot its powerful rays directly in their path—he keenly scanned the horizon.

Nothing was to be seen but the gently rippling bosom of the great mass of interminable water.

Towards every point of the compass Jack strained his eyes, but nothing save the blue and distant horizon, which appeared to blend with the sea, rewarded his anxious vision.

There he stood until the orb of day sank, like a lurid ball of fire, and the dark shadow of approaching night descended with the swiftness peculiar to the tropics.

One short leap from sunshine to darkness—no twilight to give warning of the day's close.

With a sigh of regret the young adventurer went aft, and helped to spread the sail over their resting-place, and as they sat partaking of their frugal meal, both felt anxious for the morrow.

"I know these seas," the old sailor said, "We have had fine weather upon our voyage as yet, but before morning we might be tossing about, our only hope of safety a piece of the broken boat, or, maybe, an oar."

Alone, and nothing but the frail boat between them and eternity, and that boat drifting at the mercy of the wind and tide! The sky overhead was so dark as to render each other's face barely distinguishable. These words were not calculated to inspire the young adventurer with cheerful anticipations.

But so far from feeling any despondency at his companion's words, that indomitable spirit that had hitherto carried him safely through so many perils showed itself in the midshipman's reply to this sombre speech.

"The night damps, Mr. Seedy," he said, gaily, "are not favourable to your temperament. Pardon my rudeness, but your voice was for all the world like a raven's, croaking out all sorts of ill-luck. I know what it is that makes you so gloomy; you are out of your reckoning with the latitude of the island. Come, don't let that trouble you. I question if the greatest navigator in the world could do better in an open boat, and without either compass or chart."

"Maybe you are right, my lad; but it seems strange that we should have been all this time without sighting one island. When I found you I passed a dozen between sunrise and sunset; that's what it is troubles me, lad. I fear, and every moment the fear becomes stronger, that we have gone to leeward of these islands. If so, the Lord help us! we shall never leave this boat again."

"Why do you despair to-night more than last night, Mr. Seedy?"

The old sailor bent over the side of the boat, and placed his head as near the surface of the ocean as he could.

He remained there for several seconds; then rising to a sitting posture, he answered Jack's question.

"I'll tell you, my lad," he said. "If we are where —— Ah! there it is again."

Old Seedy again leant over the side, and appeared as though listening for the repetition of the sound that had first caused him to assume this strange reticence.

Presently he arose, and, as though speaking to himself, said—

"It's nothing; yet I could have sworn I heard the same noise before."

"What is the matter, Mr. Seedy? You seem full of strange fancies to-night. What was the sound like, that caused you to listen so anxiously?"

Old Seedy again turned his head to windward, as though not being satisfied with the result of his previous efforts to make out the cause of the strange sound that had hitherto baffled his efforts.

"As near as I could judge," he said in reply

to Jack's question, "it was like the roar of a heavy broadside, though at a long distance."

Jack attempted to peer through the gloom that surrounded them, as he answered—

"If so, we shall see the flashes of the guns."

"That's what I've been thinking, lad; so, perhaps, after all, it is but my fancy. Think no more of it, lad, but turn in; you have had a long spell at the oars to-day."

"No, Mr. Seedy," was the reply. "If it is necessary to keep watch, I will do it. Last night you let me sleep undisturbed. Surely, if I am able to share your dangers, I am entitled to share the fatigues."

"Very well, lad; I will turn in. I am not so strong, I find, as I was twenty years ago; then two or three nights without sleep wouldn't hurt me, but now—well, I suppose I don't get stronger as Old Time put his mark upon my head. Good night, Jack; rouse me up if you hear that noise, or if you feel sleepy."

"Good night, Mr. Seedy. I hope to call you up with the cry of Land ahead."

"I hope so, too, lad—good night."

The old seaman was thoroughly worn out, and no sooner had he drawn the coverlet of skins over his form, than his long, regular respiration told how soundly he slept.

Jack kept within the shelter of the sail to prevent the heavy mist which was falling from saturating his clothes, and possibly laying the seeds of an insidious disease in his young frame.

Though thus sheltered, both eye and ear retained their keenest faculties, and were alive to the slightest sound.

"I cannot make Mr. Seedy out to-night," Jack mused; "it is not often he indulges in groundless alarm, nor is it often his practised hearing is at fault, yet he fully believed in that sound. I know from his manner that he did so. However, I do not—Ah."

A rumbling noise—not unlike the sound of a distant cannonade—came upon the boy's ears, and caused him to run to the bow and endeavour to pierce the gloom that hung over the sea.

The bright flashes which he fully expected to follow this startling noise were not visible, and after listening anxiously for some time, he returned to his seat, and feverish with excitement, noticed the recurrence of the sound.

An hour passed, and nothing was heard save the ripple of the waters and the sigh of the gentle wind.

"I wish the morning would come," our hero soliloquised; "this inky darkness gives one such peculiar sensations when anything occurs that seems out of the natural order of things."

The wind now began to freshen, and the boat, which had hitherto been nearly immovable, began to drift, as Jack conjectured towards the sound.

"Anything is better than this suspense," muttered Jack, as he shipped the oars; "I will hail towards the noise and set the matter clear."

Forced by the wind, and propelled by the skilful young oarsman, the boat skimmed swiftly onward.

Between each jerk of the oars the boy listened intently, but without without hearing the mystifying sound repeated.

Suddenly pausing in his labour, he unshipped the oars.

"This," he thought, "will never do. I shall possibly get between the vessels that are engaged, and receive a shot that will send us to the bottom."

There was sufficient wisdom in this proceeding to emanate from an older head; and Jack, when he had arrived at this conclusion, resumed his seat beneath the awning, his mind fully occupied by the strangeness of the nocturnal disturbance.

He had fallen into a half-conscious state just before daybreak. The soothing ripple of the water had lulled him; in spite of every effort he closed his eyes, and, though the mind was in this semi-conscious state, the nervous faculties e re alive to the slighest sound.

With an exclamation falling from his lips, sufficiently loud to awaken old Seedy, Jack sprang to his feet, and listened to a terrible roar which came from a point apparently not many fathoms from the boat.

The uninitiated might have supposed that the sound came from a contending fleet of vessels, but our hero and his companion knew too well the perils of the dangerous deep to be thus misled.

Simultaneously the words came from their lips which explained the mystery—

"Breakers ahead!"

Neither was thrown off his guard by the proximity of this unlooked-for danger, but with one thought each seized an oar, and began to turn the bow of their little craft away from the thunder of the heavy surf.

CHAPTER XXVI.

PURSUED BY THE SAVAGES.

THEY felt that their escape from certain death had been miraculous, and as they bent to their oars and increased the distance between the boat and the terrible roar, a mute prayer of thankfulness came from their hearts to Him who had once more saved them from death.

"Didn't think they were so near us," old Seedy said. "That's the first time, lad, I ever mistook breakers for guns."

"I was deceived the same way," Jack said; "but the roar of these is much louder than usual. Is it not so, Mr. Seedy?"

"Well, yes, lad. When the sea breaks upon that shore there is not so great a noise."

"What are these breakers?"

"A coral reef, lad, to a certainty."

You think that is the island?"

"I think so; but these places are so much alike, that I wouldn't like to say for certain. However, when daylight comes we shall see."

Keeping within earshot of the heavy surf, the adventurers anxiously looked for the first grey streak of dawn.

Should this turn out to be the isle where the gun-brig's hull had found a resting place, their wanderings would, for a time, come to a close.

Would they find the hull as old Seedy had left it, high and dry upon the sunken reef, or had a terrible storm swept over the island and broken the stout ship into fragments?

These and other self-put questions were asked and pondered over again and again, but without either arriving at a satisfactory conclusion.

They hailed the first beam of morning with a glad shout, and as the murky vapour began to rise from the waters, the boat was again turned towards the roaring surf, which had so nearly destroyed them on the previous night.

What a sight met their curious gaze when the island became clearly visible under the bright effulgence of the rising sun!

A sight, though it brought at first keen feelings of disappointment to their minds, each confessed was the most beautiful the eye could behold.

One glance told old Seedy it was not the island he sought, and but for our hero's wish to explore the grand yet tranquil spot, he would have put the boat about and ventured further in search of the object of their mission.

Within a quarter of a mile from the prow of their little craft, the sea was beaten into a long line of white troubled foam.

As the eye became accustomed to the seething line of water, the adventurers beheld a reef of coral, over which the blue waves sported, as though in mockery at the wish of those who gazed upon the sight to pass the beautiful but deadly barrier which stood between them and the island.

"No use that way boy," old Seedy said;

shaking his head gravely; "a whale wouldn't live two minutes in such a surge."

Jack's imagination was fired by the sight beheld, and had the danger been ten times greater, he would have risked it to have explored the lovely isle.

"Let us pull round the other side," he said, "we shall perhaps find a channel wide enough to admit our craft."

Old Seedy acquiesced, and the boat was soon skirting the dangerous coral reef, the voyagers calmly looking out for a break in the line of pearly foam.

It was with the trouble and risk necessary effect a landing, and to minds so constituted our adventurers' the danger only added a zest to the enterprise.

Beyond the line of sparkling foam a sheet clear water was visible, so little disturbed the boiling surge, that an inland lake alone could have vied with its glassy surface.

The sight of this was more than sufficient call forth the energy of so tried a seaman the master-at-arms.

"Lookee, lad," he said, suddenly; "we will have the little barque afloat in that quiet water if we have to leap over those breakers."

They had rowed round the extent of the isle before noon, but still the same formidable white line stood between them and the tantalising sheet of water which so peacefully bound the verdure-clad shore.

While thus engaged they had ample time study the general outlines of this oasis in the desert of water.

They saw the verdure-clad shore, and, rising in a gradual yet sharp pyramidal form, a tier of lordly hills, each crowned with vast numbers of the fairy-like fan palm, their graceful stems tapering upward in every fantastic yet beautiful form.

Resting for a moment upon their oars at another point which showed the opening between the vast hills, they saw a dense forest, with its giant vegetation rising hill above hill in a manner that added to its solemn aspect of impenetrable mystery and rugged grandeur.

The magnificence of the high mountain peaks which seemed to blend with the heavy sky added to this scene of beauty, and called forth an enthusiasm from the younger adventurer which peril or difficulty could not subdue.

Coasting upon another part of the romantic isle, and still looking eagerly for a break in the interminable line of foam, the sea breeze blowing from the opposite side brought with it such a fragrant odour of sweet-smelling flowers, that proved the desired spot was fraught with

RILEY SEES THE OLD ONE.

he gentle beauties of the floricultural world as well as the wild and mighty trees of forest vegetation.

The sun reached its meridian, and the adventurers, baffled but not dispirited, were compelled from fatigue to give up the seemingly endless task.

"I'll tell you what it is, lad," the old seaman said, "there is but one chance of ever taking the little bark beyond those reefs."

"What is that, Mr. Seedy?"

"We must wait, lad, and see if the tide goes down, and show us a path big enough for the boat to pass through; but even then it will be dangerous, for the sea never gets calm upon such a reef as that."

" When do you think the tide will change, Mr. Seedy?"

" Not afore sundown, lad; so we've plenty of time to try the passage. Let's pipe to dinner."

" Sundown," our hero repeated, and cast a regretful look towards the island; that is a long time to wait."

" Not long, lad; and in case there should be any red or black skins on the place, we will get ready for 'em."

Jack gave another look at the placid sheet of water between the surf and the shore, and hugging himself with the hope that the receding tide would enable them to reach land, went aft and assisted to prepare their meal.

Now that the excitement had partly died away, both felt the effects of not taking food since the preceding evening; so with appetites sharpened by the unceasing labour, they fell upon the dried shark's flesh with a vigour that looked like a fit of indigestion hereafter.

Having to wait as patiently as they could under the tantalising circumstances, they passed the time by again taking a survey of the exterior of the lovely isle.

Old Seedy put down its circumference at twenty miles at the very least; his companion, to whom the place seemed of vast size, guessed nearly twice that distance.

From this external examination they were suddenly aroused by an unexpected sight, and both, with one accord grasped their ever ready rifles.

A number of pit-pans—boats hewn out of a solid piece of timber—were seen approaching the western side of the island.

They were six in number, and each held, as near as could be seen, about ten men.

One glance was sufficient to show that the travellers were savages, and as a matter of precaution the rifles were relinquished and the oars resorted to.

" We'll pull a little round to leeward, Jack," the old seaman said, " in case they've not seen us."

Barely had the blades dipped beneath the surface when a sudden shout from the savages followed by a simultaneous movement of their paddles, showed that they were seen and pursued.

" Pull steady, lad," the master-at-arms said, " if the worst comes, we can but make a stand, and if our rifles don't put some of them out of the way my name's not Joe Seedy, that's all."

CHAPTER XXVII.

THE FIGHT.

THE adventurers soon found that in point of speed the pit-pans had much the advantage, and although both were well practised at the oars, they soon discovered that all attempts at distancing their pursuers were out of the question.

Seeing this, old Seedy, like a careful general, looked towards the island to discover an opening between the ridge of white coral.

" Once through that, lad," he said, " we can draw our boat across the passage, and make leaden bullets stop the chase."

The idea was good, and, under the circumstances, nothing better could be done.

The boat was turned towards the coral reef, and, to the adventurers' joy, they found the tide had considerably lowered, and in many places the hitherto invisible barrier was clearly visible above the white flakes of foam.

Old Seedy stood up for a moment to take the bearings of the dangerous reef, and, to Jack's delight, he said—

" There is an entrance, lad; it winds in and out very much, and at the widest point we shall have scarcely room enough to use our oars."

He was about to resume his seat, when a whizzing noise, followed by several splashes in the water, caused him to look towards his pursuers.

The leading pit-pan had considerably gained upon them—so close that the naked figures of the savages were plainly visible fitting arrows to their bows.

The noise that had attracted old Seedy's attention was caused by their first attempt to pierce him as he stood upright in the boat.

" Give me you oar, Jack," he said, calmly; " you go aft, lad, and see what sort of a mark you can make of the leading pit-pan."

Taking both rifles, Jack stood in the stern, watching every movement of their pursuers.

The savages had reseated themselves when old Seedy's body presented no further mark for their arrows, and were now busily plying their paddles.

The master-at-arms was straining every nerve to reach the dangerous opening in the reef, and the boat seemed to fly through the water.

It was of no avail.

The light pit-pans came in a straggling line in their track, and as the old sailor turned his head and narrowed the distance between his boat and the coral reef, he saw that despite his efforts, they must be overtaken.

" Lookee, lad," he said, " we don't want to kill any of 'em, but if you don't stop the leading canoe, we shall have ‗ ‗ake a stand-up fight afore we reach the reef."

The round blades of the Indians' paddles presented a glistening disc beneath the sun's rays, and to the young sailor's unerring aim a fair object for his skill.

"Yes," said old Seedy, when he mentioned the paddles, "knock a score of them out, and we may, perhaps, get inside the reef afore the rest come hand over hand upon us."

Every nerve strung to its highest tension by the imminent peril that awaited them should the Indians overhaul their light craft, Jack brought the butt of his rifle to his shoulder.

The trees, the very rocks themselves, were not firmer than the boy's arms as he held his piece and glanced along the barrel.

He chose a moment when the boat rose to the crest of the wave (for they were now in the surf), and fired.

The success of his shot was proclaimed by a yell from the Indians, and as the boy looked eagerly towards the pit-pans, he saw that two out of four paddles were gone.

Old Seedy testified his delight by a deep-toned British hurrah, and despite the precious value of every moment that passed before the reef could be reached, he threw his oars up, and said, gleefully—

"Try it again, lad—try it again. See—the varmints have stopped, and the others are gathering round."

The words were jerked out as his body swayed to and fro with the exertion of rowing.

From what our hero could understand of their previous movements, it was evident the sudden loss of their paddles had for a time confounded the Indians.

He could see the pit-pans clustered together, and one form was plainly visible handing the paddle which had been shattered by Jack's bullet from one to the other.

"That's puzzled 'em," chuckled the old seaman, as he bent completely double. "Ha, ha, ha! they won't get over it for a——By the Lord, here they come like so many vultures."

His self-congratulatory speech was cut short by seeing the pit-pans suddenly spring out and urged forward with all the speed strong arms could accomplish.

Not more than six times the length of the boat existed between the adventurers and the glassy sheet of water—their promised haven of rest and safety.

The pit-pans were a quarter of a mile away, so well had old Seedy urged the boat onward, while the savages were examining the mutilated paddles.

Although every moment decreased the distance between the pursuers and the pursued, the latter knew that unless their boat became fixed upon the coral reef they could not be overtaken.

Already they were being tossed about by the seething foam, which whirled and eddied around them, at times lifting the frail craft almost perpendicular, as the surge, forced forward by the mighty heave of the ocean, rushed impetuously over the reefs.

Both knew the crisis was at hand—one more move and their boat would be shivered in a thousand pieces, or floating in safety upon the calm sheet of water that intervened between the surf and the shore.

Our hero stood amidships, one hand grasping the mast to steady himself, and his eyes watching for the opening in the reef.

The surface of the water was one white mass of foam, and as the waves broke inward and the froth rushed over the blue bosom of the tranquil lake, it was at times difficult to detect the pathway between the sharp points of coral.

"Keep a sharp look-out, lad," the old seaman said, as he caused the stout oaken shafts to give in his strong grasp, "and tell me when she goes wrong."

Once, when the breaking of a giant wave left the particles of the sunken rock perfectly visible, our hero caught sight of the narrow winding passage.

That momentary glance was sufficient, and, keeping his keen gaze fixed upon the spot, he guided the old mariner with word and gesture.

He felt everything now depended upon his skill, and, forgetting for the time the group of savages, who were hurrying on to destroy them, he thought only of the task before him.

"So, so," he said. "Gently with your larboard oar—now pull. Quick; steady—again larboard; now give way—with a will. Huzza, huzza! We are safe!"

The roar of the boiling surf, the blinding showers of spray, the tossing of the boat—all passed away, as they shot through the opening and left the deadly entrance on their lee.

It seemed scarcely possible that there could be such a vast difference in the time and space that had intervened.

The tranquil beauty of the scene was, if anything, enhanced by the roar of the breakers from which they had just emerged, and as the old seaman paused to recover from the long and arduous pull he had undergone, he looked towards the verdure-clad hills, and exclaimed—

"Beautiful, beautiful!"

They had little time to admire the surround

ng   /iness. The angry yell, rising even
above noise of the breaking waters, told how
near the foe had come.

"We will try the shore, lad," said old Seedy.
"There is a mangrove growing there ; if we
can once get under its shade, we can fight a
hundred of those naked devils. Collect the
ammunition and be ready to spring ashore.
There is nothing else left."

The pit-pans were now in the midst of the
roaring surf, and the castaways, as they looked
back at the white froth from which they had so
recently escaped, beheld one of the boats turned
upon the sharp-pointed coral.

There came a yell of despair from the dusky
crew. The next moment there could be seen a
compound medley of broken timber and human
forms, as the angry wave bore them upward,
then dashed them upon the sharp pinnacles of
the hard coral.

"One gone," said old Seedy ; "see lad, it has
beaten them back. No ; one has passed. How
far are we from the tree ?"

"Three boats' lengths."

"God help us! if they—but they will. Fire,
lad, fire! Disable one at least, and we are safe."

The sharp report of the rifle rang out, and was
followed by a scream of pain from the Indian
boat. One had fallen by the well-sped bullet.
There was one paddle lost, but as the death-cry
rang out, a second pit-pan dashed through the
surf, and came with a speed of light after the
daring fugitives.

Old Seedy answered their wild yell with a
cheer of defiance, and as the cry left his lips the
boat's keel struck the soft muddy bank.

"The mangrove!" he said ; "this way Jack."

They shared the ammunition between them,
and dashed beneath the shelter of the famous
tree which old Seedy had struggled so hard to
reach.

Though our hero lived to become an actor in
many a scene of peril, he never forgot the feeling that swept through his heart when he followed his companion to the thickly-clustered
trunks of the mangrove trees.

It was not fear, although if his brave heart
failed him in that dreadful moment, it would
but have been human.

It was not akin to this feeling. Better had it
been so ; the suffering would have been less
acute while it lasted.

The boy's blood ran like liquid fire through
his veins, his temples throbbed, and a pale light
shone in his fixed and unnatural-looking eyes,
and with this strangely altered state of feeling,
there came over him a tigerish wish to shed
human blood.

He wanted to revel in the life-stream from
the bodies of his foes, and like an angry lion he
would have turned and grappled with them had
not his companion dragged to him to a place of
shelter.

The excitement he had undergone since the
previous night had been sufficient to cause this
strange state of feeling, and by the time they
had sheltered their bodies behind the trunks of
two large trees, the wild excitement passed
away, and he became the cool daring boy who
had stood undismayed in the centre of a den of
wild beasts.

By the time they had taken up their position
the pit-pans had run aground, and the crews,
like so many demons, sprang ashore, and with a
swift pace came towards the fugitives.

The master-at-arms was too well versed in the
crafty Indian mode of warfare to take the least
notice of this demonstration.

He knew full well that it was but a feint to
get them to expose their bodies, to become mere
targets for the arrow and equally deadly javelin
With both these weapons they saw the Indians
were armed.

There was not more than two yards between
the adventurers, and they were able to converse
freely without being overheard by the subtle
foe.

Jack brought his rifle up when he beheld the
Indians running towards the trees, and would
have fired had not old Seedy restrained him.

"Steady, lad," he whispered, " they will not
come among the trees unless we move out and
show ourselves. Down on one knee, lad, and
be ready to let drive when I give the word."

The boy dropped on one knee; the barrel of
his good rifle brought forward ready for instant
use ; old Seedy did the same, and both remained
silent, invisible, and watchful, and ready at any
moment to cut short the lives of two of their
foes.

The wisdom of this manœuvre was soon
shown, for the Indians, when they approached
the skirts of the forests, came to a sudden halt,
then quickly raising their bows, sent a flight of
arrows whizzing past the very trees where our
friends crouched.

"I thought so, the varmints," muttered Old
Seedy, as he ran his eye along the barrel of his
rifle. "They want us to take cover."

Finding this did not dislodge the fugitives,
the Indians spread themselves out and began to
advance slowly and cautiously inside the thickly
wooded forest.

The plan they had adopted promised to bring
success, for while the right and left flanks ad

vanced, the centre remained stationary until the extended line formed the third of a circle.

With the cunning of their race the warlike savages thought to drive the adventurers from their place of concealment, then by a quick movement the right and left flanks would join, and the fugitives would be hemmed in on all sides and entirely overcome.

Had this manœuvre taken place in the open ground, our friends would have had no difficulty in picking off the nearest of their foes as they advanced.

But in the thick forest, where the trees stood so closely together that in many parts there was scarcely room enough for even a warrior's naked form to pass, the matter wore a grave aspect.

To have fired would have been madness; they might have brought down two of their foes, but the smoke of their rifles would have betrayed them, and before they could have reloaded a score of swarthy savages would have pounced upon them.

The master-at-arms watched them with his keen grey eyes twinkling with an angry fire, and when he beheld the flanks begin to converge towards each other, he said in a still voice to his young companion—

"Lay yourself flat on your stomach, my lad, and creep to the next clump of trees—there, just beyond where those birds are flying."

Without disturbing the thickly-grown underwood, the young officer crept with a serpent-like motion towards the spot indicated.

He kept the trunk of the tree he had just quitted between his body and the enemy, and in this manner reached a shelter some thirty yards further away.

They reached their position without being observed, although at times the old seaman felt certain that Jack would betray them.

They had been but a few minutes in their retreat when the leading files of the foemen closed, and by this movement they passed through the very trees which had first sheltered the adventurers.

Not a living thing could have escaped them in that circle, and Old Seedy chuckled when he beheld them look upward at the branches of the trees, as though expecting to find their prey among the stout limbs of the mangrove.

They were evidently at fault, and after a few words from one who seemed to be their chief, they spread themselves out, and began to repeat this manœuvre.

There could not be a better plan than this for searching the forest, for by continually repeat-ing this movement they must pass through every part of the thickly wooded ground.

As they again advanced the adventurers again glided forward, and a second time the Indians closed without seeing their prey.

They were now upon the verge of the forest, and old Seedy began to grow anxious as to the result of the next move.

There was a tall batch of high canes some thirty yards beyond the trees, and behind this a heap of fallen rock, but before they could possibly reach the cane-brake there was an open space which must be passed.

The master-at-arms was not long making up his mind. The Indians were again standing in a circle, and he knew the next move would bring them clear of the trees.

"We must make a run for it, Jack," he said. "The varmints will close around this spot next time, and unless we are out of sight I would not give a purser's dip for our lives."

A sudden shout from their foes caused the adventurers to peer out, and they beheld their pursuers gathered round the trees which had last given them shelter.

The savages had found their trail. A few bush-spreading plants had been pressed down by old Seedy, and like so many bloodhounds they turned, and began to follow the tell-tale marks.

"Its all up, lad," said old Seedy. "they have found our trail, and will be ahead of us directly."

Jack Rawlings shook the powder in the pan of his rifle, and asked—

"What is to be done, Mr. Seedy?"

"Nothing lad, but to make a running fight of it. We must fire as we go from tree to tree, and when we clear the forest make a dash for the rocks. Be careful, lad, never to fire until I am loaded, and will do the same with you."

The midshipman understood the advantage of this, and at a single word from old Seedy he sprang to his feet.

Two of the Indians who were in advance gave a shout, and like a pack of wolves the whole number dashed forward.

Showing no more of their bodies than was necessary to use their rifles, the brave boy fired at the advancing crowd.

The sharp crack of the piece resounded in a thousand echoes, and one of the redskins sprang upwards, and then fell flat upon his face; the bullet had gone through his heart.

The whole party came to a stand-still when they reached the body of their fallen companion, and one, stooping over the prostrate form, turned it over, and sought for the weapon that had so swiftly sent the dusky spirit to the hunting-grounds.

Taking advantage of this, the adventurers dashed from the trees, passed the cane-brake, and with a glad cry scrambled over a huge piece of granite.

Never had Nature formed a better piece of defence than this piece of stone; it was about ten feet high, and with a jagged top which had broken away from a towering mountain, half stone, half earth, and between the base of the mountain and fallen fragment a distance of nearly two feet intervened.

The fugitives saw at a glance the advantages this place possessed, and standing behind this natural breastwork, they rested their deadly weapons upon the ready-made embrasures, and awaited the Indians' approach.

Though for a moment struck with dread at the strange death that had befallen their companion, the momentary feeling of fear passed away, and burning to avenge his fate, they gave a loud cry and bounded after the pale-faces.

A puff of smoke from old Seedy's rifle, and a second Indian falling to the earth with a bullet in his thigh, somewhat checked the ardour of their advance.

Though evidently unacquainted with the use of fire-arms, they seemed to know that a sudden onset would be the surest way of silencing the murderous weapons.

Drawn up two deep they stood before the piece of rock; at a single word from their chief an arrow sped from each bow, and buried themselves in the base of the hill behind our adventurers' backs.

The midshipman, like his companion, had lowered his head when he beheld the Indians placing the shafts in their bows, and when he saw them quivering in the earth, he would have returned the discharge by a shot from his rifle.

"Hold your fire!" said the master-at-arms, energetically; "they will try and take us by boarding. Be ready. Here they come!"

With long springing jumps rather than running the Indians dashed towards the little fortress.

Six of the band dashed up the face of the rock, and would have sprung down upon the adventurers, had not the terrible crack from both rifles hurled two backwards, bleeding and senseless.

The remainder paused—it was but momentary, for, urged onward by the crowd below, they were compelled to advance.

Old Seedy had by this time clubbed his rifle,

and sweeping it round his head, dislodged another pursuer.

Jack had placed his rifle on the ground and drawn his sword, and soon the bright blade was crimsoned by a red stain which proved that another of the enemy had been disabled.

Three of the attacking force were at the foot of the rock; and so swiftly had all this passed that those in rear were ignorant of what had happened until they came, breathless and panting, to the fallen rock.

CHAPTER XXVIII.

RILEY MCGOWAN A MAN OF CONSEQUENCE.

THE Indians examined the footprints on the sands, and at once struck upon Riley's trail, and when the ex-caterer saw this he gave vent to a howl.

"It's a fool I am," he muttered, "shure the biggest mad man in Kilkenny would know that these black divils only have to see where a man has put his foot to follow and find him out."

Riley prepared for action by resting his musket upon the top of the breastwork.

"It's all up with sweet Kilkenny now," said Riley, "sorra a bit of it I shall ever see more—ugh—here the divils are, take that."

Riley pulled the trigger, the hammer fell, but there was no report; alas, poor McGowan had knocked the cap off the nipple, and before he could again prime the piece, the tattooed and scantily dressed gentlemen were masters of the situation.

Not only the situation, but the ex-caterer's elegant person.

"I surrender," said Riley, "so you can keep those elegant clubs and spears for those who want them."

Riley McGowan's captors seemed to understand that no attempt to resume hostilities would be made, for they did not bind their prisoner's limbs or do him any bodily harm.

id that which caused Riley to sadly abuse them in English, and as much of the Irish tongue as he could command.

"Bad luck to ye, is it me cocked hat that ye want?—take it."

One of the islanders did so, and placed it on his head, making some signs for Riley to divest himself of his jacket, and the ex-caterer did so.

"It's but little ye have to wear," he said, "so ye are welcome to the jacket, for it's a shirt and trousers I have left yet."

The man who took McGowan's jacket put it on hind part before, and the effect was so ludicrous that Riley could not help laughing.

"It's an illigant fit," said McGowan; "would ye like it buttoned, avick?"

His mirth was but short, for another of the party made unmistakeable signs that he wished to possess Riley's trousers.

"Is it these, ye blackguard?" said the ex-caterer; "ye can have these, for the divil a bit of sate is there left, and as for the legs, ye'd not be too hot for the bit of ventilation, as Misther Rawlings would say."

Riley now stood in his shirt and shoes, and the latter was soon asked for.

"Is it the brogues ye want?—the divil mend your manners. Take them; it's but little sole there is; and as for the uppers—don't be in a hurry, ye chip of the black pot—there they are."

The shoes were great prizes, for one of Riley's captors had one, and another the fellow.

"Look at the omadhauns," laughed Riley, "it's the left foot one the spalpeen with the ring in his nose has on his right foot, and the other has the right one on the left foot—mother of Moses! did any one ever see the—— what?"

One of the islanders pointed with the blade of his spear to Riley's shirt; his only remaining ragged, and not over clean garment.

"The shirt?" said Riley. "Dacency—dacency—it's naked I can't go about—eh—use that boarding pike, thief, try if I don't; well then as Riley McGowan sees there's no help for it, he'll give it you rather than have a hole made in his illigant body with that spear—take it, ye thief, and the divil mind you."

Riley "peeled" as he spoke, and when the savages saw his naked breast they gave a yell, and began to dance sound him.

"What the devil do you mane?" said McGowan. "Is it my skin they want—eh you chuk-e-ree-loo—well the devil a sense can I make of yer. There they go again with their yer chuk-e-ree-loo, and dancing like so many mad devils."

The dance continued for some time, and the man who had expressed such a great desire for the ex-caterer's shirt made no attempt to take it but danced and howled with greater vigour than the rest.

"Look here, my lads," said Riley, "if ye want the only garment I have, and dacency would make you lave it for me if ye were not such hathens, but as ye are hathens, and would rob a poor boy of his ragged shirt, either take it or lave it, for my arm is tired of houlding it out."

As no attempt was made to deprive the ex-caterer of his only garment, he wisely slipped it over his head and remarked—

"Ye have more dacency than I thought, and it's obliged I am——What the devil now?"

Well might Riley give forcible expression to the astonishment that took possession of him, for the change that took place in the behaviour of his captors was most extraordinary.

Directly he assumed his shirt, the dancing and yelling ceased, and with one accord the islanders threw themselves at Riley's feet, and in the humblest manner not only gave him his attire, but placed their weapons and head dresses upon the ground.

Riley was not slow to avail himself of the opportunity to encase his limbs, and while he made his toilet and resumed the cocked hat, the aborigines retained their recumbent position.

"It's much obliged to ye, I am," said Riley, "for the things ye have given me back; and as ye are so polite, maybe ye will take yerselves off, for it's plenty of work I have to do by the time the master-at-arms and Mister Rawlings comes back."

The savages listened; then, flinging their hands over their heads, pressed their foreheads on the ground, and made a strange moaning noise.

"It's mad the blackguards are," said Riley; "what the divil do they mane?"

One of the men crawled on all fours close to the ex-caterer's feet, and motioned in a supplicating manner.

"I'll forgive ye," said Riley, "if that's what ye want; so get up, and don't be wearing out the skin off your knees—there, be off, ye omadhauns."

McGowan raised his hands after the manner of the heavy father on the stage, when he says, "Bless you, my che-el-dren," and the savages, as though overjoyed at the act, jumped to their feet, and began to dance round Riley.

"It's a pity," he thought, "that Terence O'Toole didn't tache me the language these haythens spake, for it's then I should be able to undherstand them; but divil a bit do I now."

The savages did their best to make Riley understand they were his humblest servants. and furthermore, were quite ready to do anything he wished.

"Well," exclaimed Riley, "it's not often that I've so many servants; so, me boys, I'll just throuble you to take me for a row on the say."

Riley pointed to the water, and the savages gave a yell and led the way, dancing like so many maniacs.

They launched their canoe, and waited until

Riley took his seat in the stern, then they jumped in and began to paddle swiftly from the volcanic isle.

"It's like an admiral I am now," thought the ex-caterer, as he lounged at his ease on the pile of soft skins; "mother of Moses, where the devil are they going now?"

The canoe was tossing about in the surf when McGowan's forcible explanation was uttered, and as he held on to the sides he fully expected to be upset.

They were not long in the surf, and when they went into the calm sea, the canoe was nearly full of water, and it's occupants were also soaked with the spray.

"Look here, ye lubbers," said Riley, "empty the wather out of the boat, and be quick about it, or it's a cold I shall have in my toes."

Riley showed them an example by bailing out the water with his cocked hat, and the savages not slow to imitate the ex-caterer, the canoe was soon emptied.

They kept at the paddles until near sun-down, then the low-lying outline of an island became visible.

"It's a prisoner I am, and it's no more of the Devil's Island or Sweet Kilkenny I shall see again. Riley, Riley, me boy, it's cooked and your bones picked you'll be."

The canoe grounded, and a multituee of dark-skinned savages crowded to the shore to examine the wearer of the cocked hat.

CHAPTER XXIX.

A FLAG OF TRUCE.

"Now, lad," said the master at arms when the Indians halted, "we must keep up a close fire or lose our lives."

His advice was acted upon and both rifles were discharged so close to the faces of the Indians that those who were not killed had their faces scorched by the powder.

The close proximity of the terrible weapons was too much for the bewildered foemen, and, obeying a signal from the chief, they retreated, keeping their faces turned to the gallant sailors.

"We can do no good here," said the old seaman to Jack, "so let us load our pieces and go up the mountain."

Loading as they went, the young chief and his companion began the ascent of the verdure-clad mountain.

From the pinnacle of the mighty hill, the castaways had a clear view of the island and the distant sea.

The midshipman's eyes were fixed upon the yellow streak which divided the dark water from the emerald tints of the luxurious vegetation.

He saw the angry Indians gathered round the boat which had brought them in safety through the perils of the deep, and as he clutched his companion's arm he gave vent to a few words which explained the painful feeling so visible upon his handsome face.

"They are destroying our boat, Mr. Seedy!"

The boy's words were too true; the Indians were breaking up the brave little craft and casting the scattered fragments into the sea.

Old Joe Seedy saw the magnitude of this misfortune, and as he leant upon the muzzle of his trusty rifle, he gave expression to the gloomy forebodings that filled his mind.

"There is nothing," he said, "that could have befallen us equal in danger, or more likely to shorten our days, than the loss of this boat."

"It is a terrible misfortune," Jack said,—"a terrible misfortune indeed."

"Ay, lad, it is. The red devils have not done this without a motive; if my suspicions are correct we have a hard struggle before us; then," he added sorrowfully, "when our ammunition is gone we shall be—— But there, boy, I will not tell you all my foolish old head would suggest. They say the darkest hours come before daylight. I hope it may be so with us, for this is a dark hour indeed."

Jack made no reply; he was fully alive to the truth of old Seedy's words, and though his heart fell at thus being cut off in the beginning of his career, he felt that the same power which had protected him through so many deadly scenes of peril would not desert them in this their hour of need.

"I should not have cared so much," the master-at-arms said, breaking in upon our hero's thoughts, "had this taken place at the island where the old bark rides high and dry on the broken rocks; but here, without the means of ever reaching the place were everything we need is to be had in abundance, it seems like the beginning of a mis—— What is it, lad?"

He broke off suddenly, and with this interrogative turned to our hero.

The boy had brought his rifle to his hip, and as old Seedy turned he drew the hammer back to full cock.

There is some new movement about to take place," he said. "I have been watching the Indians ever since they destryed our boat, and from time to time I have seen them turn their faces this way. Now, look! there is one of their number coming up the hill-side."

The master-at-arms followed the direction of

his youthful companion's finger, and beheld one of the red-skins coming towards them. He saw the man was unarmed, and by the white wand which he held above his head, knew that his errand was of a peaceful nature.

"Ground arms, lad," he said; "yon stick he carries means the same as a flag of truce."

By the brilliant head-dress worn by the stately Indian, old Seedy knew that the chief of the tribe had brought the offering of piece.

Long intercourse with the aborigines of South and Central America had made the master-at-arms conversant with their habits, and a feeling of joy sprang up in his breast when he beheld the rank of the herald.

"They don't mean fighting again, boy," he remarked, as he stepped forward to meet the Indian prince; "if they did, one of the young men would have come, not a chief."

The Indian paused when the old sailor stepped to the brow of the hill, and laying the white wand upon the ground, he bared his plumed head, and stood like a magnificent statue.

Old Seedy had time to note the peculiar tattooing upon the chief's breast, and turning his head towards Jack, he said—

"He belongs to a tribe which were once kind to me, so be of good cheer, boy; I know their lingo, and will soon make them friendly to us both."

Jack inclined his head; he was at that moment lost in admiration at the faultless symmetry of the young Indian's splendid figure, and the matchless beauty of his grave features.

Old Tom placed his rifle on the ground, and advancing to the white wand, touched it with his hands.

The Indian chief repeated this act, and extending his hands towards the adventurers, said, in the rich figurative language of his people—

"The aged white hunter and the young white brave have spoken with living fire to their red brethren. Is it right?"

"Why," said old Seedy, in the same tongue, "do the children of the forest make war upon the solitary white man who sought this shore, not to slay, but to find safety from the great waters."

The Indian chief's face wore a troubled look as he asked—

"Does my brother speak the truth? His hair is white with age. I cannot think he would lie."

"He does not lie," said old Seedy, quickly; "he speaks the truth."

"Yet," the Indian said, "when we saw the white men's canoe, and followed it to greet our white brother, as one hunter should greet another, there came the living lightning and killed one of our braves."

"Go back to your people," old Seedy said, as he at once understood that the affray had begun through a mistake on both sides, "and say that the white hunter is sorry. Tell them we feared the red men, and used the mighty weapon which speaks like the distant thunder and slays like the lightning's shaft. Go tell them that we would be at peace. Say to your chief, the Great Beaver, that the white man who slept in his wigwam in the forest of the great plain, would live on this island. Say this to him, and let him depart with his people."

The young chieftain's face betrayed the surprise and joy he felt at old Seedy's words, and rushing forward he took the old sailor by the hand.

"The son of the Great Beaver was saved from a tiger's fangs by a solitary white hunter who came in a winged canoe. Tell me, how was the son of the Great Beaver saved?"

"The old chief," said the master-at-arms, "and his braves were upon the war trail, and Tacaula, the son of the Great Beaver, was left with the women. He strayed to the forest, hand in hand with the White Fawn, and met a tiger prowling among the trees. The boy had left his spear in his father's hut, and would have died had not the white hunter slain the tiger."

"I am Tacaula," said the young chief, joyfully. "The white hunter speaks the truth, and the boy he saved is glad."

He wrung old Seedy's hands with a fervour that told how deeply he rejoiced at thus strangely meeting the man who had saved his life.

The master-at-arms returned the pressure of the Indian's hand, and asked—

"What of the White Fawn? Does she dwell in the wigwam of Tacaula?"

The young chief's eyes blazed with anger, and striking his breast, he answered—

"She does not. Tacaula slew her brother, and her heart was turned against him. Listen! she will be punished for this. Even now she is tied to a tree in the forest, that wild beasts may eat the heart that refused to love the son of the Great Beaver."

Old Seedy had known the doomed maiden when she was but a timid, prattling child, and fearful that his words would be realised, he pointed to the forest beneath, and asked—

"Does my son mean here?"

The youth bowed his head and cast his eyes upon the ground as he answered—

"It was to place the White Fawn in this peril

that we sought the island, and when her cries came past upon the wind we left. It was then we met the white hunter and his brave companion."

The seaman's blood curdled with horror, and s a plan to save the beautiful girl came to his brain, he said—

"When does my son leave this place?"

"I came," said the chief, "to ask the white men to let us bury our braves who have fallen before their weapons—to ask them not to kindle living fire as the braves are put beneath the earth; then we depart. What does our brother say?"

"Bury your braves in peace, and depart."

The young chief broke the white wand in two—one piece he have to old Seedy, the other to Jack; then bowing, awaited the conclusion of the ceremony.

"Give him a piece of your bough, lad," said old Seedy; let us get rid of them as soon as possible, or a horrid death will befall one that I knew when she was but a lisping child."

The young officer looked the surprise he felt at these strange words; not having understood the conversation, he was ignorant or the terrible death that menaced a young and beautiful girl.

He gave the Indian a portion of the twig he had peeled of its bark—a proceeding in which old Seedy readily bore a share, and the Indian youth, as he received these tokens of peace, placed them in his belt; then taking old Seedy's hand between his own, he said—

"Tacaula does not forget that to the white hunter he owes a life; he is grateful, and will return when the hearts of his people have forgotten the work of to-day. Until then he will ask the Great Spirit to watch over you, and keep you from the teeth of the Heparti's. Farewell!"

He turned as the last words came from his lips, and ran down the hill-side with the speed of an antelope, and old Seedy, looking after the lithe, manly form, repeated slowly—

"The Heparti's."

"What is the meaning of that, Mr. Seedy?"

"Meaning, lad? Man-eaters, cannibals, and e are left among them."

"Here on this island?"

"Ay, lad; they are but few, and live in the hollows of the rocks by the sea. I know them too well; but as long as we keep here on the high ground we are safe. Once go, Jack, within sight of their holes, and I would not give an inch of old rope yarn for our lives."

"What is that I heard you were saying about a horrid death befalling one whom you knew a child?"

"Sit here, boy."

The young officer seated himself beside his companion and watched with interest the movements of the Indians, as they buried their fallen companions in the valley below.

Old Seedy told the astonished boy the substance of the conversation between himself and the Indian, and when Jack heard that a young girl was in such imminent peril, he would have at once started to the forest.

"We must wait," old Seedy said. "I am almost maddened by the knowledge of the girl's peril, but we must wait until they leave the island."

"But can we——"

"You know not their customs, lad; were they to suspect our enterprise, they would return and cut the poor girl in pieces."

"We can defend her," said Jack. "If we wait until they leave, the poor girl will in all likelihood be torn to pieces."

"We must hope for the best, Mr. Rawlings· thank Heaven the prowling brutes do not come out until after nightfall, and before that time I hope the redskins will have gone."

The cool manner of the old seaman somewhat checked the boy's impetuosity; but the task was difficult, and old Seedy had need of all his reasoning powers to restrain his young companion from hurrying at once to the rescue of the Indian maiden.

The fiery nature was perceptible in the restive spirit, which could ill brook the old seaman's prudent counsel.

"The deed is inhuman!" the middy passionately exclaimed. "Is this the boasted chivalry of the red-skins, to sacrifice a girl because she cannot return the affection of one who is hateful to her sight?"

"I don't know much about what you call chivalry," said old Seedy, quietly; "but I know the red-men have some strange customs. Perhaps this is one."

"It's a disgrace to them."

"May be, lad; but all the palaver from a whole fleet of chaplains wouldn't make 'em believe so. But quiet, lad; we shall yet be in time to save her."

Jack set his teeth firmly and looked towards the dark group that were filling in the burial place of the fallen braves.

He could distinguish the noble form of the young chief who had visited them, by his brilliant head-dress, and, as he recalled the young Indian's features to his mind, he turned to the master-at-arms and asked—

"Surely that handsome youth was not a party to this horrible sacrifice?"

"I think not," was the reply; "but you see, Mr. Rawlings, though he is a chief, and son of the ruler of that tribe, he dare not go against anything that his people wish. I knew the young fellow long ago, and I know, if he dared, he would take us to the village, and we should be treated as friends. But, you see, he must not do it; it would be against their laws, and perhaps would cause his death."

"How cause his death?"

"This way, lad. The tribe would call a council, and bring it in that he had brought disgrace upon them by being friendly with the white men who had killed some of their tribe. What did he say to me as he left? Didn't he tell me that he would come when the hearts of his people were less angry with the white hunters? Doesn't that prove that he can't do anything unless the tribe give their consent?"

"It seems like it, Mr. Seedy."

"Ay, boy; so don't put the young fellow down in your log as being chief mate in this business. Depend upon it, lad, he would like to save the girl, only he dare not."

"Dare not!" Jack repeated fiercely. "Were it my case I would do so, even if I had to fight my way through the whole tribe."

"Maybe you would, Mr. Rawlings but the young fellow is an Indian, and don't forget his bringing up; it's born in 'em, sir. There they go—so you will soon be out of your misery, and the poor girl out of her's, I hope."

CHAPTER XXX.

A MYSTERIOUS DISAPPEARANCE.

In the heart of the dark forest, the master-at-arms and the midshipman found the young Indian girl, bound hand and foot to the trunk of a young mora tree.

The maiden, though so young, seemed perfectly indifferent to her fate—the contempt for death so peculiar to the Indian nature.

She expressed no gratitude for her deliverance her manitou, she said, had willed it that the old white hunter and the young brave should save her from the prowling beasts of the forest.

The master-at-arms smiled at the girl's words, and in her native tongue said—

"Had the manitou willed that you should have been torn to pieces by the wild beasts, would you not have been afraid when the darkness came on?"

"Why," she said, "is there not a happier country beyond this island, where my spirit would have been happy with the spirits of those who have gone before me to the land of joy?"

When the old sailor translated this answer to Jack Rawlings, the lad said—

"You can't wonder at the Indian's contempt for death, when their minds are taught to believe in the existence of everlasting happiness after the spirit goes to the happy land."

"Hem," said old Seedy, "I suppose it's all right, Mr. Rawlings, but I don't understand much about these things."

"What" Jack asked, "are we to do with the young girl, now we have saved her from the beasts of prey?"

"We must build a hut," said the old sailor; "that done, we can set about the construction of a boat, and continue our voyage in search of the gun-brig."

"Poor Riley," said Jack, "I wonder how he fares with his ghosts, and other sources of annoyance."

"McGowan," said the master-at-arms, "will be all right—I know him better than you do, lad; he has a brave heart, and half the fear he expressed was only assumed. Depend upon it, when we return we shall find him as happy as a king. But come on, let's find a place to pitch our hut; and mind, Jack, you don't fall in love with this pretty girl when she teaches you her language."

Jack laughed.

"Fall in love," he said, "with this brown-skinned damsel. I don't think I shall; although she is, I must own, very pretty."

"Ah!" said old Seedy, "eighteen is your age, Jack, and she is about two years younger, just the age for romantic love; but don't give way to it, lad—d'ye hear an old man's advice."

Jack promised he would not, and old Seedy shook his head as they left the forest, for the midshipman was paying the brown-skinned damsel the most polite attention.

The hut was built in the course of a week, and Jack, who was an excellent swimmer, dived and fetched up the greater portion of the arms and ammunition the Indians had thrown into the sea when they destroyed the long boat.

The time passed pleasantly enough, for the cannibals had not as yet left their caves, and the party began to hope they had left the island.

Jack made rapid progress in acquiring the Indian language, and when warned by old Seedy not to fall in love with his instructress, he still persisted in his denial of the possibility of such a thing taking place.

One morning when the master-at-arms and the midshipman left their chamber in the hut, old Seedy went to the doorway by the room where the White Fawn slept, and telling her to prepare their breakfast in an hour, shouldered his gun, and said to Jack,

"Look to your priming, lad; there was a tiger outside not an hour since—ah! see there are the tracks."

They followed the footmarks to the forest where the tiger was joined by another, and the footprints continued together for some distance then broke off in contrary directions.

"You follow this one, lad," said the master-at-arms, "I'll look after this gentleman, and we shall meet on the other side of the forest."

CHAPTER XXXI.

UNWELCOME VISITORS.

JACK continued the trail until the day was far spent, and having reached the other side of the forest, he sat upon the trunk of a fallen tree to rest.

Suddenly he started to his feet and grasped his rifle.

Within a dozen paces of where he stood lay old Seedy's jacket and rifle, and when Jack examined them, he saw on the butt of the piece the imprint of the master-at-arms' fingers, and these fingers at the time were covered with blood.

The jacket, too, bore a mute but terrible evidence of a struggle having taken place; and Jack, pursuing his investigations, further discovered the imprints of several naked feet, and following the trail, found it led to the beach.

Here he saw the marks left by several boats or canoes, evidently of more than ordinary size.

He stood for some time silently leaning upon the muzzle of his rifle, and his intelligent mind having formed an opinion respecting his friend's mysterious disappearance, he slowly, and with an aching heart, turned towards the forest and returned to his hut, faint and sorrowful, just as the sun's last rays were gilding the waves.

Early next day he was astir; he had resolved to follow the canoe, and if possible, rescue the old seaman.

He had no boat—nothing that would float and sustain him upon the water; but taking the idea from the pit-pan used by the tribe of the Great Beaver, he selected a tree, whose trunk would make him a boat.

It was the labour of weeks to fell the giant tree and prepare it for being hewn into a form that would make its exterior seaworthy, and

the interior sufficiently large to hold himself the girl, and an abundant supply of food.

Slow as the work progressed, he never for one moment flagged in his exertions. It was a labour of love, and the thought of the master-at-arms being in captivity, gave his arm giant's strength.

Thus the task, which at first seemed hopeless progressed day by day, and Jack began to look forward to the time when he could once more float on the blue water.

One morn soon after the sunbeams had gladdened the earth, and the White Fawn had gone into the forest in search of game, Jack left the hut.

He watched the girl's handsome form until it became lost among the drooping foliage of the graceful fan-like palm.

"I should be thankful," he thought. "Here I have all that would make thousands, who are struggling from day to day for their bread happy. A beautiful and devoted companion, a fertile and rich kingdom, yet I am not content No; happy as the days have been since I became a dweller upon this isle, there is a drawback to my happiness. Poor Joe Seedy's absence and uncertain fate make my life one of unceasing anxiety."

Tears came to the young officer's eyes as he thought of the kindly friend he had so strangely lost, and, as he threw his axe upon his shoulder and went towards the unfinished boat, his face brightened, and he resumed—

"I must not despair. My boat will be ready before another week has passed, and with the Fawn for my guide, all my cruel uncertainty will be at rest."

Stripped to the waist, he began his labour and save for the chattering of the birds, nothing was heard in the forest but the blows of his sharp axe.

He had been at work nearly an hour, and the rough outline of the frame of his boat was becoming visible.

He stopped to regard the effect of his untiring energy and to rest his body, which had become stiffened by the stooping posture he had been compelled to assume.

"It begins to look a little ship-shape," he said, in a pleased voice. "A little more off the cutwater, I think, will give her greater speed, besides lessening the labour of rowing."

In stepping backward his eyes involuntarily turned seaward, and in a moment he became as though turned to a statue.

His lips were parted, his breast rose and fell, and his eyes seemed as though they were about to burst from their sockets.

THE INDIANS WERE HOLDING A WAR COUNCIL.

Looking beyond the fading line of the white breakers he beheld a number of canoes filled with men.

They were different in construction to any he had seen before, being much larger, broader, and each carrying a large square sail.

In number there could not have been less than thirty, and he calcutated the crews at two hundred at the very least.

Jack knew enough from what the White Fawn had told him of the bloodthirsty nature of the tribes which dwelt on the mainland, and as he gazed at the formidable flotilla he felt that their visit to the island boded him no good.

At first he hoped they were of the tribe to which the girl belonged, but a second glance at the canoes dissipated this hope.

Tacaula's braves, he remembered, came in pit-pans, while the flotilla which came so near the isle was composed of long, narrow, pointed canoes.

"What could be the object of their visit?"

He asked this question over and over again, but he could not suggest any satisfacrory reply.

Suddenly he snatched his jacket from the ground, then ran swiftly in the direction the White Fawn had taken.

He found the girl cautiously stealing upon a herd of deer, and his sudden appearance not only caused an exclamation of surprise from the beautiful huntress, but startled the game that was almost within reach of the rifle Jack had taught her to use.

"Fawn," he said hurriedly, "there are canoes near the island. Come and behold them."

"Canoes!" she repeated, her lips faltering. "The Great Spirit forbid that my people have come!"

"It is not your people, Fawn."

She clapped her hands joyfully, and said—

"I am happy again. We shall not be parted."

When they reached the rising ground the Indian girl stopped suddenly, and in a voice of terror, said—

"Lost—lost! It is the Hepartis."

"Hepartis! Fawn?"

She clutched his arm and looked up wildly into his face, and said—

"The White Fawn speaks. It is the man-eaters, and there is no hope."

Jack knew too well the significance of her words, and though he had at first felt a chill creep over his frame, the feeling passed away, and snatching the rifle from the White Fawn, he said—

"Fear nothing, Fawn; we can yet baffle them."

"No, no. They have the cunning of the serpent. We must hide away or die."

"Neither," Jack said, resolutely. "Run for the other rifle. From this position we can sink every canoe that crosses the reef."

"No good," she said, mournfully. "The man-eaters can swim faster than the beaver. Listen to the White Fawn, who would die for you, and loves you more for being thus brave. But what can one warrior, however mighty, do against a tribe?"

Jack lowered the muzzle of his rifle.

He knew her counsel promised the greatest safety, and with many a wistful look at the canoes he took the young maiden's hand, and ran swiftly to the hut.

She would have prevailed upon him to hide among the rocks, but our hero ended the matter by securely fastening the heavy door.

"No, Fawn," he said. "These logs are proof against arrow or javelin, and as long as we have an ounce of powder we are safe."

The girl's eyes shone brightly, and, taking a second rifle from the corner, she came to the midshipman's side.

"We will die together," she said; before our spirits wing their flight to the h hunting grounds, there will be sorrow in man-eaters' wigwams."

Jack smiled sadly at the beautiful words, as he placed the whole of their amn tion beneath the loop-holes which had luckily constructed when building the hut.

The prudent course he had adopted whe dived beneath the water for the powder bag of bullets, which had been thrown into sea by the angry Indians, was a matter of congratulation in this moment of dire peril.

Yet he trembled at the knowledge tha his hands were the lives of the whole d horde that were at that moment yelling joy as they crossed the reef.

"They come, Fawn," Jack said; "but we die the beach shall be dotted with bodies."

"My brave has spoken, and it will be so.

CHAPTER XXXII.
RILEY MCGOWAN'S WIVES.

THE wearer of the cocked hat expected noti less than annihilation when the yelling cr surrounded the canoe.

The women, as usual, were foremost, and moment Riley's hat was appropriated by on the dark girls who was dressed in anything an excess of clothing.

Two damsels had begun to take forcible session of the ex-caterer's jacket, and would a few seconds have torn it piecemeal from body, had not one of the gentlemen wh acquaintance Riley had made on the volca isle interfered.

His interference was effectual, but not poli

He jumped ashore, shouting some uninte gible menaces, and with the flat of his hea paddle he floored the damsels who rushed possess our friend's jacket.

They squalled as they were knocked over, a the lady who had decorated herself with Riley cocked hat, prudently dropped it before t paddle could reach her skull.

"Manners, ye baste," said Riley, "shure they want me old clothes, why let 'em, b don't be after cracking their skulls. Here, m darlints, take the jacket and the hat, for it's b little use they are to a poor boy who will soo be roasted and eaten for yer suppers."

Riley flung the jacket and hat from him, an the wind catching his unfastened shirt-front revealed his breast.

Those who were near enough to catch sight of the ex-caterer's skin, gave a shout of joy and grovelled at Riley's feet.

The words they used were repeated by the remainder of the tribe, and in a moment every man, woman, and child, assumed a suppliant posture, except the men who brought Riley to the island.

They stood erect, and, shouting to their friends, pointed from to time at Riley.

"What the divil is the matter with the black divils?" said Riley; "first they come to tear me old clothes to pieces; then they fall down as though they wanted to kiss me foot."

One of the elders of the tribe arose and came to Riley, and, to our friend's astonishment, said in broken English—

"The great Bear come—we wait long—the wise men say he come—the many long time go past, he not come—the Great Bear is welcome!"

"It's much obliged I am," said Riley; "but maybe ye will tell me what the divil all this manes; for it's not a bit can I understand; and while ye *are* about it, old fellow, maybe ye will tell me where ye learnt to speak such illigant English?"

"Talkee Unglish?"

"Yes," said Riley; "where did you pick it up?"

"Me on board slave-ship—some long time—cook meat for sailors—get away after long time—now Great Bear's slave."

"Is it the Great Bear I am?"

"Yes—yes!—save our people—Great Bear come—wise men not lie—see, see!"

The old man exposed Riley's chest, and pointed to the blue outlines of a bear that was tattooed thereon.

"By this and that," said Riley, "it is the bit of tattooing that was done by my old messmate, Dan Sullivan, that ye all make this fuss about?"

Riley paused as the old man began to manifest evident symptoms of delight."

Bedad," he thought, "it's a lucky thing anyhow that I let Dan tattoo the bear on my chest, for these omhadhauns would have picked me bones but for that; anyhow I must find out all about it from this old thief who spakes English, but first I'll see whether they have a drop of anything to wet my throat, for it's as dry as a chip."

He made known this want to the old fellow, who said—

"The Great Bear drink—him throat dry, he have drink must."

A few words caused one of the young men to run towards the village, and he soon returned, bringing a calabash filled with the juice of a fruit not unlike the pomegranate.

"It's hot," said Riley, after a pull at the calabash, "but there's worse where there's none."

The old man and Riley had a long and rather a difficult task before them, for the former had to explain the story of the bear, and how it so strangely affected Riley.

"Maybe, thought McGowan, "he'll be dry before he's done, so I'll keep the little drop that's left by me."

After a little trouble, McGowan learnt that a man holding the office of high priest to the tribe had led them into a war with the inhabitants of a neighbouring isle.

The issue of this war had been very disastrous to the tribe, for they were frustrated every time they met the foe.

The man who had been the cause of this misfortune was seized by the tribe, and would have been put to death had he not had a miraculous visit from one of the gods worshipped by the islanders.

"This deity," so the cunning rascal said, "was very angry with his children for placing the great medicine's life in danger—so angry that he would not forgive them until the criminal was released."

Further, he told his hearers the tribe would have to remain under a dark cloud until there should come a white man who would have on his breast a sign that had been placed there by the deity.

The sign would be either a bird or a beast or letters in a language only known to the deity.

"The white man," he further said, "would lead the tribe to victory, would make them masters of as many of their neighbours' isles as they wished to conquer; but until he came, and they were to seek for him, the tribe must suffer."

Riley's eyes twinkled when he made out the points of the case; he saw at once the wonderful visit had been only in time to save the fellow's life.

He understood, too, the medicine man trusting to the by no means remote chance of an English sailor being left or shipwrecked on one of the isles, would serve his purpose.

He knew, also, that the seamen were in the habit of decorating their flesh with all sorts of peculiar tattooing, and luckily his words had come true.

The tribe, smarting under this continual promise, and believing the cunning rascal's words were, as a matter of course, delighted when they saw the marks on Riley's breast, and at once welcomed him as their deliverer and protector

"Well," said Riley, "as far as the fighting

goes, you will find me the boy for that; but is there anything else you wish me to do?"

Riley was to be made a chief, and at once a transformation was soon effected.

McGowan was now encircled with a chaplet of feathers, and he donned his costume, which was much lighter than his well-worn garments.

After the shouting and yelling was over, and Riley McGowan stepped into their midst, covered in half a dozen feathers, and a girdle of dyed cloth around his waist, his interpreter made a sign to the young women, who at once came forward.

"Bear great chief," said the man who could speak English, "Bear want wife, Bear take six."

"How many?" exclaimed Riley, aghast. "Six—and all live together!"

"Six—one, three, two, five, four, six."

The tribe yelled as Riley made his selection, and with his half dozen wives at his heels he joined in the marriage dance, and, from time to time, kept up his spirits by a sip or two from the calabash.

"Foot it," yelled Riley, "round again; go it ye divils, go on there, all the Mrs. McGowans, foot it! Arrah, it's not much money for clothes ye'll cost me, seeing as half a yard of stuff will make ye a suit."

From the combined effects of being so "very much" married, and the pulls at the calabash, Riley was seen to stagger, then fall; he was soon picked up by his wives and carried off to a mud hut that stood in the centre of the village.

CHAPTER XXXIII.

THE POISON HUNTERS.

A DEEP silence reigned in the hut during the time the Indians were disembarking, and from time to time the young officer looked at the sad face before him.

He could not calmly contemplate the probable death of the companion whose faithfulness had won his heart.

As he thought of her form stricken low by the merciless hand of a savage, an angry cry came from his lips, and the weapon he held was grasped with a firmer hand.

The Fawn heard the cry, and came to our hero's side, and placing her hand upon his shoulder, said—

"My brother is sad. Does he fear death? Surely not. One so brave will be given a place in the happy hunting grounds."

"No, Fawn," he answered; "I fear not death; too oft have I stood face to face with the tyrant to heed his approach. It was upon your account my heart felt heavy."

Her eyes glistened, and she drew closer to him.

"Upon my account!" she said; "does the Fawn's life hold any value in the heart of the young hunter?"

"More, Fawn, than I knew until this dark hour; yet it is not strange. Have we not hunted together—have we not sat beneath the mora, and listened to the whip-poor-will, and the plaintive note of the houtou and the pi-piyo? and our hearts have grown together in those moments when the forest was filled with their cries, and the pale moon shed its light over our heads. Can you ask me Fawn, if my heart would not be cold were you to die?"

"Fawn can now die, she is happy; her heart is glad."

Jack's lips touched the girl's forehead as she spoke, then raising his head to look through the loop-hole towards the cluster of dark forms that stood out in bold belief against the ocean.

"See Fawn," he said, "they disperse. Can you tell me what it is they seek?"

The girl no sooner beheld the Indians attentively seeking among the trees and long grass then she clasped her hands and exclaimed wildly—

"The death sting, they are seeking the poison, may the Great Spirit look upon us now, for we are soon to die."

These dreadful words caused even our hero's nerves to give way, and as he brought the butt of his piece to the ground, he said—

"They will gather the poison, Fawn, and perhaps leave us in peace."

The girl shook her head sadly.

"No," she said; "it is worse that we are here. When they have gathered the poison it will be a test to try it's strength upon our bodies."

"Heaven preserve us!" said the midshipman, "we have but little chance of outliving this fearful day. Quick, Fawn!" he added, "see, they come this way! Ha! one points to the hut, and they fix the poisoned darts in the blow-pipes! Here, take your rifle, and bring down that chief with the head-dress of white feathers."

The hut was seen, and fifty nude savages armed with the blow-pipes and poisoned darts, came towards them.

It may seem strange to those unacquainted with the weapons used by the half-nude savages that Jack Rawlings and his companion should have expressed so much fear, especially as they were both expert with the rifle, and they had an abundant supply of powder and shot.

A brief digression to explain the mode of

getting, making, and using the poison will, I am convinced, be pardoned by those who are anxious to know how Jack Rawlings met the savages.

To such of my readers who desire to read, for instruction as well as amusement, the following account, which I have gleaned from the most reliable sources, will be very welcome.

The poison used by most of the tribes of South America is prepared to the greatest perfection; to them no toil or danger is too great to collect the precious materials, and it was to this circumstance that the lonely island owed the sudden appearance of the nude savage forms which so alarmed the Indian maiden and her companion.

In the silent depths of the mighty forests the ingredients which form this life-destroying essence grow in wild profusion.

A pine is the first thing the Indian seeks. When he has gathered sufficient of this he digs up a dark tuberous root. Tying these two together, the next thing to be found is a bulbous plant which contains a green and glutinous juice.

After gathering a small bundle of these stalks, the searcher looks under the brushwood for two species of ants, one large and black, and so poisonous that its sting produces a fever; the second is small, and of a bright red, and stings like a nettle.

After obtaining these, a quantity of Indian pepper is gathered; then the deadly fangs from the Labarri snake are extracted, and the whole of the ingredients are in the poison-seeker's possession.

The labour is not yet concluded, for the subtle poison has to be prepared, and the task is by no means easy of accomplishment or free from danger to those engaged in the manipulation.

With the above poisons in his possession, he proceeds thus to make an essence that will combine the power of each of the above, and reduced to such a form that it can be easily carried about, either in the chase or on the warpath.

First, the pine and bitter roots are scraped into thin shavings, and put into a sieve; this is held over an earthern bowl, and water poured on them; the bulbous stalks are then bruised, and the juice squeezed by the hand into the pot; and, lastly, the venomous snake's fangs and the ants and pepper are added.

This pot is then placed over a slow fire, and as it boils, a little of the poisonous juice from the pine is from time to time added.

This is continued until the whole of the ingredients become a thick syrup, and the operator, as he pours the subtle essence into small earthenware jars, holds it at arm's length, in order that he may not inhale the deadly vapour.

So great an undertaking is this esteemed, that the hut wherein it is made is considered polluted, and either burnt or levelled to the ground; and those engaged in the operation must fast during the whole time the work continues.

The pot which is used for holding a syrup must never have been used before, or the virtue of the poison will be lost.

Though these and other precautions are taken, the Indians who attend the manufacture are ill for several days after.

So much for the preparation of this mode of death; a few words as to its use will be necessary.

The arrow is barely nine inches long, and is made from the leaf of a species of palm tree, hard and brittle, and as sharp as a needle.

About an inch of the pointed end is dipped in the poison, and the other end is exposed to the action of fire, to render it hard, after which it is bound with wild cotton; this, again, is fastened with shreds of the silk grass.

Six to eight hundred of these deadly missiles are placed in a quiver made from the dried skin of the tapir.

The Indian, to guard against being pierced by his own weapons, fastens the arrows' points downwards to a long stick by strings of cotton.

Thus, when he wants a fresh arrow, he draws he stick a little distance out of the quiver, and is enabled to handle the deadly weapon without danger to himself.

A thong enables the quiver to be slung over the shoulder, and with his blow-pipe in his hand, the savage warrior is better armed than the European with his rifle, ball, and cartridge.

The blow-pipe is, perhaps, not the least singular part of the equipment.

This extraordinary tube of death is found on the wilds of the unpeopled tracts of country near the Rio Negro.

It is of a bright yellow colour, and grows to an extraordinary length.

The Indians use pieces at the very least twelve feet long; both inside and out is as smooth as polished ivory, and of equal diameter, and without the least sign of a knot or curve. This tubular reed, which Nature furnishes in abundance to her dusky children, is too delicate to stand the risk of coming in contact with the lower branches of the trees—accidents that would happen either in the chase, or in the heat of an engagement with a hostile tribe.

To obviate this, the Indians use a case formed

from the straight lance-like shoots of a palm called the Samourah; first carefully extracting the pulp, then inserting the long delicate reed—polishing and pointing the end which goes to the mouth with silk grass, finishes the long weapon and its possessor is ready to meet the largest brutes of the forest or the fiercest foe.

Inserting one of the poisoned arrows in this singular weapon, the Indian can send the missile with one puff the enormous distance of 400 yards, and so truly that the smallest bird can be brought down while on the wing.

The effect of the poison is instantaneous; the slightest scratch or prick with the envenomed arrow-tip produces instant death.

The victim does not expire as though suffering pain, but drops to the earth, every faculty numbed, and as the subtle essence becomes infused in the blood he droops and dies, but so gently that it seems more like falling into a gradual slumber.

The most reliable travellers assert that three minutes is the usual period which elapses between the time of receiving an arrow and the passing away of the earthly spirit.

There is but one antidote, and this only known to a few of the tribes.

The reader can now understand our hero's feelings when the exulting horde of fierce savages drew up before the hut, and each having their quivers full of poisoned arrows, he will confess that the midshipman had but little chance of escape.

The smallest opening in the logs would be sufficient to send a succession of deadly missiles to the interior, and Jack, for the want of proper tools, had been compelled to permit several spaces to be left between the log walls of the hut.

CHAPTER XXXIV.

THE HIDING-PLACE.

WHEN the young sailor bade his companion bring down the Heparti chief, the tribe were running towards the hut, their blow-pipes carried in a similar position to that adopted by the soldier with his musket at the trail; but scarcely had the words left his lips when the Indians came to a sudden halt, and the chief, coming forward without his weapon, advanced to within twenty feet of the hut, and made signs that he wished to hold a parley.

Our hero would have fearlessly gone forth to meet the red man, had not his more cautious companion seized his arm and said hurriedly—

"Stay. See you not a warrior behind t[] drooping palm?"

Jack peered through the small round ho[] from which he had withdrawn his rifle, and b[] held an Indian crouching behind the pal[] leaves, his long blow-pipe pointing towards t[] door of the hut.

The Indian chief became impatient, and fol[] ing his arms, looked contemptuously at the l[] building, and exclaimed—

"Is my brother a squaw, that he fears [] come and hear the words a chief would utter [

Jack listened to this taunt with flashing eye[] and had not Fawn gently held his hand, [] would have sent a bullet through the dusk[] warrior's brain.

"Be silent," whispered the girl; "the H[] parti knows not that the white hunter dwel[] within the hut. Be silent, and he may depar[] and not know that any——"

She stopped abruptly and pointed to th[] chief, who was cautiously advancing toward[] the hut.

"Down," cried the girl "Let us burro[] like the fox; he may not see us."

Jack comprehended her motive, and thre[] himself flat upon the ground, and so close to th[] side of the hut that detection by the Indian[] prying eyes was impossible.

The Fawn crouched close by his side, he[] dark eyes eagerly watching the dusky form o[] the feathered chief.

He came with the panther's wary gait, an[] applying his eye to one of the many crevices[] looked long and carefully at the interior of th[] hut.

He saw not the recumbent forms of th[] young pair, and at last, as though satisfied tha[] nothing living was within the log building, h[] walked boldly to the door, and tried to enter.

Three stout logs barred the door, and the[] Indian, after several ineffectual attempts t[] force an entry, uttered a grunt of dissatisfaction[] and then, turning slowly away, he walked to[]wards his companions.

"He is gone," said the White Fawn; "and[] when the poison is made, it will be beneath the[] roof of this hut."

Jack Rawlings uttered an exclamation o[] horror.

"Tell me, Fawn," he said, wildly, "is there[] no means of escape?"

"None," was the sad answer; "we mus[] die, for the hut will serve their purpose."

Suddenly she paused, and pointing to th[] floor of the hut, added—

"Fear has driven remembrance from ou[] minds—see, there is a place of safety "

Jack Rawlings gave a glad cry as he understood her meaning.

Beneath the pine logs which formed the flooring of their island home, the young adventurer had excavated a square hole to contain their provisions, and to sleep in when the cold winds should sweep through the imperfectly closed walls of their dwelling; he had made it deep and broad, and now, in the hour of their need, it served them as a sanctuary.

The portion of the flooring which covered this underground chamber was movable and easily raised.

Had Jack constructed it for a place of refuge from danger, he could not have made it to answer the purpose better with the limited means at his disposal.

To convey their weapons, food, and water to this place was the work of a moment. Then Jack followed, and with his ready rifle in hand he seated himself beneath the trap.

It was a fearful time, and every moment seemed an age to the young pair as they sat in the murky light (a few rays struggled faintly through the narrow openings of the pine logs) listening to the sounds of the approaching foe.

They came—a dozen strong-limbed fellows, carrying the trunk of a small tree—a few words from the chief; then the young pair heard the crash of the falling doorway, and the Indians came through the aperture, and began eagerly searching the two small chambers of the hut.

The listeners heard their remarks as they found a hammock made from plaited grass in Fawn's chamber, and their expressions of surprise at beholding in Jack's sleeping apartment a couch of dried skins.

They were puzzled by the strange sight, and held a long deliberation respecting the occupants of the two chambers.

To Jack's relief the supposition was that they had fled to the forest, and thither a number of the Indian youths sped, hoping to capture the fugitives.

Those who remained in the hut began preparations for distilling the subtle poison, and to our hero's horror, placed the large earthern vessel over their hiding-place.

He felt the Fawn's hand, cold and clammy, placed upon his wrist, and her words sounded like a death-knell as she whispered—

"When the poison is made, the hut will be given to the flames."

He pressed her hand, and would fain have uttered cheering words, but his heart became heavy as the utter hopelessness of their position came upon his mind.

There was no hope. He felt they must die beneath the blazing timbers of the hut, or dash through the trap door and fall to the earth stricken to death by the poisoned arrows.

As the cold, clammy drops of agitation stood out upon his forehead he bowed his head, and endeavoured to meet his fate with fortitude.

The task was hard and the struggle great, for the fiery spirit to succumb to the grim destroyer without striking a blow for life, and as he heard the soft footfall of the naked feet above his head, a grim resolution came to his mind, and he determined to die with a weapon in his hand rather than perish beneath the blazing walls of his island home.

"Fawn," he said, "I cannot die thus."

"Hush! they will hear my brother's voice."

"I care not—the blow will but fall the sooner. Como, you have a rifle and can use it; let us face the—"

"Is my brother mad?—there's a chance yet for us to escape; but one man will remain with the poison, the others will go outside the hut to escape its fumes."

"Listen, Fawn," Jack answered; "the fire will be lighted over our heads, the pine logs will blaze and give way, then the contents of the boiling cauldron will fall upon our bodies."

The girl shuddered at the prospect of such a violent death, and clutching her rifle, said—

"It is better to die from a poisoned arrow, come."

Jack arose, and gathering all his strength, prepared to lift the trap.

CHAPTER XXXV.

RILEY M'GOWAN ON THE WAR PATH.

WHETHER from the effects of being so "very much married" or a desire to change the somewhat monotonous life he led on the island, Riley McGowan was as anxious as any of the tribe to go forth in quest of the foe.

He soon picked up sufficient of the language to understand what he heard, also to make himself understood.

The tribe, thinking to retrieve their former losses, heard with delight the Great Bear's order for the assembling of all who were able to go upon the war path.

"Tell the spalpeens," said Riley, to the old man who could speak English, "that its myself who will be to the fore when the fighting comes on, and if any blackguard turns his back to the inimy, I'll bate the life out of him."

The herald made a salaam, and soon afterwards a dozen conch-shells began to emit a most abominable noise.

"Bedad," said Riley, "if there isn't much

music there's plenty of noise. Come on, Mrs. McGowan number one."

Number one, the youngest of the dark-skinned beauties, came in response to her lord's mandate, and stood with her hands crossed submissively before him.

"Bring the calabash, quick, and see that its full of fixed bayonets."

The fiery spirit was very appropriately named by the ex-caterer, for its was more like drinking red-hot spikes than anything else.

During the time Riley sobered himself with the calabash, an uproar took place in the hut.

"Bedad," said the Great Bear, "they are at it again. Go it, ye devils."

It was his amiable, but short-tempered wives, who were having a pitched battle about the honour of keeping their lord's dinner.

In obedience to the warlike summons, the tribe assembled, and the old fellow, whom Riley had promoted to the position of aide-de-camp, thus delivered the Great Bear's message—

"The time has come. The Great Bear has seen the spirit of our victim—he has bid him go upon the war-path. He has told the mighty Bear there are some amongst our young men whose backs will turn towards the foe. Let them beware, or there will be sorrow and wailing in the lodges. Let the canoes be launched."

The canoes were launched, and Riley, and the rest of his followers, pulled towards the enemy's domains.

There were no fire-arms amongst the party. Riley had a revolver, but as his friends had forgotten to bring any ammunition from the pirates' isle, the weapon was useless.

Bows and arrows, clubs and spears, were sufficient for the purpose, and Riley, as he took the helm, and took a firm grip of his lead club, gave a whoop that would have done credit to a Red Indian.

"Now, my boys," he said, "it's no skulking behind bits of stones when ye see the enemy, lads, go on at 'em at once."

The braves yelled with delight; they did not understand their leader's words, but the fact of his shaking his cloak spoke volumes.

Riley did not like the mode of warfare adopted by these petty tribes.

It was nothing more than a system of dodging from tree to tree and bush to bush; the beaten party being those who were not clever enough to out-manœuvre the foe.

Riley had resolved to alter this.

The news was not received with the ardour it ought to have been, for the dusky warriors knew a tree or a stone was not a bad protection against an arrow or a flying spear.

Towards sunset they came in sight of the foeman's isle, and the latter answered the yell of defiance by launching canoes and preparing for battle.

The enemy made no attempt to prevent the landing of their foes, but resorted to their old practice of lodging behind trees or stones.

Riley had drilled his tribe to charge *en masse*, as Suwarrow, the great Russian General, used to drill his recruits to charge mummies dressed as Turks.

"Now, me lads," shouted Riley, as he jumped ashore, "Ould Ireland for ever. Whoo! Faugh-a-ballagh."

Flourishing his club he made a dash at the enemy, the tribe following close at his heels.

The foe unprepared for this change in their adversaries' tactics, were taken at a disadvantage, and being brought in closer position became suddenly flustered, and before the sun had set they were flying full speed towards the villages.

Riley led the pursuit, and when they reached the huts there would have been a murderous attack upon the women and children, had not the leader put a stop to it by cracking the skulls of some of his followers who had begun to use their knives.

The old men of the conquered nation came forth with peace offerings, and after much talk a lasting peace was made, and the late foes embraced each other, and——drank themselves speechless.

This victory did much to establish Riley's popularity, and when he returned to the isle with his victorious army there was great rejoicing.

Great shouting, great blowing of shells, and great drinking of "fixed bayonets," and in the midst of the uproar Riley's aide-de-camp came and told him the tribe, out of gratitude, had resolved to make him a present of six more wives.

Riley asked to be excused, but his admirers were inexorable.

"The divil take ye!" growled Great Bear; "its row enough I have now, and fighting too for that matter, for there's hardly a bit of hair left on me head; for the swate craturs all pitch into me at once. Give the others to some one else."

"Great Bear, great chief—great chief have plenty of wives—cook meat for him—chop wood—hunt game for him—"

"Yes," said Riley; tear his hair out and scratch his face—never mind it, I'll take 'em, but by this and by that, the first chance I get, it's take my hook I shall." Riley kept his word.

CHAPTER XXXVI.

AN OPPORTUNE ARRIVAL.

BEFORE Jack Rawlings could raise the trap and boldly confront the Indians, the latter gave a yell, and, seizing their blowpipes, rushed from the hut.

Jack emerged from his place of concealment, rifle in hand.

One glance through the open door showed the cause of this sudden movement on the invaders' part, and the adventurer, when he beheld the unexpected sight that met his gaze, called upon the Fawn to come forth.

She came in obedience to his voice.

"Tell me, Fawn," he said, "are not these the pit-pans of your people?"

She looked towards the smooth sheet of water inside the breakers, and clasping her hands, said—

"It is! They come! The Young Beaver and his tribe. May the great spirit be merciful to my people!"

Jack looked at the excited girl, and asked—

"What dire misfortune is this my sister fears?"

"See you not the Heparti's, like a dark cloud hovering near the brink of the water?"

"I do."

See you not my people fitting arrows to their bows?"

"I see that also."

"Can you, a white man, not tell the meaning of these things?"

"By Heaven! yes. There will be a battle between the tribes."

"My brother has spoken true. There will be a battle."

"I knew not," Jack said, "that your people were at war with the Hepartis; tell me, Fawn, why is this?"

The girl's eyes flashed angrily as she answered—

"When our chief, whose hair is as white as the snow of winter, was a young brave, aye, as young as you are, there came to our wigwams one of the accursed Hepartis. He loved a maiden of our tribe, and would have taken her had not the chief—then not even a warrior—cleft his skull in twain with a tomahawk. From that day to this there has been war between them, and, though so many moons have passed, and many braves have fallen, they will fight until one tribe has gone from the earth."

Jack knew the fierce passions of the warlike Indians were aroused against a hostile tribe. Neither would give in until one tribe would be so reduced in numbers that it would be impossible to take the field.

This result attained, the victorious tribe would compel the vanquished to become their slaves.

The girl's people were a brave, hardy tribe, more numerous than the Hepartis, of more robust frame and constitution, before the long and fearful war broke out between them. The many sanguinary engagements had somewhat reduced their numbers, for although they at all times fought like heroes, the subtle weapon wielded by the Hepartis gave them an immense superiority over the arrows and tomahawks of their foes.

The meeting upon the lonely isle was a surprise to both parties, but no sooner did they behold each other than they both made preparations for the coming strife.

The Heparti chief drew his men up in a semi-circle upon the bank, and with their deadly blowpipes held ready to send forth a flight of envenomed arrows, they crouched waiting for the signal to begin.

The warriors of the Great Beaver, except those who were using the paddle, stood up in the fore part of their pit-pans, their bows bent, and their loud cries of defiance bidding the Hepartis fire.

In the foremost pit-pans Jack beheld the Apollo-like form of the Young Beaver.

His heart throbbed violently at the thought of the noble savage being slain by one of the envenomed barbs from the blow-pipes.

"Fawn," he said, "is your heart turned from your people?"

The dusky maiden's form shook for a moment, and her large eyes filled with tears as she answered—

"I could not love the Young Beaver, yet his was the only voice that spoke against the cruel order for me to be bound to a tree, and left for wild beasts to devour."

"I am glad to hear it," our hero said, "and you, Fawn, in memory of his kindness, bring the rifle I have taught you to use, and we will aid the Young Beaver's men in their fight against the Hepartis.

The girl's eyes sparkled, in spite of the cruelty of her people; her heart was yet warm towards those among whom her early days had been passed.

The warlike fierceness of her nature showed itself in the sudden clutch she made at the rifle, the trusty weapon that had once been in the possession of Joe Seedy.

"Come," she said, "I am ready; and when the living lightning goes forth from this tube of death, each time shall a chief of the Hepartis fall."

Our hero uttered an exclamation of delight.

"Fawn," he said, "your woman's wit has suggested a plan by which we can aid the men the Young Beaver leads to battle. Yes, we will pick off the chiefs and scatter dismay in their ranks. Ha! there is the signal for the battle to begin."

A shout from the tribe of the Great Beaver came upon their ears. At this moment a shout of mingled rage and despair as the poisoned barbs of the Hepartis dealt death among the band the Young Beaver commanded.

The young chief saw his warriors, stricken by the poison, fall forward as they madly urged their pit-pans through the water, their teeth firmly set, and their massive muscular chests heaving with excitement.

In spite of the showers of poisoned arrows they kept up their swift pace, and in obedience to their young chief's command, did not discharge a single arrow in return.

The Young Beaver, conspicuous by his circlet of black feathers, stood in the bow of the foremost pit-pan, his superb form was drawn erect, and as he bent his dark fiery eyes on his hereditary foes, he gripped his glittering tomahawk, and said—

"Forward, men of the Great Beaver, the Heparti is a dog—a coward—a squaw; he cannot fight but with poisoned shafts. Forward, and let your tomahawks drink their blood."

He was answered by a yell louder and fiercer than any that had yet left their lips, and the light pit-pans sprang out of the water beneath the vigorous arms of the excited rowers.

The Young Beaver had spoken the truth in one respect.

The Hepartis were not armed; but in warfare they relied solely on their blow-pipes and spears.

A charge with the keen tomahawk was to them a matter to be avoided.

They had no weapon to contend against a close combat, so they unwillingly retreated before the muscular tribe of the Great Beaver, taking refuge behind trees, and from thence sending forth their deadly missiles.

They saw the purpose for which the young chief and his braves kept the bows unbent; saw the gleam of the terrible tomahawks in their hands, and they tried with might and main to keep the foe from effecting a landing.

Shower after shower of deadly barbs greeted the advancing braves; time after time the rowers were struck by the deadly poison and

fell forward dead—the paddles held firm in their death-grasp.

Not a word was spoken, as the bodies of the fallen were thrown into the sea, and the places taken by others, who, excited almost to madness by the fearful havoc the enemies' arrows were making among them, soon made up the distance lost by the change of rowers.

They were within a dozen feet of the beach. The Young Beaver, who had singled out the chief of the Hepartis, gave the war-cry of his nation, and waved his gleaming axe above his head.

The signal was understood.

As though by magic, a hundred dusky warriors sprang to their feet: the paddles were abandoned, and the braves, turning toward the Hepartis, sent a flight of arrows in the midst of the closely-packed tribe. So sudden had this movement taken place that the enemy were, for a moment, taken by surprise.

Twenty of their number bit the dust as they were in the act of applying the blow-pipe to their lips.

Their yelling disturbed their companions' aim and before they could reply to the arrows which had caused this change in the aspect of the fight, the Young Beaver gave a second whoop and, at the head of his fierce warriors, dashed ashore.

The Hepartis feared those gleaming axes, and knowing that the advantage they possessed by fighting with space enough to use their long weapons, they broke, and fled to the cover afforded by a dense clump of trees.

The Young Beaver, though he panted to be avenged upon his foes, gave the signal for his men to also take to cover.

The young chief knew that in crossing the open ground to engage the enemy, he would run the risk of losing a number of his men before he could come hand to hand, and knowing that every wound, no matter how slight, produced death, he wisely, but reluctantly, gave the order for them to disperse.

The wand of a magician could hardly have produced a more startling effect than this order caused.

The band of warriors seemed to melt away and none but the dead and wounded strewed the ground.

Jack Rawlings had watched these movements between the hostile tribes with flushed cheek and blazing eyes.

He longed to place himself beside the Young Beaver when he saw that noble-looking savage start from the shore and rush towards the forest.

He could scarcely restrain the hearty British hurra which rose to his lips at the sight, and, had it not been for his companion, he would have rushed from the shelter of a clump of cane brake and joined the warriors.

"Stay," she said; "does my brother wish to reach the happy hunting grounds, his spirit taken from him by the tip of the poisoned arrow?"

"I can pass round them, Fawn."

"My brother is mistaken; he knows not the cunning of the Heparti dogs."

"The trees," Jack said, "will hide me from their sight."

"The trees," Fawn answered, "will be used by the Hepartis when my people bear down upon them, as the jaguar springs upon the deer. The Hepartis are squaws. They will run behind the trunks to hide from the warriors of our nation. See, my brother, the Fawn speaks the truth."

As she spoke the Hepartis separated, and ran behind the protecting verge of the forest.

When she saw her people imitate this movement she said—

"See! the tribe of the Beaver behave with the wisdom of trained warriors. They hide their bodies from the foe."

Jack could not help smiling at the girl's words.

When the foe ran behind the trees she likened them to cowards, but when her people imitated the movement, she likened it to the subtle tactics of Indian warfare.

The parties remained for some time under cover, the chiefs alone daringly exposing their bodies, and hurling the bitterest taunts at each other to bring on the engagement.

"The Heparti," said the young chief, "skulk like squaws. Let them come forth, that my young men may see the colour of their faces."

"Let the men of the Beaver seek the hiding-places of the Heparti, not hide like women or old men. Faugh! ye are dogs!"

The young chief's eagle eye blazed with fury, but his handsome face, schooled to hide the workings of his mind, seemed immovable as he calmly answered—

"Many moons have come and gone since the Heparti first met the men of the Great Beaver. Many scalps have been brought from the Heparti, yet more shall be taken. Come from your hiding places——"

The sudden report of a rifle stopped the young chief's speech, and to his surprise, one of the hated foe fell from the branch of a tree

The Young Beaver saw the Indian grasp madly at the air as he fell—saw a throe pass through his frame as he reached the ground, and the bronzed limbs became rigid.

The Indian had fallen within a few feet of the young chief, and as he bent his dark eyes upon the small circular wound, he muttered—

"The white hunter is abroad. He has saved the Young Beaver's life."

He knew that the skulking form hidden by the thick foliage of the giant trees, had crept there but for one purpose, that purpose, to strike him with an envenomed dart.

In spite of the danger which the act incurred, the superb warrior sprang from the shelter of the tree, and, with a loud shout of defiance, he stooped over the yet warm body, and quick as thought, cut off the reeking scalp; then waving the bloody trophy over his head, he darted back to his place of shelter just as the Hepartis sent a shower of poisoned arrows, with unerring aim, to the very spot he had just vacated.

The taking of the scalp caused a shout of joy from the chief's followers, a shout that was answered by a yell of savage anger by the enemy.

For some minutes after this not a glimpse could be seen of the lurking warriors.

Our hero, from his place of concealment, had seen the Indian creep from his companions and ascend the tree.

He watched him until he reached one of the upper branches, and as he levelled his blow-pipe at the young chief, the boy fired and brought him down.

The shot had somewhat astonished the Heparti, and the sudden scalping of their companion had taken place while their attention was distracted looking for the daring hand that had fired, as it were, from their very midst.

Not a sound disturbed the stillness of the primeval forest for some time; the deadly rifle had awed the poison-hunters, and the tribe of the Great Beaver feared to raise their arrows until they knew the exact position of their white-skinned friend.

CHAPTER XXXVII.

A DESPERATE BATTLE.

WHEN the Heparti saw the Young Beaver wave his trophy above his head, and when he darted back among his followers, they had only recovered sufficiently to use their long deadly weapons.

A council was held, and the dusky braves, burning to avenge this insult, began to move from tree to tree to get nearer the foe.

They did this with such cunning that at times

only the outline of their forms could be seen, shadow-like, among the small openings in the forest.

But, cunning as they were, not a vestige of their bodies was distinguishable, but the whizzing of an arrow told the men of the Great Beaver were on the watch.

A dozen of this party had been more or less hurt by the time they had glided to the verge of the forest, and when all were covered by the trunks of the trees and the thick foliage, they began to fire into the hiding place of the Young Beaver's band.

Save for a smothered cry, now and then escaping a fallen warrior's lips, there was no perceptible sign that the peaceful place was tenanted by upwards of two hundred savage men, each eagerly thirsting for each other's blood.

Closer and closer they crept to each other, until not more than a dozen yards of the clear green sward intervened between them.

Jack's heart beat wildly as he crept from bush to bush, following closely the steps of the hostile tribe.

He saw the crisis was at hand, and the dusky bands would soon be engaged in close and deadly conflict.

Oh, how ardently he longed to place himself beside the graceful form of the young chief, but the straggling band of the Heparti prevented this.

He knew that to pass them on either flank would be to expose himself to the deadly poison, and thus for the time he had to wait and watch for an opportunity of obtaining his wish.

A mass of cane-brake and dwarf palm rising from a little hillock was reached by our hero and the Fawn, at the very moment the Young Beaver gave the loud signal for his band to rush upon the foe.

The dusky warriors, like hounds relased from the leash, bounded from their place of concealment.

The gleaming tomahawks shone beneath the sun's bright rays, then came a sudden shout as the fore rank of the Heparti seized their spears and rushed to meet the bounding warriors of the Great Beaver.

There was a second rank yet of the Heparti.

These kept among the trees, and as the foe advanced they sent forth shower after shower of poisonous darts.

Many of the Great Beaver braves fell under the deadly fire, but the young chief, who was now fighting like a lion at bay, remained unscathed.

Jack and the girl held their rifles ready, waiting for an opportunity to fire, when they could do so without injuring their friends.

At present their aid would have been as fatal to the Young Beaver's band as it would have been to the foe, for the dark forms swaying to and fro under the fierce fight were so mixed together that it became hard to distinguish friends from foes.

In spite of the superhuman exertions of the young chief and his braves, they were compelled to retreat and seek refuge from the deadly fire which the foe kept up from among the trees.

The Heparti gave a yell of triumph when the men of the Great Beaver fell back.

Like so many demons they rushed from their cover to follow in pursuit.

Their joy was soon changed to despair.

When they reached the small open piece of ground which divided the tribes, the men of the Great Beaver suddenly turned and sent a flight of arrows among their foes.

The Indians' aim was true to the mark, and many of the Heparti fell, an arrow quivering in each of their hearts.

The thick-wooded forests gave Jack's friends the advantage the Heparti had hitherto enjoyed.

The Young Beaver formed his men in two ranks; the front rank down upon one knee, the second standing close behind.

In this manner they received their advancing foe.

First the front rank discharged a flight of arrows, and while they were preparing for the next discharge the standing rank emptied their bows.

Thus checked in their onset, and too brave to retreat, the Heparti stood their ground for some minutes, vainly endeavouring to use their blowpipes against the Young Beaver's band.

Foaming at the mouth with passion, the chief of the Poison Hunters tried every inducement to urge his men forward.

The attempt was futile.

The close, deadly discharge of the foemen's arrows was too much for them, and with a yell of savage despair they broke and fled to cover.

The Young Beaver saw the confusion he had thrown them in, and calling aloud upon his warriors, he dashed in close pursuit.

He was too close upon them for the deadly blowpipe to be used, and the Heparti thus left with their spears, turned and met the tomahawks of the foe.

The fight was carried on with all the ardour of savageness inherent in the warlike tribes, and the Heparti being nearly double the

JACK HOLDS A COUNCIL WITH HIS BRAVES.

umber of their foes, soon forced them back to he open space.

The ground was by this time strewn with the dead and dying of both parties, and it seemed that nothing short of a total extermination of one tribe would end the fight.

The long-cherished hate of over half a century was concentrated in the hearts of those remnants of the two tribes.

Both the chiefs were young braves, and felt that the honour of their nations rested in their hands.

The men under them were actuated by similar feelings; thus the battle was more desperate and bloody than it would have been had the whole of the tribes been engaged.

Had such been the case, there would have been men among them whose years might have been reckoned by their snowy locks.

As it was, they were all young, and each felt how great would be the honour to return from the red field of strife and tell how they had exterminated the last of the hated foe.

The Young Beaver's tomahawk became reddened from the blade to the tip of the hilt.

Like a panther thirsting for blood, he de-

8

stroyed all who came within reach of his valorous arm.

Blinded by the fierce passions that filled his breast he saw no danger; and once, when pursuing the foe, he was himself surrounded by a dozen of the enemy.

Twice his keen tomahawk struck in twain the shafts of the foeman's spears.

Twice he struck down those who would have taken his life.

The third time he followed two stalwart warriors who were retreating before his murderous weapon, and in aiming a downward blow at their heads he missed his mark, over-reached himself, and stumbled forward.

His tomahawk fell from his grasp, and he was at the mercy of the remainder of the foe, who were following close upon his footsteps.

He turned like a tiger at bay. A short hunting knife hung by a leather thong to his wampum belt, and seizing the weapon, he opposed it to the long spears his foes wielded.

With a glad shout they rushed upon him, and the brave warrior, whose name was a terror to the Heparti, stepped back to evade the thrust made at his breast.

The step was nearly fatal.

His foot caught in a tuft of fibrous oot, and he stumbled and fell upon one knee.

"Yield, dog!" said the foremost of the foe, drawing back his hand to give the fatal stroke; "yield to the Heparti thou squaw!"

The young chief hurled his hunting knife far away from him, and baring his breast, replied—

"Never! strike the son of the Great Beaver! He dies as a chief should die!"

The foe whirled his long-handled weapon high above his head, and lowering the point was about to slay the gallant youth.

Another moment, and the young chief, the pride of the Indian nation, would have been no more.

But before the barbed point could enter the brave heart, the terrible crack of the white man's rifle was heard, and the Indian, with a stifled cry, sprang upward, then fell forward upon his face dead.

He was shot through the heart, and the bullet came from the rifle held by the *ci-devant* midshipman, Jack Rawlings.

CHAPTER XXXVIII.

INDIAN GRATITUDE.

THE Young Beaver wrenched the spear from the stiffening grasp, and with the terrible fury of a wounded panther, he sprang to his feet, and threatening the foremost of his foes, cried out—

"The spirit of the Young Beaver shall never be sent to the happy hunting grounds by the hands of a dog."

He made the boast somewhat too soon, for in his fury he drove the spear so far through his opponent's body that he could not extricate it before the remainder were upon him.

Undismayed by this fresh misfortune, he seized one of his foes by the throat, and, despite the captive's struggles, held him up as a shield.

He had noticed the clump of cane-brake from which the puff of smoke came after the bullet struck his foe, and, covering his body with the writhing form of the Heparti, he returned, step by step, to their new sanctuary.

He judged, and judged rightly, that the friendly hand which had twice saved his life would use the terrible rifle upon his foes should they follow him.

One by one he saw the pursuers fall, and from the rapidity of the firing he guessed that more than one rifle was at work.

By the time he reached the clump of thick brushwood he was left with only the Indian he had seized and used as a shield.

The rifle of Jack and the beautiful girl had rid him of all but this one of his bloodthirsty foes.

Hurling the half strangled Indian from him, the Young Beaver was about to enter the cane brake when Jack came forth, and pointing to the still savagely fighting tribe said—

"Our place is there."

The young chief made no reply, but seizing the boy's hand, he pressed it warmly and said—

"My brother has twice saved my life, the Young Beaver is grateful."

"When the men of your nation," said Jack, adopting the figurative language of the tribe, "have driven from the island the hated poison-hunters, then we will talk, not until then."

"My brother is right; he is a brave, and although young, many scalps should hang at his belt."

With this word falling from his lips, the young chief stooped and picked up his tomahawk, and bounded towards the combatants.

The battle was renewed with but little advantage on either side, and though many fell both parties kept their ground.

The arrival of Jack and the fierce young chief upon the side of the tribe of the Great Beaver, produced a change in the aspect of affairs.

Jack handled his rifle with a dexterity that struck terror into the hearts of the Heparti, and caused them to fall back.

Fighting savagely to the last, they retired

towards their canoes; and as the setting sun glanced upon the waters, they jumped aboard and pulled madly from the island.

Five of the ten canoes which had arrived filled with armed men were now empty, and the fragments of the band pulled as though a legion of fiends were upon their track.

The Young Beaver's followers plied their arrows upon the retreating tribe, and Jack's rifle did good service.

Once the beaten tribe paused in their retreat. It was their last effort.

A shower of poisoned darts came from their long weapons; then they dashed towards the boiling surf, and disappeared beyond to reappear upon the blue waters.

This last discharge brought grief to the heart of the Young Beaver, for his friend, the gallant midshipman, lay prone upon the earth, a poisoned arrow quivering in his breast.

The Young Beaver gave a mournful wail when he saw the brave boy fall, and the tribe gathering round at this cry from their chief, gazed strangely at the plumed head, bent so calmly over the stricken boy.

He saw their glances and guessed the thoughts in the dusky warriors' minds' and placing one hand upon Jack's head, he said in a voice husky with grief—

"The warriors of the Great Beaver have a heavy grief upon their hearts. Behold the great white hunter who has twice saved me from the dogs of the Heparti! Behold him dying! The poisoned fang eating away his young life, and not all the great medicines of the tribe can save him."

The boy that had twice saved the life of their beloved chief had earned a debt of gratitude, and the dusky braves would have defended him to the last man; and when they found his life was slowly passing away, they gave vent to their grief in a low cry.

The Indian chief held the boy's head upon his knee and tried to induce him to speak.

"But one word," he said "ere your spirit wing its flight to the wite hunter's paradise; but one word more would be music to the soul of the Young Beaver, and balm for his bruised heart."

The rapidly glistening eyes were fixed upon the chief's handsome face, and the blue lips tried to give utterance to a few words.

It was in vain; the grim destroyer's fingers, cold and crushing out his young life were closing around his heart; and those who knew the subtle nature of the poison, knew that he had but a few minutes to live.

With the last effort of his failing strength, Jack Rawlings grasped the Indian chief's hand and gasped—

"Must I die?"

The Indian chief started—he had forgotten until that moment the antidote to the poison.

There was but one—that to draw the venom with the lips.

"He has saved my life," thought the Young Beaver; "is it our Indian gratitude that he should die? No; I will save him."

The warrior cautiously applied his lips to the wound, and drew therefrom the venom.

The change that took place seemed miraculous.

The eyes that were fast closing in death opened.

, The fixed, glassy look left them, and as he beheld the young chief he gave him a glance that spoke more than words.

His limbs, too, which had been listless and limp upon the ground, now began to regain their wonted vigour.

He made an attempt to raise his right arm.

Joy! Once more the sinews, were of use, and with a glad cry he regained his feet.

He was saved, snatched from the very jaws of death, and the dusky braves rent the air with their shouts of joy.

But the chief who had saved our hero's life? He had gradually sunk into a state of listless torpor, and our hero beheld with anguish this fatal sign.

He called to the braves, and in accents of the most thrilling nature, said—

"Will he die!—my preserver! Will he die?"

The Indian girl placed her small dusky hand upon the troubled boy's shoulder, and said—

"Unless the poison enters the blood through a wound, there is no danger. Be of good heart, my brother; he will sleep and wake to life."

Jack bowed his head in mute thankfulness, then bent over the senseless form.

He was to all appearance asleep. So placid, so gentle was the expression upon his features, that it seemed as though he was under the influence of a sweet and soothing vision.

CHAPTER XXXIX.
JACK RAWLINGS IS MADE A WARRIOR.

OUR hero and the young chief's liking for each other had by their mutual obligations become refined into a brotherly affection.

The wounded Indians had been attended to, and the English sailor and his dark-skinned friend walked towards the tree from whose boughs Jack's rifle had dislodged the skulking Heparti.

"Brother," said the Indian chief, breaking a small twig from the tree, then separating it in two he gave one part to Jack, "keep this; it will remind you of the debt the tribe of the Great Beaver owe to one who has done so much for them."

Jack took the small twig, and placed it in his belt.

"I will keep this," the chief said; "it will remind me how much I have to remember the visit of the young brave to this island; but"—he stopped abruptly—"where is the aged hunter whose form is as upright as the trunk of yonder tree? he is not here."

Jack uttered an exclamation of grief.

"He has gone," he said, "and by the strange trail. My heart is heavy when I think of what may have befallen him."

"Gone!" repeated the Indian. "He went not with my people."

Jack drew his Indian friend towards the forest, and pointed out the strange marks that were yet left.

He told him of the red stain upon the rifle, and how the imprints of many feet were visible upon the sands.

The Young Beaver paused for some moments over the strange story, and, when he spoke, his words caused our hero's heart to fill with grief.

"The trail," he said, "points to the Heparti. They alone have taken him from you."

"The Heparti!"

Jack repeated the words and his lips went white.

He knew that there was but little hope of ever beholding Joe Seedy again had he fallen into the power of this accursed tribe.

They were the most savage nation upon the coast, and loathed even by the red men.

The ate human flesh, and their horrible rites filled the minds of those who beheld them with the deepest loathing.

"The aged hunter," the chief said, "shall be found, if alive."

Jack shook his head despondingly.

"Nay, my brother, the tribe of the Beaver are now upon the Heparti trail; the pipe of peace has been buried, and until the Beaver's tomahawks have drunk the last of the Heparti's blood there will be no peace between us."

"My friend," Jack said, "I will accompany you on the war trail; my rifle is at the service of your nation."

"I would take my brother, but the great chiefs have had a vision that a white man will bring misfortune to our tribe. Thus my braves would not go upon the war path with you. I would be too happy, but I have but one voice; the chiefs have many, and all bow down when they speak."

Jack knew after this speech it would be impossible to alter the chief's determination, so, hiding as far as possible the disappointment he felt, he said calmly—

"My brother will come to the isle when he returns from the war path, and if the old hunter lives, he will also come."

"He will; until then farewell. See, my people are waiting for me, and the chief must not be the last upon the trail of his foes."

He wrung our hero's hand, then bounded in the direction of the beach.

Jack watched the pit-pans leave the island and skim over the deep waters of the ocean.

Then, as the last boat disappeared like a speck in the distant horizon, he turned from the sight, and walked sadly towards the Indian girl, who stood beneath a tree awaiting his return.

A fortnight passed before Jack heard anything of the Young Beaver, and he had almost begun to despair of ever gaining any tidings of the old master-at-arms.

One sunny eve, as he passed to and fro on the sands, he was equally surprised at the sight of a couple of pit-pans bearing towards the lonely isle.

He recognised the occupants by their tattooing and features, and hoped the chief he saw in the stern of one of the pit-pans was the Young Beaver.

He was disgusted when the party landed, for the chief was a man of less note than the Young Beaver, and there was a sinister expression in his face that warned our hero not to trust him.

The Young Beaver had sent the Great Elk, such was the chief's name, and a score of braves to protect Jack and the Indian girl against the enemies or any straggling parties of the poison-hunters.

The Great Elk had a message from Jack's friend; the tribe had been successful in meeting the Heparti, and had signally defeated them in a stubborn battle.

The Great Elk also told Jack Rawlings that from intelligence gleaned from the prisoners they had taken that old Seedy had been captured and sentenced to death for slaying two of the tribe when he reached the Heparti lodges.

But the night before he was to be executed he strangled the sentinels placed over him, then escaped, and had not since been seen or heard of.

The news was somewhat comforting. It did

away with the dread uncertainty that hung over the faithful old fellow's fate.

So thought Jack until the chief told him that in the fastnesses of a thick forest the Heparti found a portion of their escaped prisoner's jacket, and as it was not far from a den of lions they abandoned the search, thinking he must have been torn to pieces.

"But," he added, "the aged hunter was as cunning as a fox; he must have left his jacket among the trees to throw dust in the eyes of the Heparti, for they are but squaws."

There might be some truth in this, yet the chances were so much against an unarmed man escaping from the prowling beasts, that Jack felt as sad as before, and looked upon his friend as for ever gone.

Our hero felt pleased with the Young Beaver's friendly act.

The addition of the band of young and well-armed braves gave him a feeling of security, and he felt proud when the Great Elk placed a circlet of richly coloured feathers on his brow, and laid before him an exquisitely carved tomahawk and shield.

He accepted these symbols of authority with a swelling heart, and then, placing a belt of wampum round his waist, he motioned for his little army to draw near.

They came, and Jack said—

"Men of the Great Beaver, you have made me your chief. Until the dark wings of the spirit of death hover near me, may I be worthy of the trust."

Great Elk answered for his followers.

"The young brave," he said, "whom the men of the Beavers love, and speak of as the Young Tiger, can command us to the death. He is a chief—a brave chief, and may his heart never be turned against us."

Jack's eyes sparkled with pride.

The title given him was one that none but the bravest warriors ever received.

"The Young Tiger," he said, "will not forget he is white, and be a brother to his braves."

A shout of joy came from the Indians, and many rushed forward and prostrated themselves before their youthful chief.

"Go, my brothers," he said; "the Fawn will give you the flesh of the deer. You are hungered and would eat."

His word was law with them, and, led by the Great Elk, they filed past their chief, their weapons lowered, and went towards the hut. Jack watched their stalwart forms until they disappeared, then glancing at the symbols of command, he soliloquised—

"Fortune plays strange freaks with us poor mortals. Here am I, a chieftain of a band of as brave men as ever trod the earth. Would that old Seedy and Riley M'Gowan could see me now! I am sure they would be proud of their countryman."

Jack little thought that Riley was a great chief, and was at that very moment making his escape from his subjects and his wives.

It was indeed a great change, and well might the boy walk with a prouder step, and head erect, as his circlet of gorgeous feathers waved over his brow.

When he neared the hut he found his men seated upon the ground before the door, partaking of the food Fawn had placed before them.

He passed among the dusky warriors—a smile upon his handsome face—as they arose, and paid him the same homage they would have paid to a chief of their own colour.

Fawn clapped her hands with delight when she beheld her lover arrayed in the showy symbols of chief, and placing her arms upon his shoulders, she said—

"Men who have fought the Heparti, men who have battled with the wild beasts of the lonely forest, speak of their chief, the Young Tiger, as a great and mighty warrior. Fawn heard this, and her heart was glad."

"The braves of the Beaver," he said, "speak too well of me. I do not deserve it."

"My brother is wrong. Did he not save the bravest chief of a great tribe? Did he not help to drive the Heparti from the isle, and made many a wigwam sorrowful by the wonderful tube which speaks with the lightning's flash, and the roar of thunder? Why does not the Young Tiger wear the scalp of his foes? He is a warrior and a chief?"

"My people," said Jack, "are not cruel, even to their foes; they do not scalp them, neither do they torture their prisoners."

"My brother forgets he is no longer one of the white braves, who cannot be better than the squaw, not to take the scalp of their enemies."

Jack tried to explain to the forest maiden the difference between the habits of his country and the savage tribe to which she belonged.

She listened with exemplary attention to all he had to say, and when he had finished she shook her head, and said—

"The Young Tiger must forget that he belongs to a nation who knows not what it is to fight; he must be a brave and wear the scalps of his foes."

Jack smiled as he answered—

"I'll be hanged if I do, if I have to resign my new dignities for it."

The Indians soon built themselves a cluster of dwellings within sight of the young chief's hut.

And when the sun sank they would gather in the open space and amuse Jack with an exhibition of their warlike dances and the use of the tomahawk.

Many were the wondrous feats they performed with the deadly weapon, and soon was our hero called to join in their sports.

He found the Great Elk of great assistance to him in learning the various modes of the Indian warfare, and it became his chief delight to exercise them as though they were upon the war-path of a coming foe.

CHAPTER XL.

IN SEARCH OP THE BIG CANOE.

THE time passed quickly in the charm of this new phase in his wild life, and Jack for a time forgot all about the object of old Seedy and himself leaving the Pirate's Isle.

Forgot, until a trifling circumstance recalled it to his memory, and caused him to at once conceive a plan whereby he could bring such articles as he stood most in need of.

The chief of them were powder and ball, for the late fight had caused a woeful havoc in his little magazine.

He had the large pit-pan which brought the Elk and his followers to the island, and with this he determined to go in search of the gun-brig's hull.

One morning, when he was about to start for the forest, he called his men together and made known the object in view.

"In the hull of the large canoe," he said, "I shall find enough of the lightning tubes to scatter far and wide the braves of the Heparti; the journey is not far, and when my young men return, each with a tube of death in their hands, they will be glad."

Jack's weapon was venerated by his followers for upon more than one occasion, when they were throwing the tomahawk and using bows, Jack had startled them by the fearful accuracy of his aim.

He had seen them set up a mark for their arrows—a log of wood—and though they were expert marksmen, not one shaft in six even struck the target.

It was then Jack brought his trusty rifle, and cutting a small notch in the trunk of a tree, returned about two hundred yards and fired.

It spite of their stoicism, the red-skins could not help running forward to the mark, and when they beheld the notch split by the bullet, th gave vent to their surprise.

Jack knew enough of the Indian character make him cautions in the use of his weapon.

Many of the braves manifested much curiosi in the construction of the rifle, and would fa have taken it from the boy's hand to try th skill.

Once when it was not loaded, he gave it the Great Elk.

The Indian, to Jack's surprise, drew the ha mer back, brought the piece to his shoulder, a pulled the trigger, thus showing how narrow he had watched the boy when using the rif

To the red-skin's surprise, the hammer f without causing any report or smoke or iss from the muzzle.

The Indian stared with astonishment, a lowering the butt peered down the bore, a then handing it to Jack said—

"When the Young Tiger points the wonde ful weapon, fire comes forth, and unseen shaf strike the smallest mark. Will the Young Tig tell his servant why these things are?"

Jack determined to inspire the minds of h followers with his powder, and after slily drop ping a charge of power in the barrel, he brougl the butt to his shoulder and fired.

The charge was rather a large one, an being dropped loosely in, the report was rathe subdued, but a sheet of flame came from th muzzle.

At this sight Great Elk stepped back with cry of fear, and covered his face with his hand

It was some time before he could approac the formidable weapon again; when he did s our hero quietly assured him that the whit man alone was given the power of causing th lightning to pour from the dark tube of death.

From this time the Indians had become po sessed with a desire to obtain a rifle each, an many attempts had been made to fashion similar weapon from pieces of hard wood.

With untiring perseverance, and great skil with the primitive tools used, they made som wooden rifles, but found that they were useless

Thus, when Jack held out the hope of findin the wreck, and supplying them all with rifles they were mad to go upon the search, and two ran to the beach to launch the pitpans.

Our hero called them back.

Throwing aside his feathers and tomahawk as the heat was oppressive, and then ordering the little band to assemble, he addressed them thus:

"Many moons may pass before we find the great canoe; my people will be tired and there are no hunting grounds upon the surface o the great ocean, and they must eat. Let us hunt to-day in the forest and kill plenty of game; to-morrow we will go in search of the big canoe."

The hunting party was soon formed, and until nightfall Jack's rifle and his followers' bows were at work.

They returned to the huts heavily laden with the day's spoil, and by the quiet moonlight birds were plucked, cleaned, and cooked.

The young deer were also cut up and smoked, until the exterior of the flesh became sufficiently hard to withstand the action of the sun's rays: thus prepared it would keep good for many weeks.

The next morning at sunrise the party left the island; the Great Elk and his braves staying behind.

The Fawn pleaded hard to accompany the adventurers, but Jack was inexorable.

"I don't know how it is," muttered Jack, as the pit-pan danced over the surf, "but there was something in the look that the Elk gave the Indian girl when I told her to stay on the island, that I do not half like."

He would have turned back but the rowers had begun their peculiar monotonous chant used by the aborigines of South America to keep time to the strokes of their paddles.

Jack's heart was light, and he joined in the chant, much to the delight of his dusky followers, and when they came to a close Jack gave them an English song and tried to get up a chorus, but his audience would not venture a word of what they termed the Young Tiger's bad tongue.

CHAPTER XLI.

AN UNEXPECTED MEETING.

THE weather was fortunately favourable to the search for the big canoe, and the adventurers were able to continue their voyage day by day, and being in the midst of a cluster of islands, slept on shore at night.

From island to island they went, hoping at every new place to behold the remains of the big canoe.

The search lasted for nearly a week, and still no signs of the gun-brig; and one evening when they had reached a covering to protect them from the night dews, Jack was startled from his sleep by an exclamation from the look-out.

He sprang to his feet and ran to the water's edge, and for a moment he could scarcely believe in the truth of his eyes.

Seated across a log, and drifting towards the island was the well-known form of his friend the master-at-arms.

After a warm greeting between old Seedy and the young sailor—chief, I suppose we must term him now—the old fellow said—

"This is an unexpected meeting, Mr. Rawlings; you are the last person I should ever have thought of seeing."

"The same to you," said Jack; "but come, pitch into the grub, I dare say you are hungry."

Old Seedy needed no second invitation, and with his mouth full, he asked—

"How the deuce did you come here, and what is the meaning of your feathers and tomahawk, and—"

"First," said Jack, "let me hear how you escaped, and explain the meaning of those marks you left."

When the master-at-arms had finished his meal he replied—

"Right, lad. But first tell me what you saw."

"On the sands," Jack said, "I found the marks of your shoes; near them were the prints of about a dozen naked feet."

"Right, go on."

"A little farther off, I saw that three canoes had been grounded."

"Correct, lad; what else?"

"When I returned towards the hut, bewildered by your sudden disappearance, I saw the broken feather from a chief's head-dress lying at the foot of a tree."

"Yes, lad, correct again."

"Not far from this, I found your rifle, hidden under the brushwood, and, on the small of the stock, and near the muzzle, the weapon bore the imprint of two bloodstained hands."

"Ah, ah," laughed old Seedy; "I suppose that scared you a bit, lad."

"It did; I made sure you were slain."

"Not yet, boy, though I ran a pretty good chance of being eaten afterwards, as you shall hear; but first, I will explain the peculiar appearance my trail presented."

"This is how it happened, lad," old Seedy continued. "You remember when we parted to go in search of the tiger?"

"Yes."

"Well, when I reached the point I had marked out to enter the forest, I was a trifle scared by hearing a jabbering among the trees. Monkeys, I thought; but with the thought came the sounds in a louder key, and I knew that a party of Indians were not far off.

A minute's listening told me they were not of the Beaver tribe, and to my horror, when they suddenly burst forth, I knew by the white paint on the devils' breasts, that I had walked into a nest of the Heparti."

"A nest. How do you mean, Mr. Seedy?"

"Thus," the master-at-arms said; "the party were concealed by a clump of dwarf trees, and knew not of their presence until I found myself surrounded."

"Not a pleasant position."

"Far from it, Jack; you may be sure I was more surprised than pleased."

"I can believe that."

"And," old Seedy continued, "I did my best to get clear of the trap; but, bless you, they were upon me in an instant; and, though I knocked several of them down with the butt of my piece, I had to give in through an unlucky chop I received from a tomahawk; it was here."

Old Seedy raised his cap and showed Jack a red seam, a little above the forehead.

"From this wound," he continued, "the blood trickled down into my eyes, and, as a matter of course, blinded me, and gave the devils a chance they would otherwise not have had. It was from occasionally cleansing this from my eyes that my hands became stained, and left the marks upon the rifle."

"But," Jack asked, "how came it under the brushwood."

"Under the brushwood?"

"That's where I found it."

"Of course, now I remember, when I found that resistance was of no use, I put the piece out of sight, and just then I heard the report of your rifle."

"It was in the middle of the forest then," said Jack, "I fired at something, but forget now what it was."

"Of course when I heard the report I did my best to get away; it was useless, but for all that, I pretty well damaged some of their faces with my fist; they settled me with a blow from a tomahawk, then carried me from the forest."

"This accounts," said Jack, "for the absence of your footmarks between the forest and the shore."

"Exactly, lad; for I did not recover until we were close upon the canoes, then I had another set-to with them; but I might have saved myself the trouble, for they bound me with deer-skin thongs, and pitched my old carcase in the bottom of a canoe, then pulled from the island."

"Something must have startled them, Mr. Seedy."

"Yes, lad; it was the second report of your piece. Well, the beggars were not long in reaching the mainland, and when they did so, I knew my doom was settled."

"Why?"

"Because in place of taking me to their lodges, I was taken to a stockade, and two fellows left to watch over me, until the time came for me to be killed and eaten."

"A pleasant prospect!"

"Yes; but as it did not agree with my notions of a comfortable death, I knocked my sentinels on the head and escaped. You have heard how I put them off the trail by leaving my jacket in the forest?"

"I have, Mr. Seedy; but as there is the first sign of the coming day, we will have an hour's sleep before the sun comes upon us.

Old Seedy was quite agreeable to this. He was weary and in pain when our hero first beheld him on the floating log.

CHAPTER XLII.
HOW THE INDIAN KEPT HIS WORD.

THE Great Elk watched Jack Rawlings and his followers until the pit-pans had passed the reef and were upon the ocean.

"The Young Tiger," he mused, "has gone and left the Fawn to my keeping."

He walked to and fro the sands, his eyes blazing with passion; he followed every movement of the pit pans, and when they had disappeared, he exclaimed—

"The Great Spirit is good, I have but to throw dust in the eyes of the two braves, then the beautiful Fawn is mine!"

He turned slowly from the beach, and went towards the little villages, which seemed so strangely dull and deserted.

The level greensward, which had so lately been trodden by the absent braves and their young leader, was now untenanted, save for the ludicrous pair of tame monkeys who were walking about hand in hand and jabbering as though holding an argument.

The creatures had been taught by our hero, and with that aptitude for imitation which is so strongly inherent in this species, they were walking, or rather hopping to and fro, in uncouth imitation of the manner in which Jack and his beautiful mistress were wont to enjoy the cool evening breeze.

A number of tame birds were perched upon the roof of Jack's dwelling, among them were two paroquets of the most brilliant plumage.

These birds our hero had taught to speak with tolerable distinctness, and whenever he appeared at the door of the hut they would scream out his name, and hop to the ground to be picked up and placed either on the wrists of Jack or the Fawn.

When the Great Elk passed to his hut, these were silently watching the closed doorway, and evidently wondering at the unusual quietude which reigned around.

He cast many a wistful look towards the closed door which hid the fawn from his sight.

The door opened at last, and the Fawn came from her dwelling, stood under a drooping tree, and as she looked out towards the water, her eyes filled with tears, and her head drooped upon her breast.

Great Elk watched the lovely girl, bowed down by the grief caused by her separation from the handsome boy.

The picture was not pleasing to the Indian's mind, and he ground his teeth angrily when he thought how fondly she was attached to the gallant midshipman.

The two young Indians came towards the angry plotter, and seating himself by his side, one said—

"My brother looks sad. Is his heart heavy when he thinks of the braves who are upon the great waters?"

"Ulaio," said the crafty Elk, "has spoken; he has asked why I am sad. Does he never feel sad when he thinks of the beautiful maidens of his nation, and how they pine for the young braves who are far away from the land of the Beaver?"

"My brother speaks true," Ulaio said. "My heart is sad when I think of our happy hunting-grounds, and the dark-eyed maidens whose eyes are like stars, and whose voices sound like the music of falling waters."

"Good," said Great Elk, "my brother knows the cause of my sadness."

Ulaio looked towards the hut and said in a low hushed voice—

"Many moons will pass before the Young Tiger and his braves will return. Why does not my brother visit the land of the Beaver?"

"The Young Tiger," great Elk said, "has left the Fawn to my keeping—can I leave? No; but my brothers can; Great Elk will watch until they return."

The crafty words had the intended effect upon his hearers, and looking into each other's faces they gave a grunt of satisfaction.

"Great Elk speaks as a brother," Ulaio said.

"We will go to the land of the Beaver, and return before two moons have passed."

A gleam of joy shone in Great Elk's eyes. This was all he wanted—the Indians away. He would be alone upon the island with the handsome girl.

"When the Young Tiger," Great Elk said, "returns to his hut, he will find the Fawn. But my brothers are alone here while the maidens so loudly lament the absence of their braves."

"It is true," said Ulaio.

"Go, then, my brothers," Great Elk continued. "In the forest there is a pit-pan which the Young Tiger has fashioned from the mora tree; in it you can cross to the land of the Beaver. Return before the second moon has waned and all will be well."

The Indians unsuspectingly fell into the snare the cunning chief had spread for them.

Had they suspected the sinister motive which caused him to wish them away from the island they would not have gone.

They had sworn by the Great Spirit to protect the Young Tiger and the Fawn—sworn this before the great council of the tribe, and they would have died sooner than broken the oath which they believed, by so doing, would shut them out from the happy hunting-grounds when their spirits appeared before the great Maniton.

The pit-pan which our hero had been at so much labour to construct was soon finished by the young braves, and at sunrise next morning they dragged the heavy craft to the shore, and tried its floating capabilities.

Great Elk was with them. His heart filled with exultation when they took their seats, and began to slowly paddle from the isle.

He watched them until they had crossed the foaming coral reef, then turned quickly away, and went towards the hut.

"Now," he muttered joyfully, "we are alone upon the island."

The girl was sitting near the door with her hands crossed over her breast, and her dark eyes fixed mournfully upon the broad expanse of water.

A large tear trickled slowly down her cheek, and showed how sad and lonely she felt at the absence of her companion.

From this pensive attitude she was aroused by the hasty footsteps of Great Elk, as he crossed the open space which divided the men's huts from their chief's.

She raised her sad face when he approached, and said mournfully—

"Does my brother bring news of the Young Tiger's return that his steps are so quick?"

"He does not," Great Elk answered, "but comes with a heavy heart to the Fawn."

She looked inquiringly at his handsome face, and asked.

"What is the sadness that weighs upon the heart of a great brave?"

"Much sadness," he said. "Heard you not

the whip-poor-will's plaintive cry when the sun sank beneath the waters ?"

The girl started.

She had heard the bird's peculiar note as it sat among the branches of the very tree which now sheltered her from the sun's bright rays.

A chill crept over her frame at the significance of this warning note, and in a startled manner she looked across the sea, her breast sad, and filled with gloomy foreboding.

The bird mentioned by Great Elk is believed by the Indians to contain the departed souls of those who have lately passed away from earth.

Her mind filled with this strange superstition and the fact of the bird having perched upon the tree which overshadowed the door of Jack's hut was sufficient to cause her the most poignant anguish.

Her lover had perished. and his spirit passing to the body of this strange, but beautiful bird, had made known his death by the low plaintive cries, which are not unlike the moaning of a human being suffering the most exquisite pain.

The girl's head drooped upon her breast and from her lips there came a sharp, long cry of woe, and swaying her body to and fro, she cried—

"Yes; it was the spirit of the Young Tiger that came to his love. He came when the sun was hiding its bright face beneath the waters, for then was the hour that he sat beneath the mora-tree, speaking to the Fawn with the soft music of his voice."

"It was so," said Great Elk, " and my young men who saw the whip-poor-will, and heard his cry, have gone to the land of the Beaver to tell the chiefs that Young Tiger is no more."

Fawn raised her eyes while he was speaking, and a faint cry of alarm escaped her lips.

She saw by the passionate expression upon his face that he was regarding her with feelings that awakened her to a sense of danger.

"Alone !" she said ; " are we alone upon the island, Great Elk ?"

"The Fawn has spoken," he said ; " it is true. We are alone."

"The Great Spirit protect me," she murmured, "from this man ! There is evil in his glance, and danger in his presence."

"But why," Great Elk continued, "does my sister look so strangely ? Can she not dwell here as she has dwelt with the Young Tiger ? Great Elk is brave, and will give the Fawn his wigwam."

She clenched her hands, and the fire of her race shone in her dark eyes at those words, yet no sound came from her lips.

"Great Elk," he continued, "will be kind to his squaw. For her he will slay the beasts of the forest; for her shall the softest couch be spread, for he is a brave. Say, will you become his squaw ?"

She rose to her feet, and fixing her flashing eyes upon his face, she said, scornfully—

"Is it thus a brave should speak to one whose heart is sad, and whose lord is far away ? Go! Fawn will not become thy squaw. She can die, but never live with you."

The passion he had hitherto subdued while speaking to the lovely girl now burst forth, and with a mocking laugh of triumph, he answered—

"The Fawn speaks to the winds. Great Elk has said she shall share his hut. We are alone, and she must do as he wishes."

The girl looked piteously around as though expecting aid would come, but when she fully realized her helpless condition, she sprang to her feet and ran to the hut, followed by the Great Elk.

CHAPTER XLIII.

THE FAWN IN DANGER.

To snatch the rifle was the work of a moment, and with her finger upon the trigger, the Fawn stood defiantly until the baffled Indian sought safety by closing the door of his hut after he had passed inside.

She stood like a marble statue until his form was no longer visible. Then she raised her hand to her burning forehead, and, closing her eyes, tried to shut out the terrors of her position from her brain.

The first few moments were passed as though she had just awakened from a horrible dream, but soon she became calm, and prepared to meet the danger that threatened her.

"Young Tiger," she murmured, "would not rest in his grave beneath the water were he to know that the Fawn became the squaw of the chief. No; she that has been beloved by the Young Beaver and turned her heart away from the music of his voice, she who has been beloved by the white hunter, can never open her ears to the words of this man."

She paced hurriedly to and fro, thinking over many plans to escape from her persecutor.

"The whip-poor-will," she murmured, "may not speak the truth; Young Tiger may yet live. I will wait until the moon wanes before she dies, if he does not return, I will know he has gone to the happy hunting grounds and will join him there."

The Indian girl's firm belief in an after state of eternal happiness with the youth she so fondly loved made the prospect of dying by her own hand one of joy rather than one of bread.

She had some days to live, for the moon was yet young, and when her mind was resolved upon thus baffling her persecutor, she began to plan a scheme whereby she could live in safety until the time came for the knife she wore at her girdle to end her young life.

A smile irradiated her face when she at length hit upon a scheme to escape the Indian's persecutions, until all hope should have passed of Jack's return, and leaving the hut she took her way sadly and slowly to the yellow sands.

Seated upon a piece of rock, she gazed on the spot yet marked by the keel of the boat in which Jack and his braves had left the island.

She remained there until nightfall, then wearied with her grief she began to retrace her steps to the hut.

When passing the clump of palm, which marked the entrance to the little settlement, the young girl gave a startled cry.

The cry was succeeded by the crackling of dried twigs, and to her horror she beheld the lurking form of her admirer emerge from the bushes.

He had watched the girl as she sat by the waters, and well knowing that all chance of compelling her to be his wife was useless, while she was in the hut he had waited until she came forth.

It was a hard matter for the treacherous Indian to refrain from giving vent to a shout of joy when he saw the girl in his power.

The cry of exultation changed to one of surprise, not unmixed with terror as he turned and gazed seaward.

The Fawn heard the sounds, looked out towards the boiling surf, and beheld six of the Heparti's canoes cross the coral reef, and shoot forward into the clear space.

It needed no wizard to tell either the Indian or the forest maiden, the meaning of this visit; both knew that the Heparti had come to wreak their vengeance upon the young white hunter and his dark-skinned mistress, for the share they had borne in the fight between Young Beaver and their tribe.

Their common danger, for the time, made the Indian girl and her suitor friends.

He came from his place of concealment, and began to prepare to defend his hut.

In the midst of his labour he was startled by the well-known war whoop, and before he could escape to the forest the foe were upon him.

One gleam of the tomahawk and the Indian rolled to the earth a corpse, then the exultant redskins seized the trembling girl, and uttering a loud shout of joy dashed onward to the centre of the forest.

CHAPTER XLIV.
THE MASTER-AT-ARMS' ADVENTURE.

THE adventurers left the island soon after sunrise, and old Seedy, as he sat beside Jack Rawlings, finished the story of his adventures after his escape from the Heparti.

He found his way to the sea-shore, and every yard of the way was fraught with danger.

In the jungles lurked the tiger and the deadly Lebarri snake; in the forest and on the plains he was in momentary danger of being discovered by hunting parties of his foes.

At last, after travelling until he lost all reckoning of the days, he came upon the confluence of several rivers, and had just thrown himself upon the brink to bathe his blistered feet, when a yell from the rear broke on his ears, caused him to start up, and fearing to fall into the power of the cannibals, he walked into the water.

Old Seedy's first intention was to commit suicide, but fortunately the surface of the river was strewn with trees and other vegetation, torn up by a hurricane.

Lashing two logs together with bush rope, he seated himself upon them, and the current swept him out to sea, where he was seen by the middy and his braves.

The pit-pan was tossing about close to the coral reef when Joe Seedy ceased his interesting narrative, and as the light craft shot through the spray into the deep blue water, Jack suddenly exclaimed—

"Canoes on the beach! What can be the meaning of that, Mr. Seedy?"

The old sailor took his rifle from the bottom of the boat, and quickly examining the priming, answered—

"That yellow streak round the bows of the strange crafts, tell me they belong to the Heparti tribe, and the meaning of their being there, lad, we shall soon find out."

A foreboding of the evil that had fallen upon the Island Maiden, caused the blood to run cold through Jack's veins.

"The Heparti!" he repeated his name with compressed lips and kindling eyes. "They have come here but for one purpose."

"A purpose," Joe Seedy said, "which is soon guessed. They have not forgotten the share you took in the late fight, my lad."

Jack made no reply. His eyes were fixed with an eager searching look upon a clump of dwarf palms.

He saw by the waving of the leaves that

something was behind them to cause the foliage to be thus disturbed.

Standing erect in the bow of the pit-pan, his left hand grasping the barrel of his unerring rifle, his right shading his eyes from the glaring noon-day sun, our hero called upon the Beaver braves to put forth their strength to run the pit-pan ashore.

The dusky warriors bowed their plumed heads to the command of their chief, and bringing every sinew into play, they fairly lifted the light craft out of the water.

"The Heparti dogs," Jack cried, adopting the mode of speech which his dark-skinned followers were wont to hear from the lips of the gallant Young Beaver; "they have come when my young men were away looking for the winged canoe,—come when but three of my braves were on the island; and by this the Heparti tomahawk has drunk our brothers' blood, and the huts which our young men built are now level with the earth.

Incited by these words, the Indians' fiery passions were aroused, and compressing their lips they pulled madly to the isle.

Borne upon the wings of the soft westerly breeze, came the joyful cry of the Heparti.

The sound was like the blast of the trumpet to a mettlesome charger, and the Indians with glaring eyes and dilated nostrils bent lower to their task.

"Do my young men hear?" Jack resumed, "it is the cry of the foe. Hark! again it comes! They shout with joy at the thought of my brothers being away."

The Indians gave a loud cry of anger and turned their heads towards the shore.

"My brothers," Jack said as he noticed the effect his words produced, "think with me the Heparti are dogs, and dare not wait to see the Beaver tomahawk gleaming in the sun."

A growl of pleasure came from Jack's followers as he threw in this compliment.

"My brothers are pleased," the youthful white chief continued; yes, the Heparti must fly before the heroes of Beaver, and their canoes will beat them from the land. Say, shall it be so?"

The Indians turned their faces towards the speaker and looked confused. The expression upon their dusky faces told that his words were not fully understood.

Jack pointed to the canoes.

"My young men," he said, "are strong of limb, to them the canoes will be as reeds. Let their tomahawks splinter them and throw the fragments to the sea. Thus the Heparti cannot escape our vengeance!"

Then a shout of approval passed their lips and the prow of the pit-pan was turned towards the canoes.

Old Joe Seedy had been a quiet but interested listener to the words Jack had said to excite the young Indians' anger; and as Jack bent eagerly forward vainly trying to make out the cause of the strange commotion among the clump of dwarf palms, he arose in the stern and said—

"Brave lad! a red-skinned warrior could have done no better; where did you learn this lesson?"

"From the Young Beaver."

"You are an apt scholar. Oh, curse the fellows! they nearly upset me."

The Indians maddened by Jack's words, drove the pit-pan with such force into the boats that Joe Seedy had he not clutched one of the rowers by the hair of the head, would have been pitched overboard.

Like demons the Indians fell upon the Heparti canoes, and with their sharp tomahawks, split their timbers into a thousand pieces.

Jack waited not until the enemy's flotilla was destroyed, but with old Joe Seedy following close upon his heels, he started swiftly in the direction of the clump of dwarf palms.

Fully expecting to come upon a group of the foe, holding high revel at their victory over the few braves he had left in charge of the island, Jack kept his eyes towards the upper branches of the trees, running not more than six feet high.

Joe Seedy found it was as much as he could do to keep up with his young companion, and as they ran side by side, he jerked out spasmodically—

"What's the matter? They are not among the dwarf palms?"

"See," Jack said in reply, "how the leaves sway to and fro! There must be—"

Before he could finish the sentence there was a crashing noise, as though he had trodden on a heap of dry twigs, and to his companion's surprise Jack disappeared.

Joe Seedy halted in time to prevent himself falling into the trap the cunning Indians had dug for the Young Tiger.

Mr. Seedy knew not for some moments what had occurred.

His companion's disappearance was so sudden that it seemed as though he had been swallowed by a huge chasm in the earth.

Joe Seedy fancied he heard a half smothered sullen growl from the depths of the pit into which Jack had fallen, and not knowing what

RILEY M'GOWAN ON THE LAGOON.

enemy might be there, he pointed the muzzle of his piece downward, and yelled out—

"Stand clear, my lad; I'm going to fire!"

"Hold!" cried Jack, as he made an attempt to scramble up the side of the pitfall; "I'm alone."

Joe Seedy knelt at the edge of the pitfall, and held his rifle at arm's length for Jack to clutch, and at length his head became visible.

Joe Seedy threw every branch and twig he could gather into the pit and after much labour he had thrown in sufficient to raise Jack within four feet of the level ground.

Gathering his branches well beneath him, he sprang from the pitfall

Our hero and Joe Seedy dashed through the underwood, and went in the direction from which came a succession of joyful cries.

Suddenly a turn in the tall cane-break revealed a sight which, for a moment, caused the boy's heart to turn cold, and his older and less impulsive companion to give vent to an oath.

Beneath the giant limbs of a mighty tree, were grouped together between thirty and forty of the Heparti braves.

In their midst was the beautiful Indian *girl,*

her arms and legs fastened by deer-hide thongs to an upright piece of wood, and scattered around her feet were several bundles of dry branches.

Jack and Joe Seedy took in these details at a glance, and the former. as a cry of mingled rage and horror came from his lips, brought the butt of his rifle to his shoulder and fired at one of the Indians, who was in the act of applying a live torch to the heap of dried branches and tufts of sun-scorched grass.

The blazing brand fell from the Indian's grasp, and, springing upwards, he clutched madly at the empty space, then fell forward a corpse.

The Heparti gave a yell, and seizing his spear and poisoned arrow, turned in the direction of the report.

Jack, reckless of the consequences, threw his rifle from him, and drawing his sword, bounded forward and stood beside the Fawn.

The Indians shrank back as, meteor-like, he dashed in their very midst, and with feelings of more than ordinary ferocity, they stood in a semi-circle around him, looking from the glittering blade he grasped at his fearless face.

Joe Seedy had only time to utter a cry of alarm before the boy sprang from his side, and stood thus, calmly defiant, his graceful, well-knit form, a mark for a score of poisoned weapons.

The old seaman lost no time in the attempt to overtake his young companion, but dropping upon one knee, he brought his deadly rifle to his shoulder, and, motionless as a stone figure, he waited to slay the first of the Heparti who should make a hostile movement towards the gallant youth.

He had not long to wait.

The Indians, though first astounded at the report of Jack's rifle, and the swift death that had come upon their companion, soon recovered their wonted hardihood, and, uttering a fierce cry, they nearly closed upon him.

Two of the foremost spear-shafts were shivered by the bright keen-edged sword, and as one of the foe was stooping to pick up the fallen blade, another shot from Jack's rifle despatched him.

One of the fiercest of Jack's foes—a chief of the tribe and a Colossus in form—sprang forward to grapple with the boy.

Jack turned his sword's point to the savage's naked breast, but before he could drive the point through the painted skin, the Heparti's fingers were entwined round his throat; and another of the tribe, standing behind, struck him senseless with one blow from his club.

Jack fell to the ground; the gigantic chief the same moment toppled forward—a bull from Joe Seedy having entered the back of h skull.

Then came a shout of joy from the Hepar as they bound the gallant boy to a tree; an Joe Seedy's blood seemed to freeze at the fea ful doom which threatened the boy he loved well.

CHAPTER XV.
A NARROW ESCAPE.

So strong was the spell upon Joe Seedy that h could not steady the rifle in his grasp.

Those iron sinews which had stood him such good need in all quarters of the glob were for once relaxed, and though he behel the Heparti warriors poising the fatal spear transfix the gallant boy he was powerless save him, and Joe, closing his eyes to shut ou the fearful sight, covered his face and crie aloud in his agony.

There seemed no hope for the poor boy.

With that thirst for blood, which is so in herent in the race, the angry Indians drev closer and closer to behold the fatal strok given.

The keen blade gleamed in the sombre ligh and the frail shaft quivered in the Heparti' strong grasp as he drew back a second time t take a surer and a better aim.

This saved Jack's life.

The Island Maiden, with a smothered cry sprang towards a fallen brave, and with won drous strength, wrenched the weapon from the dead man's hand.

Like a lioness defending her young the gir stood over the body her lover, and, as quick as the lightning's flash, her weapon found a sheath in the Heparti's breast.

Buried in the dusky savage's flesh was the long spear; and the shaft swayed to and fro with the force of the blow.

It was well aimed, and the man fell without a cry, his heart cleft in twain.

The girl's eyes sparkled brightly as she beheld the Indian fall to the ground, and before a hand could be put forth to slay her, she snatched up Jack's bright sword, and turned quickly round to the dark cluster of men.

"Behold!" she cried, "how a Beaver maiden makes war with her foes! Behold a Heparti dog! how she can defend the white hunter, whose hand has sent many of your accursed race to the endless fields of eternity!"

They levelled their weapons and pressed closer, and the girl with a savage laugh, gazed at the bristling line, and said—

"Back! There's a devil within me, that will send your cowardly spirits to the black guardian of your race. Back! I say."

The men, awed by her voice and manner, paused and looked into each other's face.

Then the chief of the Heparti spoke.

"Men of the land where the tiger lurks!" he said, "make not war upon a woman."

The men gave an angry growl.

"We are braves," he continued, "and men of a great and mighty tribe; keep your weapons for the Beaver dogs. This woman who has slain a warrior, let her die with the white hunter—let the flames reach them—let it eat away their bodies, and the wind carry their dust upon its wings. I have said. Are my brothers content?"

They gave a glad shout, and despite Fawn's attempt to save herself and lover from their impending doom, she was disarmed, and again a prisoner.

They would have bound her to the form she so well loved, had not a mighty shout at that moment startled them.

It was the men of the Beaver tribe with Joe Seedy at their head, who were now bounding forward to avenge their white chief's fate.

The chief of the Heparti pointed with his spear towards the depths of the forest and said:

"Take your prisoners hence, and while our spears are being reddened with the blood of the Beaver dogs, let the flames go upwards as an offering to the god of battle."

They answered him with a yell, and from among those who stood near the captives some seized them, and started at a swift pace towards the spot indicated by the chief.

Scarcely had they disappeared among the trees when Joe Seedy and the Beaver men dashed through the cane brake.

The Heparti quickly formed under their leaders, and with levelled spears prepared for the onset.

Jack's followers, furious at the loss of their leader, and goaded to madness by Joe Seedy's cries, bore down upon the bristling line.

There was a short and stubborn conflict for a few seconds, then the Heparti line swayed to and fro, and then beaten back by the heavy tomahawks wielded by the Beaver braves, they broke and fell back upon the confines of the forest.

Joe Seedy, who was well versed in the Indian mode of warfare, urged his men forward to cut off their retreat.

It was craft against craft—redskin against redskin; and the Beaver warriors, though a swift in their movements as the eagle in its flight, were too late to intercept the foe.

Once among the trees the Heparti disappeared as though by magic.

Joe Seedy glared savagely at the giant trees, and raising his clubbed musket above his head, he called out in the Indian tongue—

"Forward, men of Beaver! drive the skulking devils from their cover."

He led the advance bravely; and his braves, taking a firmer grasp of their reddened weapons, dashed after him.

From tree to tree the Heparti were driven, but not without laying low some of the Beaver tribe.

The Heparti also suffered severely in their retreat; the slightest portion of their dusky forms visible only for a moment, would be followed by the swift flight of a tomahawk through the air.

So true was the aim that every weapon slew or maimed one or more of the foe.

Far into the sombre stillness of the mighty forest, pursuer and pursued kept up the fierce struggle.

The chief of the Heparti knew that they had either to conquer or die, for the young men of the opposing tribe, with biting words which the Indians know so well how to use, taunted their foes with the intelligence that their canoes were now broken to fragments, and no mode of escape existed unless they conquered those opposed to them.

The Heparti hurled their taunts back as bitter.

They told how they had landed and slain the Indian, and how the island maiden and her pale-faced lover were at that moment being consumed by fire.

Joe Seedy sheltered by the broken stump of a tree plied his rifle with deadly skill. But when the Heparti told the fate to which they had given his young companion, the old man's eyes become dim and his limbs trembled with the throb of agony which passed through his frame.

The cunning Heparti saw the old seaman's agony and heard the yell which came from the men of the Beaver when this intelligence came. They knew also that the foe would brave everything to rescue the young chief and the island maiden from the funeral pile, and with devilish subtlety retreated in a direction contrary to that which had been taken by Jack's captives.

Joe Seedy looked eagerly around for the smoke which he knew would be visible should the fiendish work have begun.

He saw nothing to mark the spot.

The blue canopy of heaven was unclouded, and so far as the eye could gaze, the green waving foliage met it.

He began to think that the Indian's words had been used but to taunt him and his followers.

With the thought his nerves became steady, and catching a glimpse of the man's face who had sent forth the dire words to him, he pulled the trigger of his unerring rifle. The Indian sprang upwards and then fell forward upon his face.

One convulsive contortion of the muscles, an effort to rise, and the red skin's spirit fled to the mystic realms of eternity.

Joe Seedy quickly reloaded, and in a voice that thrilled friend and foe, he said—

"The Heparti is a liar, and with the lie upon his tongue he has gone face to face with the Great Judge."

The chief of the hostile band stepped boldly out from the shelter of a tree, and poising his long spear he dashed it at Joe Seedy.

"Dog!" said the warrior, "The Great Judge never lies! His voice came to my ears and bade me slay you. Thus do I obey!"

Joe Seedy had only just time to throw himself flat upon the earth, when the spear came whirring through the air.

It struck the ground a few feet beyond his prostrate form.

"Well aimed!" muttered Joe Seedy, as he turned on his back and fired at the retreating chief.

The ball sped onward and struck the Heparti chief in the leg.

In spite of his stoicism and the stubborn spirit which actuated the aborigines to suffer the most excruciating agony in silence, he could not help a low cry of pain escaping his lips.

The Beaver tribe yelled derisively, and one pointing towards the tree behind which the wounded chief had taken his refuge, said—

"Listen to the cry of the squaw! Behold men of the Beaver, how your foes cry when they are wounded."

A second yell followed these words, a yell that was again repeated; old Joe Seedy pointed where, with outstretched hands, to a thin spiral column of light blue smoke, which was slowly ascending among the trees.

"To the rescue!" shouted the old seaman, clutching his rifle. "Behold ye, men of the Great Beaver, the work of the Heparti!"

They understood the significance of these words and look, and suddenly leaving the bush, they bounded after the old seaman.

The Heparti were close enough to hear old Seedy's words.

And the chief, following in the direction of his outstretched fingers, saw that his men had begun the work of vengeance.

It was now impossible to keep Jack's friend in ignorance of the spot where the sacrifice was about to take place.

Knowing this, the Heparti turned and fled before the resolute attack made by the foe as they rushed towards the place of execution.

Keeping well in advance of their pursuers the Heparti reached the spot where the funeral pyre was beginning to blaze, a few yards only were between them and their pursuers.

But ere the men of the Beaver could pass over this small pace, the fire had encircled the helpless victims, and one powerful ruffian sprang upon the pile of logs, and flourishing his scalping knife above his head, pointed with his left hand towards Jack and the Fawn.

Old Seedy saw the ruffian's purpose, and regardless of all save the desire to be avenged on the dusky devil, he broke through the phalanx that surrounded the pyre.

With one bound he stood beside the Indian.

There was a short but deadly struggle.

Then the brave Young Tiger snatched the scalping knife from his foe.

Like a flash of lightning, it descended up to the hilt in the Indian's breast, and the man fell backward into the living flames. The Beaver braves drove back their foes, and with a glad shout, began to scatter the pine logs and dry brushwood on every side.

The scalping knife cut the captives' bonds, and the Fawn and her lover fell forward upon the charred wood to all appearance dead.

CHAPTER XLVI.

DEFEAT OF THE HEPARTI.

JOE SEEDY sprang like a leopard among the dusky forms that secured the captive pair.

Passion gave the old seaman the strength of a giant, and with his clubbed musket he dashed the Heparti to the earth as though the stout warriors were but reeds.

Right and left the butt of his rifle fell with a dull thud upon plumed heads, and with every blow the men of the Beaver and their white ally numbered a foe less.

Jack's dusky warriors were close upon Old Seedy's heels, and their gleaming tomahawks did savage execution, until the Heparti, awed by the prowess of the little band, broke from the position they had taken up and fled wildly towards the forest.

The last of the Heparti, a young brave, whose

wampum belt was as yet unadorned with a human scalp, gave a longing glance at Jack's clustering curls; and before the boy's followers knew what had taken place the young savage sprang upon the heap of dried brushwood and plunged his left hand among the cluster of dark curls which adorned our hero's head.

He gave an exultant cry as he drew his scalping knife and flourished it above his head—that cry was his last.

While its echoes were yet repeated among the mighty trees Joe Seedy seized him by the throat, and with Herculean power hurled the exultant Indian many feet from his intended victim.

The Indian tried to rise and follow his retreating companions, but ere he could do so one of the Beaver braves cleft his skull in twain.

A wild cheer came from the conqueror's throats, and with one impulse they brandished their crimsoned tomahawks and dashed after the foe.

Old Joe released the captive pair, and as he wept tears of joy over his young favourite, he blubbered out:

"Don't mind an old man's weakness, Jack, I can't help it."

Jack pressed his friend's hand; then drawing the Fawn from the smoking pile, he said, and a shiver ran through his frame as he spoke—

"Look, Joe! you were not much too soon."

He pointed to the flames which were rapidly ascending.

"Not much, lad. But hark!"

The two listened to a distant shouting, and the Indian girl clasping her hands, said joyfully:

"It is the cry of victory! The men of my Beaver tribe are scalping the foe."

"That must not be," Jack said; "come Joe, let us save the poor wretches from being murdered."

"Right, lad," replied Joe, "though the red skin devils would have roasted you, we would not, as Christian men, let them be butchered."

The Fawn placed her hands upon Jack's shoulders, and looking into his face said softly:

"My brother forgets he is chief."

"How so?"

"He talks with the aged hunter," said the Fawn, "who knows the white man's tongue bears words that the chief of all great men would use."

Jack looked first into the girl's face, then into old Seedy."

"Lor!" said he, "how different are the feelings of this girl to the women of our nation."

"Nature lad—nature!" responded the old sailor. "It is born in 'em, aud what's born in the flesh——you know the rest."

Jack smiled, and he pointed in the direction of the hut as he said:

"The Fawn's place is beyond the mighty Argla. Let her go. Young Tiger will behave as a warrior. But come on, or we shall be too late."

They dashed among the trees, and guided by the fierce shouts of the victorious Beavers, soon reached the scene of slaughter.

Jack's fear had not misled him; the men of the Beaver tribe were slaughtering the foe with that keeness for blood which belongs to the red men of the forest and the fiend for their tribe.

Bravely had the Heparti stood in a small open glade in the vain hope of staying the pursuit.

There was a momentary struggle as weapon met weapon, and a swaying to and fro of the dusky phalanx, then the Heparti broke and fled towards the trees.

Their foes surmised their intention, and they spread themselves out like a fan, and intercepted them, and being in small bodies, they could make but feeble resistance.

The tomahawks of the Great Beaver gleamed in the air like flashes of the brightest light, then they fell with crushing force upon the skulls of the unfortunate foe.

Their pit-pans destroyed; pressed in the rear by the victorious Beavers; no escape for them save by plunging into the tranquil sea, the Heparti threw down their arms and sued loudly for quarter.

The reply was a deep yell, and the red weapons were plied even more fiercely.

Another five minutes, and not one of the Heparti braves would have been alive.

Bounding to the spot, and placing himself between the excited victors and their cowering foes, Jack, with flashing eyes, called upon them to stay the red work.

Their passions were too much excited to readily obey their leader, and, save from one or two, the tomahawks continued to gleam in the sunlight, and each stroke sent a red man's spirit to the mystic regions of eternity.

Jack snatched a tomahawk from the stiffening grasp of a dead Indian, and placing himself before the Heparti, he sternly waved his followers back.

"The men of the Beaver," he said, and his dark eyes blazed with passion as he spoke, "are braves. They make not war with a foe whose hands are empty, and whose weapons are thrown away. They would not be braves if they did so; and as surely as the sun streams through yon trees, will I slay the next hand that raises a weapon."

Two-thirds of the Beavers shrank back as Jack raised the threatened weapon, and the determined aspect with which he wielded it.

But four of the band, disregarding his words, dashed towards a group of the beaten foe.

Jack observed the act, and before their weapons could be used, he was amongst them.

"Dogs," he said, "is it thus you obey your chief?"

"Die!"

He struck one to the earth with his tomahawk, while the remainder, awed by their companion's fall, immediately lowered their weapons.

Jack followed up the advantage he had gained over the fiery band by saying:

"You have sworn before the great council of your tribe. Sworn by the great spirit to serve and obey the Young Tiger. Is it thus you keep that oath? Go, ye men of the great Beaver! Seek your lodges, and when the wild brutes' thirst for blood shall leave your hearts, come to the hut of the Young Tiger."

The Indian race, so quickly aroused to demoniacal fury, are as easily subdued by a judicious appeal to the really honest depths of their nature.

I use the term honest because the red men, until they became polluted by their intercourse with the white traders, travellers, or settlers in their country, were really honest, sober, braves and chivalrous; quick at anger yet as quickly appeased.

But now these traits one by one left them as the mighty forests and endless savannah, became peopled by the flow of emigration which poured out from the cities of the Old World.

The ring of the settler's axe in those vast regions awoke echoes that sounded strangely upon the ear of the simple forest children!

They saw mighty trees cut down by the strangers' hands; they saw the game—their only wealth—driven far away by the surging crowd of pale-faced strangers!

Tract after tract of land was taken from them; their hunting grounds were given to the axe or to the flames; and because the Red Indians resented this wholesale destruction of the lands they and their's held from time immemorial, the needly adventurers had laid aside their axes and took up the rifle against the naked and poorly-clad natives.

CHAPTER XLVII.
JACK MEDIATES.

WHAT was the result?

Wholesale massacres on either side; then falsified reports reached the old country respecting the red man's ferocity and cunning.

Reports originated with the very men who had robbed the Indians of their birthright, and driven them with fire and sword from their hunting ground.

With such chronicles there can be but little wonder that the simple forest children were classed among the most degraded of God's creation.

The small band which served Jack were free from the evil traits so unjustly attributed to the Indian's character.

Naturally brave, they loved the boy for his gallantry, and would have followed him to the death on any enterprise, no matter how rash or hopeless.

The Young Tiger was to them a superior being, and they worshipped, admired, and loved him.

Nor was the disobedience they had shown when he ordered them to desist in the terrible slaughter, through any disrespect of the feelings of their young leader.

It was simply an uncontrollable impulse of their untutored nature, and the example he made of one of their number, in place of exciting angry feelings in their breast made them love the boy for his strict sense of honour.

The Beaver men, with bowed heads, slowly left the field of slaughter, and went towards their lodges.

Then Jack, still holding the bloodstained tomahawk in his hand, turned towards the Heparti.

"I have saved you," he said, "from an ignominious death; my young men were angry when they saw that the foe had come to the island during their absence, and killed all they left. And, with worse than the ferocity of the tiger, they took a poor helpless girl and gave her to the flames. Are such things right? Are they the promptings of warriors, who boast as being of a great and powerful tribe?"

The Indians were silent, and gazed from the youthful speaker to old Joe Seedy's statuesque form.

The old tar was leaning upon the muzzle of his fatal rifle, listening with pleased astonishment to his favourite's words.

"I've seen many a redskin chief," he thought and heard them speak, "but this boy is a wonder, considering the little he knows of forest life. It's nature, I suppose."

Old Seedy was not far adrift in his surmises.

"Listen, men of the Heparti," Jack continued, finding that none of the tribe answered; "the great forests, the mighty plains, and the troubled waters are large enough for all to dwell upon."

An exclamation of approval came from one of the listeners.

"It is," Jack said. "Why then do the Heparti seek to slay the men of the Great Beaver?"

"Many an Heparti's scalp," said one of the tribe, "hangs in the Beaver's lodge."

"Is that a reason that you should thus war with each other?"

"An Heparti warrior," said the Indian, proudly, "is ever on the war path with his foes."

"Nature, Jack," Old Seedy cried out in English: "you won't change it, lad?"

"I'll try in this instance, Joe."

"Push a-head, lad."

Jack turned to the Indian, who had spoken for his companions.

"Does the Heparti warrior," he asked, "always return from the war-path?"

"Many," was the reply, "go to the happy hunting grounds."

"But they would sooner live."

The Indian's reply was characteristic.

"They die as warriors should die."

"You can't get over that, lad," cried Old Seedy, this time, quietly; "better give in with the argument."

"So I think," Jack said, "for my dusky friend seems quite able to hold his own."

"Ay, lad, he'd do that against a fleet of petticoats, and they love to show a good amount of jawing tackle."

Our hero laughed, for the comparison, though vulgar, was nevertheless all a sailor.

"But what in the name of all that's good?" said Old Joe, "do you want these fellows to do that you talk about from point to point?"

"I should like," Jack said, "to put an end to this war between the tribes."

"Whew!"

Joe's whistle of astonishment would have excited the envy of a bo'sun.

"What are you whistling for, Joe?"

"Nothing, lad—nothing; exercise, that's all."

Jack looked straight at the old fellow, as he said—

"You are quizzing me, Joe; but never mind. I will try my hand at peace-making."

"Do, lad, do; it will save many a poor devil's scalp if you can get them to bury the war hatchet and take to smoking pipes of peace."

Jack felt that Joe was not very sanguine about a successful result of his mediation.

Hopeful, however, himself of the issue, he again addressed the Heparti.

"My brother tells me," he said, "that the braves of his tribe die as warriors should die."

The Indian bowed his plumed head—a token of acquiescence.

"Does my brother forget the empty lodge, the sorrowing woman he leaves behind when the spirit wings its way to the happy home beyond the sun?"

"An Heparti squaw," said the Indian, "lives to repeat the brave deeds of her husband."

"Go it, darky," chuckled Old Seedy.

"Does she rejoice that he is dead?" Jack asked.

The Indian was silent; he could not tell a lie.

"She does not," Jack said. "Neither do the young men of the tribe when they lose a brother."

"Young Tiger forgets," said the Indian, "that the Heparti have many braves, and their young men can be counted by many hundreds."

"I do not forget," said Jack, "but the life of every brave is precious, and should not be wasted in this long war with the Beavers. What say my brothers—will they bury the war hatchet and be friends with those who have so long and nobly fought?"

There was a few minutes' silence, and Old Seedy chuckled out—

"Why don't you try to wash their skins white, Jack?—it would be quite as profitable as the palaver you indulge in, and which is wasted upon your hearers."

"Have patience, you tantalising old sinner! I shall bring them round to my way of thinking, yet."

"Perhaps you will, lad; but not this side of a score of years."

Before Jack could reply, the Indian answered his suggestion.

"Young Tiger," he said, "is a mighty man for one whose years are but few."

"That's soft soap, Jack, and—"

"Let him go on, Joe."

The old tar grinned as the Indian proceeded.

"When he speaks," said the Heparti, "his voice is as soft as the dew upon the flower."

"That's—"

"Do be quiet, Joe."

"When on the war-path," continued the Indian, "his bound is like the panther's. We listen to the words of so great a warrior, and find them to be good. Thus do we bury the hatchet of war; thus do we ever become friends !"

They hurled their weapons from them; and breaking a bough from one of the trees, each took a portion and laid it at Jack's feet.

The boy with a triumphant look turned towards Old Joe, and, raising his bugle, formed from a conch-shell, blew three loud notes.

The sound was answered by the Beaver braves suddenly appearing from among the trees, and Jack, when all were present, told them of the termination of the long war between the tribes.

The men of the Beaver tribe soon followed the example of the Heparti, and broken branches were exchanged.

At the conclusion of this ceremony, the rival tribes began to fraternise and embrace each other, as though they were brothers meeting after a long absence.

Jack and old Joe left them, and walked slowly towards the tent; the old sailor thoroughly astounded at the miraculous change the boy had effected in the hearts of the angry savages.

Arriving there Joe saw his friend enter, and retired to take a short survey of the place.

He was not long away, but on his return, on entering the tent, he was startled by hearing an angry cry from the boy's lips, then followed the report of fire-arms, and Jack dashed through the doorway, with a rifle in each hand.

"What on earth is the matter ?" old Joe began, when he saw the boy's face blackened and charred with gunpowder.

Jack grasped him by the shoulder, and in wild, thrilling accents said :

"Come, Joe—the island is no longer a home for us. Let us go."

"Why ? Bless the lad ! Why, what's gone wrong ?"

"Ask no questions now," Jack said; "but come, let us once more see the lonely waves beneath us."

"But—but——"

"For heaven's sake, Joe, do not seek any explanation now. I will explain hereafter."

He turned towards the boat as he spoke, and ran as though pursued by a legion of furies.

Old Joe shook his head sagely, and putting one of the rifles Jack had dropped upon his shoulder, he closely followed.

When he reached the margin of the great ocean he found Jack wildly pushing the boat out from the land.

Old Joe, still lost in wonderment, gave him a helping hand, and they were soon afloat.

As the boat glided from the shore Jack threw himself on the pile of skins, and remained for many hours silently watching the single mat-sail as it flapped against the mast, or bellied out before the wind.

CHAPTER XLVIII
THE GUN-BRIG AT LAST.

THE lovely isle had long sunk below the dim and misty horizon before Jack spoke to his companion.

When he did so old Joe was struck by the change in his voice and the glitter in his dark eye.

"Joe," he said, "come and sit beside me."

The old seaman went aft.

Jack said—

"I feel, old friend, as though my blood had changed to liquid fire. Come, can you not find something to turn my thoughts from the fearful scene I have—but then you shall know all when I am calm enough to tell you."

"Worthy lad, what can I do to calm you ?"

"Recite some of the wonders you have beheld —anything is better than the mental torture I endure. Come, Joe, grant me this favour."

"I will, lad. I will try and keep your mind from thinking upon the strange matter that has so upset you. Though I fear you have exhausted my powers of amusement, still I'll try, and if I am prosy you must excuse it."

"I shall not have to do that," Jack replied, a faint smile flitting across his pale face.

"We shall see, lad ! Put that skin round your shoulder, the evening is cold."

Jack did so, and Old Joe went amidships to fasten down the sail, one end of which had become loose.

When he returned to our hero's side he drew a warm skin over his shoulders, and after a few moments' silence, and two or three long side looks at his companion, the young hero hurriedly ejaculated—

"See, Joe; what is that ?"

"That, lad ?" responded the old sailor, attentively watching a small black speck floating in the distance, "appears to me very much like a piece of wood."

"Wood! and here ?"

"Ay, lad, and there ain't much to be surprised at in that, considering we are in the stream that runs direct from a cluster of more than a thousand small islands."

"A thousand islands !"

"Ay, lad; a thousand wonderful places that have come up out of the sea's depths. Belched up with large bodies of smoke and flames, which the mighty waters could not extinguish."

"Volcanic islands, Joe ?"

"Ay, lad, so they are termed."

"You said there was not much to be surprised at in seeing this log of wood here?"

"Nothing to be surprised at, lad, certainly, when I tell you that hundreds of vessels strike upon the hidden pieces of coral islands which are rapidly sinking again into the bed of the ocean."

"Jack pondered for a few minutes.

"Joe," he inquired at length, "are none of these islands inhabited?"

"None, lad, except by goats and birds; and when a few men may escape from shipwreck in the whirling waters. You have passed them, lad, upon your voyage out from England, and——"

He paused, and as the piece of wood which had attracted their attention rolled over and over, added:

"A piece of the Albatross, by heavens!"

It was a fragment of the jolly boat, and in white letters stood out the name Albatross.

Jack looked the astonishment he felt, as he said—

"We are not far from the place where we were wrecked."

Old Joe shook his head.

"As for that, lad," he said, "we may not be a hundred fathoms, or we may be a hundred miles."

"The promised hope," Jack said. "We have been long hoping to behold the remains of that beautiful vessel."

Old Joe was silent.

The well-practised young eyes were watching the rippling waves, in the somewhat wild hope that a second piece of the ship would serve to guide them to the spot.

The boundless water, as far as the eye could reach, was without a speck save for the fragment of the Albatross jolly boat, which, by this time, was slowly drifting past the boat.

At length Joe, startled, spoke—

"Look here, lad," he said, "the stout craft has not gone to pieces, lad."

Jack looked on interrogatively.

"I mean it," said Old Joe, "and unless I am very far from the mark, the ship has been boarded since I left her."

"Boarded! by whom?"

"That," Old Joe said, "remains to be seen. It may be a shipwrecked crew. Again, a party of Indians from the mainland may have come across the old hull; or, what is as much to be feared, a gang of pirates, driven by stress of weather, may have used the spars for fire-wood."

"How do you know all this, Joe?"

"All what, boy?"

"That the vessel has been boarded since you left her."

"It's very simple, lad. The jolly boat, of which this is a piece, was half way down the hold when I left the Albatross, and so fixed by the force with which the waves broke her from the fastenings, that it would have been necessary to cut away part of the hatches to have loosened her"

This explanation satisfied Jack.

"By the way," he asked, "what were you so intently gazing across the water for just now?"

"To find out the way that piece of the jolly boat came."

"You are a strange fellow, Joe," said his companion. "Is finding a pathway across the ocean possible?"

"Ay, lad; when I know the maelstrom is the point of attraction for the fragments of the wreck."

"The maelstrom, Joe?"

"Yes, lad; the place where there are two or three currents meet, and such is the attraction power of the vortex that vessels have been drawn into it before now."

"Your opinion is," Jack said, "that this piece of the wreck is being drawn slowly towards the whirlpool?"

"Yes, lad; and if I am right, we are going direct to the cluster of islands we have so long wished to find."

"I hope so, Joe."

"So do I, lad, for we shall be able to live more like Europeans, if we find the vessel, than we have done lately."

"We have a few hours of daylight left," said Jack, "and with this wind we shall see the islands before dark."

"I hope so, lad, for I should not like to face a rough sea in this cockle-shell."

"It would not be very safe, Joe, certainly."

"I should think not, lad. Now, come, as we have talked enough to calm your mind, let me know the cause of the strange sounds I heard inside the hut."

The Young Tiger's head drooped as he said—

"Not now, Joe."

"Look, look, what is that?"

Old Joe sprang to the bow of the canoe (they were now close upon the rocky shore of a large barren isle), and his eye followed the direction of Jack's finger.

He gave an exclamation of astonishment as his eyes fell upon the singular sight which had attracted Jack's attention.

Within the space of a dozen fathoms from the beach lay the massive form of a dead elephant.

Across the fallen leviathan's side a large crocodile had taken up his position, and overhead a flock of hideous-looking vultures screamed and flapped their wings, evidently scared from their repast by the huge crocodile's presence.

To complete the picture, the form of a man could be seen, rifle in hand, crouching behind a fallen rock.

"Well, lad," old Joe said, "this beats everything. What on earth can that fellow be crouched there for?"

Jack answered by telling him that during his sojourn amongst the haunts of the forest dangers and the savage tribes who came from time to his domain, he had learnt the value of being prepared for any emergency.

During the time Old Seedy was gazing upon this strange scene, he had been loading and priming both rifles.

One of them he handed to his companion, declaring his object to be that of waiting to have a shot at the crocodile.

The words were barely uttered when the sharp crack of the stranger's piece rang out and the crocodile fell backward, cleaving the ground, and lashing his tail with rage and pain.

"A good shot," muttered Joe Seedy, as he handled his piece; "that bullet went in just above the scaly one's fore-leg.

The crocodile's death-agony was by this time over, and he lay beside the huge carcase he had come to feast on.

The stranger, when he beheld the scaly brute roll down, gave a joyful cry and sprang to his feet with the intention of examining the dead brute.

But as the cry escaped his lips, the pit-pan grounded and old Joe sang out—

"Ahoy! messmate, ahoy!"

The crocodile-slayer turned, then stood like a stone figure, and gazed wildly at the strangely-clad forms of Jack and his companion.

He waited until they reached the shore, then, as though seized with sudden fear, uttered a wild shout, turned, and dashed madly from the spot.

"Well," old Joe said, "that's one way to give us a welcome to be sure. What ailed the fellow?"

"Perhaps," our hero replied, "he has gone to give the alarm to his companions, if he has any."

"True, lad, such may be the case; so before we go any further suppose you go aloft and look out.'

Jack selected one of the tallest trees for his post of observation, and with an agility a squirrel only could have equalled climbed its summit.

Then he had a clear view of the island, and after a long and searching look became certain that, but for the crocodile-slayer, the island was completely deserted.

He was therefore about to descend, when a dark-looking object upon the opposite side attracted his attention.

At first he thought it was some mammoth rock which some mighty convulsion of nature had dislodged from the almost perpendicular cliffs which surround the isle.

By degrees the outlines of this strange form became clearer to the boy's eyes, and little by little he made out the battered but still distinguishable form of a dismasted ship.

"The Albatross!" he exclaimed, "the Albatross at last!"

Slinging himself off from the upper limb of the tree he soon reached his companion's side.

"The Albatross, Joe! the Albatross!" he sang out, lustily.

Old Joe looked upwards among the branches of the trees.

"Where, lad, where?"

"On the opposite side of the island!"

"Glad to hear it, lad; but what about the fellow and his companions?"

"Can't see a soul," replied our young hero. "The place seems as deserted as when it was first created."

"Well, well," the old seaman mused, "it you didn't see any one, why it's my opinion that the fellow you saw took us for cannibals and started off to save his life as he supposed."

"I'm pretty much of that way of thinking myself," added Jack: so let us go to the vessel and see whether there is anything yet on board likely to be of service to us."

Jack made a forward movement as he made the proposition, and started off as though intended to go across the island.

"Come back, lad!" was the old tar's caution, "we can sail round to the spot, which is much to be preferred to going round on foot, perchance to encounter some more crocodile-killers

Jack saw the force of this reasoning at a glance, and immediately turned back toward the boat.

His impatience, however, could not brook the delay necessary to hoist the sail; and, jumping in, he took the rudder, asking Old Seedy to the paddle. ——

CHAPTER XLIX.
ABOARD THE WRECK.

JOE SEEDY smiled at the impatience of his com

sion, and as he paddled from the beach with a wish to quell his impetuosity, took the opportunity of saying—

'By the way, Jack, you have not told me the cause of your sudden flight from the island; this is a good time to redeem your promise.

Jack was very thoughtful as he replied. For a few moments he was evidently conning over the subject, which as evidently was not pleasing to him. Feeling, at length, his comrade had a right to the information, he went on.

"Well, Joe, you shall know all things. When I started I had made a resolution not to tell you, and—"

"But would that have been kind, lad?"

"Perhaps not, Joe; indeed, so I have concluded. Still, when you know all, you will no doubt respect the feelings which prompted my decision."

"Well," rejoined old Joe, warmly taking his companion by the hand, "you don't mind me; why should you wish to conceal anything that interests you from one who loves you so sincerely as I do?"

"It shall be so; you shall know all," and the hot blood reddened his cheek as he thought of the revelation he had to disclose of the scene in the hut.

At the conclusion of the strife apparently so happily brought about between the hostile tribes, the Indian girl, who had been watching Jack as he acted the part of peacemaker, gave a savage cry and went inside the hut.

Rage, contempt, indignation—all filled the maiden's heart; and, tearing off a circlet of gorgeous feathers which her lover had given her, she tramped them under her feet.

"Young Tiger," she soliloquised, with unbounded scorn, "is a squaw, and the Fawn, a princess of the Great Beavers, will close her heart against him."

Scattering the feathers of the circlet with her hands as she said it, and throwing them out of the window.

"This act," said Jack, " was scarcely completed as I entered the hut.

"Amazed with astonishment I gazed at the girl, and somewhat sternly addressed her with the question—

"'What is the meaning of this?'

"She turned her angry face towards me, and answered—

"'Young Tiger is a squaw; and the men of the Great Beaver are made squaws by his words.'

"Can you wonder at it Joe? Hearing this my eyes kindled with anger as well."

"The Fawn continued, 'When the Heparti

lay beneath the Beaver's knife, and twenty scalps were ready to be taken, the pale-face dog told them to bury their knives and be at peace.'

"'I did so, and they obeyed.'

"'They are cowards, and afraid of the pale-faced chief, whose blood is but water,' said the Fawn, derisively.

"'And it is the Fawn who speaks?'

"'Aye; and you can show anger to her. Go where the foe stands with their red spears; show it to them.'

"Joe, with these words I felt a curse rising to my lips. To prevent its utterance I bit them.

"The Fawn construed my silence into an admission of the cowardly feeling, which she attributed as the cause of the peace which had just taken place between the warlike tribes.

"'My brother,' she continued scornfully, 'feels that he is no longer a brave, or feels that he should become a squaw, and stay in the hut to chop wood and cook the game which——'

"With this, Joe, I was struck beyond endurance. I knew the words used by the Indian girl were the most insulting that could be addressed to a warrior.

"With indignation I held out my hand to imply she should be silent.

"The action was clearly misconstrued by the over-excited girl.

"She imagined I was about to strike her, and actuated by a sudden frenzy, she seized a rifle from the wall and fired point blank at my head.

"The bullet whistled closely to my ear—so closely that I felt it as the smoke and flame shot across my eyes.

"Snatching the weapon from the island maiden I reeled backwards.

"'Fawn,' I said, and my voice was full with bitterness, 'we part at once and for ever.'

"She would have spoken, but whether in tones of sorrow for her past act, of of further defiance, it is hard to say; but ere another word escaped her lips the door of the hut was dashed open and you entered."

CHAPTER L.

A SLEEPLESS NIGHT.

"Well," old Joe said, as Jack had then given him the particulars of the scene in the hut, "well it's nature, Jack. The girl was savage because you deprived her countrymen of the chance they had of obtaining a few scalps."

"Yes; but——"

"Wait a minute, lad. She knew nothing about what we term mercy; there ain't such a word in the dictionary of their lingo. So, perhaps after all, you've no particular right to blame her so much."

"Not blame her, Joe?—not blame her for firing point blank at my face?"

"Well, no," old Seedy answered, "certainly not; or that shot may not, after all, have been premeditated."

"It was within a hair's-breadth of settling me, at any rate," replied Jack, somewhat nettled; for he felt the cool way in which Joe Seedy evidently accepted the spirit of the scene he had narrated. But Joe's love days were over.

"Poor lad!" retorted Joe even more provokingly. "Well, do you feel sorry at the loss of your dusky mistress?"

Jack was silent for a time.

"I'll speak the truth," he said at last; I am not particularly sorry."

"Just so; the hey-dey of love, that's all."

"Not exactly that, Joe; still I did not care for her as she cared for me, I think; and I have often felt that I was playing the hypocrite by encouraging her passion."

Old Joe rested on the paddle for a few seconds.

"Well," said he at last, "everything, Jack, happens for the best, they say, and perhaps this has been so."

"Perhaps it has, Joe,"

Standing out boldly against the clear blue heavens was the massive hull of the stranded ship, and Jack, as they glided slowly under her bows, was struck by the melancholy grandeur of the sight.

Already was the keel disappearing with the effects of the many storms that had swept over the island since the vessel had become fixed in her final resting place.

"It is a sad sight," the boy said, "a very, very sad sight Joe; the vessel left thus to the mercy of the raging waters; sadder still is it to remember that the gallant fellows who trod her deck are at the bottom of the great deep."

"It is indeed a sad sight, lad."

By this time they had made their boat fast to a rope which hung over the side; and Old Joe, breaking open one of the lower ports, scrambled through, closely followed by his youthful companion.

The port hole led to the captain's cabin, and when Joe Seedy had entered, he uttered an exclamation of surprise.

"What's the matter, Joe?"

"The ship has been ransacked, lad. Look here!"

He pointed to a locker, the lid, though strongly bound with iron, had been smashed open.

"Perhaps," Jack suggested, "the man we saw slay the crocodile, has done this."

"Not likely, lad. There has been more than one hand in this business; and unless I am very much mistaken, the old barque has been visited by pirates."

"Why do you think so?—a ship may have touched here, and an examination of the papers may thus have been made."

"Honest sailors," old Joe said, holding a pirate's creese towards his companion, "do not carry such as this."

Jack examined the deadly-looking weapon attentively.

It was the first time he had seen a blade fashioned in the serpent-like form of that murderous creese.

"A murderous implement," he said; "to what enemy does it belong?"

"To the pirates, lad."

Jack placed the weapon in his belt.

"I'll keep it, Joe," he said; "for in close quarters it would be most useful."

Old Joe nodded, and proceeded to further investigate the ship.

Every locker and chest had been broken open, but nothing appeared to have been carried off.

A pile of arms stood in the rack, just as old Joe had left them when he started in quest of the Young Tiger.

Cutlasses and pikes were still on the hooks they had occupied when the stout crew stood full of life and strength ready to seize their weapons.

Old Joe shook his head at the sight.

"I don't like it, lad; I wish they had taken the arms with them."

"Why?"

"I'll tell you why, lad. The pirates have been here and searched the old bark for money, which they have not found. You see, the cargo and arms are safe. So, to my mind, this is how the matter stands: they have been disturbed by a sail appearing off the isles, and if that sail were the merchantman, they have captured her; if she were a man-of-war, which I hope, they have been taken. If this is not the case, mark my words, lad, they will come back, and as sure as you stand there, we shall have a visit from them before long."

"You said, Joe, that they had not found the treasure on board—how do you know that?"

"Because, lad, our skipper was too wide awake to keep his gold where a pirate's officer could find it. I know the spot," he said, "and

JACK MAKES A DISCOVERY.

if we live to see the old country again, we shall have more money than we can comfortably spend in an ordinary lifetime."

"There must be a vast amount then."

"There is, lad. Come below and you shall see it."

They went below to the lower deck, and at the end of a tier of water casks Old Joe paused.

"Give me a hand, lad," he said, "with this crowbar."

Jack obeyed; and Old Joe, after removing a square piece from what at first sight appeared to be a ponderous cross beam, thrust his hand inside the small opening.

He brought out a canvas bag, from which came the musical chink of gold.

"There, lad," he said, "there's a sample of the hoard, and there's plenty more up here."

"Useless stuff to us, Joe."

"Ay, lad, just now, perhaps; but we shall not always be here, I hope."

Jack smiled. He felt the romance of his ideal life wearing off day by day, and like Old Joe he earnestly longed to behold the busy world again.

"What a strange hiding-place!" he remarked, as Old Joe closed the aperture. "They would have sought long before looking here for gold."

"'Tis a strange place, lad, and the man who used it was a strange man."

"How did you find it—for surely he did not entrust this secret to the whole of the crew?"

"Not exactly, lad;—trust the skipper for that. I don't believe, with the exception of myself and the captain, that a soul knew of this goodly store."

"You were his confidant, then?"

"No, lad. I found it out this way—it was quite by accident. When we were off the bay of St. Aubin, the Albatross overhauled a French ship and captured her, on board of which there was a quantity of bullion.

"Well, we had scarcely cast off from the Frenchman, when a three-decker, with the French colours at her mizen, came down upon us."

Jack's eyes lit up at the prospect of a sea-fight being narrated by old Joe; but he was disappointed.

"There was no time for escape, and no chance of a successful issue had we fought. Well, I happened to be down here, just about this spot when a gun was fired upon us and a boat sent to board us."

"There was no fight after all then?"

"No, lad, no! Well, I was busy about my work, when I heard a noise just above my head."

"'Rats,' I muttered.

"But no. The noise continued, thump, thump, thump. I hastily, in search of the cause, cut out this little square piece of wood from the beam, and closely following it came a bag of gold."

"A prize, Joe."

"Yes, lad, had I wanted it. Well, I took the bearings of the case, and soon found out the secret."

"What think you it was, lad?"

"Don't know, Joe."

"Well, just this. The skipper had a small shaft leading from his cabin to this hollow beam, and when he had tied the gold in canvas bags he dropped it out of sight. That was a knowing move, Jack."

"Yes, it was so, and by its means he was saved from the clutches of the three-decker, who made a stiff search for the gold the Frenchman had lost, but the skipper's hollow beam was too much for them."

"So I should think. Now, Joe, we will go back to the cabin and turn in, for I'm tired,

and a comfortable bed is too much of a luxury to be easily dispensed with."

"It is so, lad; and as I know where to find plenty of preserved meat and the captain's wine, it will be our own fault if we do not make ourselves comfortable and jolly for the night"

"It will, lad, so let's steer for the cabin."

Old Joe soon found the preserved provisions, and with several bottles of good wine they regaled themselves to their heart's content.

After supper old Joe slung a hammock in the cabin, and Jack took possession of the dead captain's luxurious couch.

They fastened the doors, not so much because they feared intrusion, but the habit acquired of living in a state of continual danger had become a second nature.

Jack tossed and turned about on the soft bed, and somewhat spitefully listened to old Joe's deep breathing.

"Hang it," he muttered, "I cannot sleep half so well as when I had only a bed of leaves."

He indulged in several impatient turns, first on one side, then on the other; then began mentally counting until the total exceeded some thousands.

Growing tired of this, and finding that sleep still kept away from his aching eyes, he jumped out of bed and pulled the soft bed from the cot.

"That's it," Jack thought; "I shall sleep better upon the hard mattrass."

He found himself little benefitted, however, by this change.

Do, indeed, what he would, no sooner had his eyes closed than he woke up with a start.

The fact was, Jack's mind was overmatched by the day's excitement, and, unlike his tried companion, he could not easily calm it.

At length he fell into a light slumber, and found himself surrounded by a legion of dark-skinned pirates.

He thought he stood in their midst, armed only with the deadly creese he had found on the deck of the Albatross.

The weapon, he fancied in his dream, was knocked from his grasp, and in a second the pirates were upon him, and he felt the cold, sharp blades enter his breast.

With a shout of despair he sprang up in bed and awoke.

The noise roused Old Joe, who in an instant was upon his feet, his trusty rifle ready for action.

Finding everything quiet the old tar said—

"What's the matter, lad, what's the matter? —I thought we were attacked by a legion Indians."

Jack told his dream, and the old tar, clambering to his hammock, said—

"Glad it's no worse, lad; had it been those devils you would never have seen another day, curse them! I once nearly lost my life by their treachery, but go to sleep, lad, perhaps I may tell you of it another time."

Jack tried to follow his companion's advice, but it was to no good purpose, and Old Joe, thoroughly aroused by Jack's sudden cry, found he could not again win the drowsy god to his pillow.

After listening to Jack, as the lad turned from side to side, he remarked—

"Well, lad, it don't seem you can sleep?"

"No, Joe; I can't get those fellows' faces from my mind. They are always standing peering into my eyes. I wish I had never touched that crease. I believe it was thinking about that caused my unpleasant dream."

"Very likely, lad, very likely. Lie perfectly still and think of something else, you'll soon drop off again."

"Not to-night I shall not, Joe, I'm sure; so if you are in the humour you may as well tell me about your brush with the fellows who have so scared me to-night."

Old Joe filled his wooden pipe with dried leaves, and when he had succeeded in making them burn until his pipe bowl looked not unlike a small furnace, he began and finished a short yarn. This was it—

"In due time we entered the rivers on which stands the large and flourishing city."

Old Joe paused.

He thought he heard a snore from the neighbourhood of Jack's pillow.

"Asleep, lad?" he inquired.

No answer came to his inquiry.

"I thought so. By Jove, I thought so," muttered the old tar. Well, it hasn't been a very long yarn if I've been spinning it all to myself."

"Jack."

No answer, his supposition was correct, it was Jack's snore he had heard.

Old Joe carefully placed his pipe under his head, and drawing the blanket over his nose, he soon fell asleep, and, I will add, in unison with his young companion.

CHAPTER L.

A SURPRISE.

Song birds perched upon the summit of a mighty tree welcomed the first blush of the new day with their clear varying notes.

Flying from tree to tree were numbers of gaudy plumaged macaws.

When their noisy shrieks subsided, for a moment the sweet plaintive song of the beautiful Legu could be heard like the sound from a flute as it floated away on the gentle morning breeze.

These sounds and the gentle rippling water washing the Albatross's side greeted our hero and his companion when they awoke.

Old Joe opened his eyes and listened with much inward satisfaction to the well-known music; then dropping from his hammock to the deck called out—

"Are you awake, Jack?"

"I am," was the answer, "I was just listening to the strange sounds."

"That's more than you did to my yarn last night, lad."

"I must apologise for that, Joe, for I fell asleep in spite of all I could do to the contrary."

"It doesn't matter lad; I am glad you did."

When they had dressed old Joe suggested breakfast, and Jack agreed.

They again partook of the good things the skipper had taken on board for his own use.

The meal over, they took a fresh rifle each from the hooks of the cabin wall, and old Joe said—

"Now, lad, I think the first thing we had better do is to go in search of the man we saw yesterday."

"I think so too," said Jack.

The sun had reached its meridian when they came in sight of the object of their search.

The stranger, in the company of a strange object like a monkey, was paddling his canoe across the narrow neck of a lagoon.

He was evidently on the look-out for some place to land, for on that side the bank was lined with tall rushes.

"I wish he'd look this way," said Seedy feeling half inclined to shout.

"Let us lay down our rifles," answered Jack, it will gain his confidence."

They had scarcely done so when the reeds were suddenly put in motion and a dozen alligators rushed into the sluggish waters and made for the canoe.

Quick as thought the stranger took a rifle from the bottom of the canoe, and aiming steadily at the foremost of his foes, wounded the huge animal, and thus saved his own life; for as soon as the water became tinged with blood the fierce monsters turned upon their wounded companion, and the stranger swiftly swept his light craft round in an opposite direction.

So busied was he in making good his escape that he did not see Jack and Seedy watching him, nor was he aware of their presence until his canoe was near the shore and the alligators were in chase of him again.

As the canoe struck the bank Jack and Seedy ran forward to assist him to land, when The stranger evidently regarding them as foes, stood on the defensive, his rifle at his shoulder and his finger on the trigger.

"Come the least bit nearer," he said, "and by the powers I'll fire."

Jack and old Seedy drew back in astonishment, and exclaimed—

"Riley McGowan!"

"Whurroo!" said the ex-caterer coming nearer; "and who may ye be?—och, by the powers, but its Mr. Seedy and Mr. Rawlings, how the divil did ye come here?"

The re-united trio shook hands, and the monkey took to his heels, and then having walked to a safe distance from the inhabitants of the lagoon, they briefly related their several adventures.

Riley was the last to speak, and when he came to the event of his return after the conflict with the hostile islanders, he said in conclusion—

"Bedad, it was time for me to get away, for them divils of wives of mine fought like Kilkenny cats, so when I found a canoe it's not a moment I lost in wishing them good-bye without saying a word, and I didn't look behind me until one night my canoe ran against the old hull of the brig, and here I have been ever since."

Thus they talked over their future plans, and Jack and the master-at-arms came to the conclusion that Riley should be reinstated into his former position as cook.

"Bedad," said Riley, "it's a cook I'd sooner be any day than a chief, so I'm willing to take the duty; but look here, Misther Rawlings, suppose ye go out and look and see if any of the black divils are coming this way?"

Leaving Riley sitting on the trunk of the tree, engaged in his own reflections, Jack ascended a neighbouring peak, and took his seat upon its extreme point, gazing admiringly out upon the broad sea.

He was shortly joined by Joe Seedy.

The island, our readers should be informed, was one of that sequestered archipelago called by Joe the many islands, all of which were of volcanic origin, and surrounded by those dangerous rocks and coral reefs which had been the doom of so many ships.

Seated upon the high promotory that jutted out into the many-coloured ocean, Jack contemplated the boundless and beautiful prospect which his new territory revealed to him.

Never had Jack in all his travels beheld a scene so lovely and so enchanting, and even old Seedy, with all his immense experience of nature in all its phases and varieties, expressed his admiration.

But Joe had seen the islands before; consequently their beauty did not produce so great an effect upon him as they did upon Jack.

The latter could not repress his admiration.

"How beautiful!" he exclaimed. By Jove this is glorious, Joe. Oh, how glad I am that we have found these islands."

"I thought they would astonish you," the old tar answered. "Didn't I tell you there were myriads of wonderful places, and I'll warrant a closer acquaintance with them will not lessen your admiration?"

"No Joe, no. I feel that I could live here for ever."

"Ah, my lad!" replied Joe, chuckling. "What! so soon forgetting our last resting-place, with your glory and power as a chief, and the beautiful Indian girl into the bargain, eh?"

Jack looked rather embarrassed at those words.

"Do not talk about that, Joe," he answered. "You know the reasons why I left the island. As for the Fawn, she will be far happier when away from me."

"Not by the signs I saw she won't," returned Joe; "but you know best."

"At all events, I did well to get away," Jack replied; "I did not want to chain myself completely to her, and the happiness of both of us will be enhanced by the steps I have taken."

"And your late subjects?" asked the old tar.

"Must look out for themselves. I have done all I could for them, and now, Joe, suppose we change the subject."

Here we are and here we must remain for some time to come; it will be long before we have explored this island."

"Suppose we set about it at once," suggested Joe.

"That's it—a romantic fit—but not more romantic than my life has been—just think of it—ashore on an island where fate has made me a warrior chief, and now——"

CHAPTER LI.
THE MYSTERIOUS VESSEL.

"WELL, what is your highness's present state and condition?" asked Joe, good-humouredly.

"Jack, the king of the many islands," said Jack, suddenly starting up, his face flushed with enthusiasm and excitement, "that is what I am now, or, at least what I will be."

"Capital; but see, being king ain't much good to anybody in your situation. Where your subjects are to come from, in the first place, I don't see; Riley and me won't make a very big nation."

"Are you quite sure that all the islands are totally uninhabited?" inquired Jack.

"I should be as much surprised," answered his companion, "to see a man of any kind as I should to see a mermaid in the water yonder, or a fine lady's kid glove lying on the beach."

"Well, at all events, there must be some birds, beasts, and fishes in the islands which I will make my subjects. Adam and Eve, who ruled all the world, had no others. Or even failing this, the islands are a kingdom in themselves."

"Yes, my lad, but a king without mortal subjects is like a gun without powder. But stow this tack," the old salt continued, "I think we have been at it long enough. Let's turn to and make ourselves generally useful. We shall want some breakfast, so get up, my lad, and help me to see about providing it."

Thus exhorted, Jack reluctantly quitted his post of observation.

Joe and he then started to take preliminary observations of the island, for the purpose of shooting turtles, and chopping wood for a fire.

After their breakfast, accompanied by Riley, the two friends set out on an exploring expedition through their wonderful island.

So far from being barren, as it at first sight appeared, the island on which they had landed was a delightful region.

In extent it was little more than three miles a circumference, but for fertility and beauty it was a complete fairyland.

Cocoa-nuts, sago, the castor-oil plant, and a variety of seeds—all probably washed ashore, in the first place, from distant lands, and taken root in the island—abounded in all parts.

These, together with the turtles, the swarms of fish, the eatable lizards, and the birds and wild goats that inhabited the high rocks, gave ample evidence that our hero's new dominion was a land of plenty.

"No need to starve—eh, Joe?" he cried, as he delightedly stood on the centre eminence and surveyed the rich prospect before him.

It seemed to Jack a wonder that some of the South American States had not taken posession of them, and formed colonies on them.

But Joe, to whom he had expressed this opinion, replied—

"They would be little use for that, Jack. They are too small to support large numbers of people, and besides you forget," he added, "that having been in the first place cast up by volcanoes, they are liable at any moment to go down in the same manner."

Jack started, and felt suddenly uncomfortable to think that all this glorious scene could possibly sink into the sea and be devoured. And above all the idea of sinking down with it—that was a particularly unpleasant reflection.

"No, Jack," remarked Joe, " the worthlessness of these islands is their only safety, and though they might support you and me, and perhaps a few dozen more, they would be despised as a colony by any of the great neighbouring Governments, so, knowing they don't belong to anyone else, you have every right to call yourself, as you have done, king of the many islands."

The whole day was passed in exploring the island and the neighbouring ones; all of which possessed the same features and general character.

Jack and Joe used their pit-pan, and Riley one of the boats from the Albatross, which he had reserved and mended for his own use.

Riley had, during his solitary stay on the island, lived in a small hut he had built on the shore, not far from where lay the wreck of the Albatross.

To this hut he invited them in the middle of the day to partake of a repast consisting principally of turtle and many of the fruits and vegetables of the island.

It being a fine day, the companions had a glorious trip among and around the various islands and the coral beds that encircled them.

Jack had fine sport in one of the islands, where he shot a magnificent turtle through the neck, killing it instantly, just as it was scuttling into the water.

When night came, as it was fine weather, the party resolved to sling their hammocks upon the branches of a couple of strong spreading trees, not far from the captain's habitation.

This impromptu sleeping place was constructed without much trouble.

By the aid of ropes the adventurers securely fastened their skin cloaks to the trees in the position most comfortable for sleeping in; and spreading under and over their bodies their other garments, contrived, as Jack expressed it, "to make as good bed as you could get at a first-class hotel."

When once comfortably settled, they found little difficulty in going to sleep.

They were weary with their day's adventures.

And all around was quiet and calm as the grave.

The night was delightfully cool.

Jack, Joe, and Riley were very quickly as fast asleep as so many dormice, and there seemed no reason why they should not sleep undisturbed till morning.

For a moment Jack did not know where he was, and in his bewilderment nearly tumbled out of his hammock.

What was the cause of that peculiar feeling of mental oppression that overcame him, and seemed to indicate some impending danger?

Jack could not tell.

He only knew that he experienced it, and that a feeling of wakefulness had come suddenly over him.

Hark!

Voices! Can it possibly be the sound of voices at this silent hour, and on this, to all appearance, uninhabited island?

Jack started up, his brain throbbing, his heart beating quickly.

He listened.

Yes, it was evidenly voices in rough, angry converse, and seeming to proceed from the opposite side of the island.

These wafted sounds were accompanied by a harsh, grating noise, like that of dragging a boat along the beach.

Jack now fancied he could hear the plash of the oars.

How near it sounded, too!

A thousand vague conjectures chased each other through Jack's mind, but none satisfactory.

He was completely puzzled.

What should he do?

Wake his companions, and acquaint them with what he had discovered, and accompany them to ascertain the cause of it?

But Jack at length determined not to wake his messmates.

So he silently slipped out of his hammock, and, armed with his sword, stole cautiously in the direction of the sound.

Wherever an open eminence presented itself, an uninterrupted view of the sea on every side was to be obtained.

Jack at length reached the top of a rising ground, covered with thick clumps of trees, at the foot of which a grassy slope stretched down to the shore.

Selecting one of the tallest trees, he quickly clambered to its summit, from which elevation he had an extensive view to seaward.

There a most unexpected sight appeared.

A large bay, or natural harbour, evidently of deep water, and capable of sheltering craft of a considerable size.

Beyond that the dull grey leaden ocean clothed in the early morning's gloom.

But, above all, Jack could distinguish the outline of a large vessel having the appearance of an English schooner getting up sail, about a quarter of a mile from the shore, seemingly slowly making her way from the island.

No other boat was to be seen, and it was clear the one he had heard launched belonged to this ship.

Jack was sorely puzzled.

He stood watching the vessel, which, with a light breeze springing up in her favour, was making rapid head way, until she grew less and less, and ultimately faded away in the distance.

There was no deception there.

Some persons had visited the island during the night, but who were they?

No strangers to the island would have landed under such circumstances.

It was evident, too, that the crew of this mysterious ship knew the island well, and were accustomed to put ashore on it, either for water or some other purpose.

But choosing the night to do so looked suspicious and rendered it all the more a mystery

Who and what could they be?

While pondering all this the vessel gradually disappeared.

Jack felt it was no use pondering longer; he turned again into his hammock, and slept until four in the morning.

When Joe awoke the morning sun was shining in all its splendour, and far over the vast expanse of the golden ocean was gemmed with innumerable islands and islets of great beauty.

Jack sat up in his hammock and gazed around him in a half-bewildered manner.

Joe was engaged a short distance off in chopping wood to make a fire.

The ex-caterer was making breakfast in the hut.

"Come, my lad," was the old tar's exclamation to our hero; "this won't do, to lie sleeping in the morning like a land lubber after a night's spree. I've been up ever so long, and been out hunting for our breakfast."

"And what have you got for breakfast, Joe?"

"Well, in the first place, using this skin bottle, I got some water from a stream out on the left yonder. Then I began hunting for turtles, of which there appear to be thousands. I felled this chap here and am going to cook him in his own shell. Why he weighs at least two hundred pounds."

While Joe was thus employed with the tortoise

the fire, Jack had gone to perform his ablutions at the spring spoken of.

It was a fine stream, falling from a low cliff about thirty feet high, and thus forming a beautiful waterfall, encompassed by high rocks, covered with luxuriant vegetation.

The thought, however, of the mysterious ship engrossed his mind, and he determined, if possible, to solve that mystery.

Arrived at the hut the ex-caterer was serving out breakfast upon the shells of the turtle which used as plates.

While engaged on their repast, Jack thought high time to acquaint his friends with the strange circumstances of the ship.

Accordingly he said :—

"Joe, you complain of me lying in bed a long time this morning, but I did not sleep quite so long as you. I was up and walking about upon the island at early dawn.

"And what were you doing, lad?" asked Joe.

Our hero answered with emphasis—

"Looking at a ship."

"Looking at a ship?" exclaimed Joe; "however, you must have been dreaming."

"Not a bit of it. I saw it as plainly as any body can see anything when it is half dark. It seemed like a schooner fully rigged, and had evidently been at anchor, some of the crew coming ashore in a boat."

"At least, I'm certain that I heard the sound of voices and afterwards the boat putting out."

"The vessel bore away to the west with the wind in her favour."

Both Joe and Riley were beyond measure surprised at this recital, but neither was able to fathom the mystery.

"Such a thing has never occurred here before," said old Seedy.

"They must have been well acquainted with this island to land safely at night on a coast so dangerous. But what did they come for? No vessels would visit such islands as these for trading purposes. There must have been a pirate."

"A pirate! Do you think so?" asked Jack eagerly.

"I do. Nobody but pirates and smugglers would act in that manner. They have evidently their secret harbours where they may easily deposit their plunder. And in case of her being a rover we must keep a sharp look-out, for our stay here won't be a very safe one."

"They can't murder us for our riches, at all events," said Jack.

"No; but if they use the island as a hiding place for their treasure," answered Riley. "it

will be hard with us if we are discovered here."

"We've got some adventures in store for us, I'll warrant," remarked Joe, "and precious tickling ones too. I should not wonder!"

CHAPTER LIII.
AND THE LAST.

LATER in the day the ship bore up for the island, and by sunset dropped anchor in the bay.

Jack, the master-at-arms, and Riley, were perched on a jutting rock, watching with excitement the approach of a boat as it came towards the shore.

"Bedad!" said Riley, "it's anything but pirates they look, anyhow."

The ex-caterer referred to the boat's crew, who were, to say the least, anything but ferocious in their appearance.

Small in stature, and evidently ill-fed and suffering from scurvy.

"I'll tell you what it is, my lads," said the master-at-arms. "These men belong to a ship that has been becalmed in these latitudes, and for want of proper food they have been attacked by scurvy."

When the boat reached the shore the men gave a start of surprise, and dropping their oars seized the arms that were under the seats.

"Ahoy!" shouted the master-at-arms. "Ahoy! don't be in a hurry with those muskets."

"Countrymen!" said one of the new-comers. "Blessed if they don't look more like savages."

"Bedad!" said Riley, it's savages that ye would look if ye had been sarved as we have been."

The ship in the offing turned out to be a merchantman, blown by contrary winds out of her course.

She had been for some time becalmed, and, as the master-at-arms had supposed, scurvy had broken out amongst the crew.

After these explanations had taken place, Jack and the master-at-arms were taken aboard the vessel, and told their story to the captain; Riley meanwhile showing the boat's crew where the turtles were to be found, also the valley where the scurvy grass grew in abundance.

The whole of the crew came ashore, and an awning was made by stretching one of the gun-brig's sails under the tree.

Jack Rawlings had hoped to take the gun-brig home, but that idea had to be abandoned when the ravages worked upon the hull by the storm had been ascertained

The vessel must be abandoned, but all that was worth being removed was taken on board the barque, and at the end of a fortnight the sails were spread and the island gradually sank below the horizon.

"Bedad," said Riley, "it's the top of the morning to ye, and a dacent good-bye, for it's a chance at sea to get back to the sweet little town in ould Oireland again."

"You forget, Riley," said Dick, "that we are going to the Pirate's Isle again."

"Going there, an' for what, Mister Rawlings; why not keep on and leave the place to the devils and the sulphur?"

"Because," said Jack, "we want the treasure there is in the cave."

"Leave it alone, Mister Rawlings, leave it alone, no good ever comes of—"

"Riley," said the master-at-arms, "the captain of this vessel thinks we ought to leave some one on the island to give an account of the gun-brig's loss to the first vessel of war that passes this way."

"Well, Mr. Seedy, an' is it yourself that's to stay?"

"No, Riley, I proposed you."

"The devil a stay—what, stay there and nobody knows the minnit but all me wives may come over there in canoes, and tear me bit from bit."

"I think, said Jack, entering into the spirit of the joke, "that you've a right to stay, Riley."

"For why, Mister Rawlings?"

"Because you have seen more than we have."

"The devil a bit of anything have I seen, it's black I have been ever since we came to the place."

Much to Riley's disappointment, the master-at-arms and Jack kept up the joke until they came in sight of the Pirates' Isle.

Then Riley disappeared below, and the search after him was futile, for the ex-caterer had taken refuge in an empty water cask.

The merchant ship hove to well out of reach of the coral reefs, and Jack and the master-at-arms were about to go ashore when a terrible roar from the island caused them to pause.

The sound was followed by a cloud of black smoke and a shower of stones, then the sea became ruffled, and for many fathoms around the vessel the water hissed and bubbled like cauldron.

"It's all over with the treasure, lad," master-at-arms said, "the slumbering volc beneath the isle has burst, and in a few ho there will not be a mark left to denote wh that island stood."

The volcano raged for twenty-four ho then, save for a fragment of blackened ro nothing was left of the Volcano Isle.

"The works of nature are, indeed, wond ful," exclaimed the midshipman as the ves left the strange scene, "and the destructi and disappearance of these islands is not t least of her wonderful works."

"Right, lad ; but these sights are comm enough here at times."

When Riley was induced to leave his hidin place, Jack told him of the disappearance of t islands.

"It's a lucky escape ye had," said the caterer, "I told ye the Old One was there, a now maybe, ye will believe me."

The master-at-arms and Jack endeavoured make Riley understand the cause of the islan disappearance, but Riley's faith was not shaken.

"Maybe," he said, "ye are right, but, an how, when I get to the ould country the divil a foot will I stir out of it again. Please t pigs! I'll spend the little bit of money I ha in a cabin and a bit of ground, and attend to t praties all the rest of my life, and maybe Bid McShane will not turn up her nose at the b with a pocket full of shiners."

Biddy did not, we are happy to say, and after years Riley told the little Rileys all abo the island, the ghost, and the sulphur, and t young rogues behind their father's back wei wont to not only disbelieve him, but to mak fun of the recital. As for Biddy, she used say—

"Go on wid ye ; it's dhraming ye were, Rile my man."

Jack and the master-at-arms were thanked b the authorities for clearing up the mystery o the phantom ship, which, as our readers ma remember, was but the reflection of a vessel i another sea.

Jack spent a few months at home, then wi Old Seedy went upon the African coast, a saw many adventures in suppressing the sla trade, but none so varied and exciting as tho they met on "Pirates' Isle.

www.ingramcontent.com/pod-product-compliance
Lightning Source LLC
Chambersburg PA
CBHW081156170626

46813CB00009B/3213